▚▚▚ BOOK 3 *in the* **Guild of Truth Series** ▚▚▚

LOCKED out of LOVE

Mary K. Norris

CRIMSON ROMANCE

F+W Media, Inc.

Published by
Crimson Romance
an imprint of F+W Media, Inc.
10151 Carver Road, Suite 200
Blue Ash, OH 45242. U.S.A.
www.crimsonromance.com

ISBN 10: 1-4405-9535-6
ISBN 13: 978-1-4405-9535-6
eISBN 10: 1-4405-9533-X
eISBN 13: 978-1-4405-9533-2

This is a work of fiction. Names, characters, corporations, institutions, organizations,
events, or locales in this novel are either the product of the author's imagination or, if
real, used fictitiously. The resemblance of any character to actual persons (living or dead)
is entirely coincidental.

Cover photo © iStockphoto.com/beijingstory and iStockphoto.com/feedough.

*This book is for my brother and sister, Sean and Kathleen.
You guys are my very best friends. Love you both.*

Chapter 1

Joel took another swig of his drink. He'd lost count of how many he'd had. Too many, if he was to fancy a guess. But hell, he wanted to take Felix out to celebrate. It was a sort of pre-bachelor bachelor party.

"I really am happy for her," Joel insisted as he took another swallow of rum.

He hadn't meant to bring up Sydney, but he couldn't help himself.

"I know," Felix said consolingly.

What was there to be angry about? Sydney had loved him, in her own way. It wasn't her fault that she found her Mirror Mate, the one person in all the world who was meant for her. Only a jackass would hold a grudge against her. And Joel was not a jackass.

Okay …

Maybe he was a little bit of a jackass.

"It wouldn't have been so bad if she hadn't hidden the truth from me for three months. Three months she suspected who Merrick was to her and she kept it from me."

"Look," Felix said as he rested a hand on his shoulder. "There are plenty of beautiful woman around this bar. Just take your pick."

Joel continued to stare into his liquor. He didn't want to look around. The women only reminded him of Sydney. If they didn't have golden blonde hair then they had green eyes or small frames. He sighed.

"And don't look now," Felix said in a hushed voice, "but our bartender keeps glancing your way."

Joel had been so distracted with his own thoughts, he hadn't even realized their bartender was female. Hadn't there been a dude filling his drinks earlier? He couldn't remember. Maybe it was time to stop.

He finished his drink and pushed the empty glass away from him. "I appreciate the effort, Felix, I really do. But tonight is about you, not me, and I need to stop moping. It's been nearly six months. I'm over it."

Felix shot him a sympathetic look.

"I am over it," he repeated, stiffening his spine. "It's the stupid alcohol in my system turning me into this whiny bitcher, I swear. Watch, I'll prove it to you." He spun around on his barstool and scanned the bustling area. His gaze caught on a woman who smiled seductively and waved. Joel's eyes instantly jumped to her hair. Golden waves.

Fuck, getting sucker punched in the gut hurt less.

He spun back around before he threw up. He dumped his head onto his forearms where they rested on the bar top. "Fuck my life," he said miserably.

Felix laughed.

At least one of them was enjoying his misery.

"Don't worry," Felix said. "Your face only turned a mild shade of green. Maybe next time you'll be able to last long enough to smile and wave back."

"Shut up."

Felix laughed again and clapped him on the back. "You want me to scout you out a nice dark-haired girl? But I have to warn you that you don't get to bring some bimbo from a bar to my wedding. Got it?"

And wouldn't that just be great? Joel was going to have to attend his best friend's wedding stag, watching the woman he'd dated for three years bounce around on the arm of another man. His life was now complete.

He needed another drink.

As if summoned by magic, a napkin was placed down in front of him. A few seconds later another tumbler filled with rum was set on the napkin. "On the house," said a pleasant, feminine voice.

Joel looked up and locked gazes with the most beautiful pair of crystal blue eyes he'd ever seen. A jolt went straight through his body. The woman inhaled sharply as if she'd felt the same thing, her eyes widening in alarm.

No fucking way ...

Joel's eyes darted down to the nametag on her left breast. Fern. Fern looked ready to flee. On pure instinct Joel grabbed her hand before she could pull away.

Instantly there was another shock of awareness that made his whole body hard, followed quickly by a strange numbing sensation, like his hand was slowly falling asleep.

Alarm turned to terror on Fern's face. Her other hand instantly dropped to the counter as if she could use it as leverage to pull herself free from him, but as soon as her hand touched the hardwood top, Joel heard the distinct *clink* of a Lock.

Startled cries rang out as people struggled to lift glasses, purses, money, and body parts from the bar top around him.

Joel stared open-mouthed. He whipped back to Fern. Together they looked down at their touching hands. Fern ripped hers free and fled behind the bar.

"Wait!" Joel shot off his barstool. The world spun. Shit.

Too much alcohol.

Felix grabbed him by the shoulder. "What the fuck was that?"

Joel shook his head to try and clear his muddled thoughts. "That woman. She just absorbed my powers." At least that's what it felt like. "I also think she's my Mirror Mate."

Felix swore. Together they raced from the bar, Felix throwing down a hundred-dollar bill to pay for their drinks.

"I was supposed to get that, you know," Joel said on their way out.

"Pay me back later."

They circled the building as fast as possible and caught Fern bursting out of the backdoor like a bat out of hell. She collided with a man in a dark suit, her slender hands on the man's chest to steady herself.

Joel ground his teeth, a sudden stab of jealousy going through him.

"I'm so sorry," Fern said to the stranger. Her eyes dropped down to where the man was trying and failing to pull his arm away from his chest.

She'd Locked him.

If what Joel saw at the bar didn't confirm it, this did. Somehow Fern had borrowed his powers. The tingling sensation when their hands touched must have been his ability going into her. He was a LockSmith, a supernatural with the power to Lock anything and everything to anything else, and he didn't mean doors. Well, he *could* Lock a door, but no key would be able to open it—only he'd be able to. He could Lock shoes to the ground, cars to the street, or even a heart in a human chest to keep it from beating. Whatever he Locked froze, stuck in place until he chose to Unlock it or he got far enough away that his ability stopped working. He'd never met another LockSmith, but he doubted Fern was one. Tingling sensations during contact was not the usual MO. And now she'd accidentally Locked that man's arm to his chest when she'd touched him. She had no idea what she was doing.

He quickened his pace.

As if sensing his presence, Fern looked up and spotted him. Her lips parted, and he noticed the slight hesitation in her body before she turned and ran down the alley.

"Hey!" the man called after her. He pulled frantically at his arm. "What the hell did you do to me?"

Joel ran up to him, Felix hot on his heels. "Don't worry, sir," Joel said with forced calm. His heart was beating a mile a minute.

Every instinct screamed to go after Fern, but he couldn't leave this man. He grasped the stranger's arm in what he hoped was a friendly manner. "She's been getting everyone all night," he lied glibly. "The honey exploded on her." He focused his attention and had a moment of apprehension when his powers didn't come to him when he first called. A few seconds later he felt the familiar tingle at the back of his neck. He Locked the man's arm to his chest in an attempt to override Fern's mistake before Unlocking it, hoping like hell his plan would work.

It did.

The man's arm dropped away and he stared down at it. "I don't smell honey," he said.

Joel shrugged and scanned the alley. A mop of silver blonde hair caught his eye. Fern. She was watching him. Her head disappeared behind the wall and Joel knew she was gone.

He clenched his hands into fists.

Chapter 2

Melanie shot into the first cab that stopped for her, not caring about the cost or the fact that she had just left work without telling anyone.

"Where to, miss?" the cab driver asked.

She threw out the address to the community center and fell back against her seat, eyes closed.

The back of her neck still tingled. Her hands trembled where they rested atop her thighs.

And here she'd spent all day thinking she might be coming down with some kind of flu, worrying about the cost of the doctor's visit and how she couldn't afford to take any time off.

But it wasn't the flu.

It was so much worse.

She hunched over and dropped her head into her hands.

"Is everything okay, miss?" The cab driver was probably afraid she was about to puke on his upholstery.

No. Nothing was okay.

"Everything's fine," she lied.

A few minutes later, the cab driver pulled up to the front of the community center. "Are you sure you want to be dropped off here? It doesn't look open."

Melanie's shoulders slumped. He was right. It was too late for the center to be open. What had she been thinking?

That I don't want to go home.

And now she'd wasted even more money having the cab driver bring her here. She was tempted to get out and simply walk around aimlessly, but there was no point. She'd only be stranded.

"Actually, would you mind taking me elsewhere?" Melanie gave him her home address and cringed inwardly at how much the fare was going to add up to.

...

"Oh, Melanie, there you are." Her mother threw her arms around her neck and gave her a huge squeeze as soon as she was through the door. "I called the bar looking for you, but they said you ran off. I feared for the worst. Are you all right?"

So all her co-workers at the bar had witnessed her flight? That wasn't good.

"I'm fine, Ma." She extracted her mother from around her. "I thought I saw Alexander and I fled."

Her mother's clear, blue eyes widened at the mention of her ex. "You should have called the police. You have a restraining order on him, don't you?"

She hated lying to her mother, but she couldn't tell her the truth. "I wasn't sure and I panicked. Why did you call the bar looking for me?"

Her mother turned around and plucked a small sticky note off the cluttered side table. "The people you found to help Nathan called earlier looking for you, and because you turn your cell phone off at work, I told them where they could find you. I wanted to check in to see if they'd contacted you yet. I know it's late, and I know you can't be disturbed at work, but I thought ... " She drifted off and Melanie offered an understanding smile.

Ma thought she was helping her son.

All this time Melanie had been trying to find ways to help her brother, and now it turned out she was just like him. The thought sent a sickening lurch through her stomach.

Cursed.

"How is he?" she asked.

Her mother's gaze dropped to the floor. "Your father and I were at work; so was your aunt and her boyfriend. No one was here to watch him. I think he had a stash of drugs hidden somewhere in his room. He's been out of it since I got home."

The wrinkles in her mother's face seemed harsher against her sad eyes and graying hair pulled back into a neat bun. She looked so tired.

She's too old to have to worry about this stuff.

Melanie gathered her mother's frail form into her arms and gave her a quick squeeze. "I'll go check on him."

She slipped down the narrow hallway, mindful of all her aunt's precious vases and safari animal figurines that cluttered the tables, along with books and glasses resting on coasters. It was a tight squeeze with six of them living in the two-bedroom home, but somehow they made it work. She stopped at the end of the hall where her parents had given up the second bedroom to her and her brother. She raised her hand to knock and paused. *What for?*

She pushed open the door.

The room was a mess. Clothes were thrown everywhere, some with fresh rips in the fabric, including hers.

"Nathan, no," Melanie moaned as she picked up two of her favorite tops. She'd been lucky enough to find them on clearance and now they were ruined. She threw them into the wastebasket in the corner.

Nathan was right where Ma said he'd be. One of his legs dangled over the edge of the bed, his arms were spread wide, and he stared unseeing at the ceiling.

Melanie swallowed the lump in her throat. Was this to become her fate? All this time she'd thought she was the lucky one. Her neck tingled and she felt an answering sting of tears in her eyes. When Nathan had first started getting his visions, he complained about an itch at the back of his neck. The doctors had diagnosed him with narcolepsy, but Melanie knew better. Now, six years later, he turned to drugs and alcohol to escape his visions.

Was it only a matter of time before Ma would find them both like this?

No.

Melanie straightened her shoulders. There was still hope. Ma said the people who could help Nathan had wanted to talk to her. She wouldn't give up until she'd exhausted all avenues. If these people could help Nathan, then perhaps they could help her as well.

Besides, I'm not getting visions like Nathan.

So what did that leave her with?

Suddenly, her thoughts flipped to the man at the bar, the one drowning his sorrows with alcohol. Her heart quivered in her chest and she rubbed at it.

He had powers. He knew what he was doing. Knew how to control them.

Somehow when she'd fled the bar, she'd trapped that suited stranger's arm to his chest, but never-want-to-see-the-bottom-of-my-glass man had simply walked up, grabbed him, and undone whatever Melanie had done.

I absorbed his ability.

She dropped down on an empty corner of her brother's bed. Her mind swam; hours ago she had only her brother to worry about and now it turned out she had some strange power, too, one that she put on display without meaning to, one that could draw unwanted attention to herself.

One thing at a time.

Say she had absorbed some of the drunkard's ability. All that meant was that he lived with powers, and he hadn't looked mentally unstable. Drunk and depressed? Yes. But crazy? No.

Something about him had drawn her curiosity at the bar. His dark mahogany hair flirting between sexy and shaggy, those defined brows half hiding a pair of midnight-blue eyes, and his hands … working hands, covered with scars like a map with too many trails to follow. What would they feel like under her fingertips, against her skin, teasing … ?

Melanie's breath caught and she instantly shook the thoughts away.

Where had those come from?

Her eyes darted to Nathan. Had he witnessed her getting all hot and bothered over some stranger?

No.

Any lustful feelings evaporated as she stared down at him. She took one of his hands in both of hers. "I'm going to help you," she promised him. "I'm going to help us both."

• • •

"Miss Vyntra?" Melanie turned. A young woman with wavy, brown hair and studious blue eyes stood before her. She was a good few inches shorter than Melanie and wore black pants and a black blazer that emphasized her curves. She thrust out her hand and smiled. "I'm Juliet Arden. I'm here to talk about your brother. Shall we?" She motioned for them to start walking down the boardwalk.

Melanie tightened her father's worn windbreaker against her as the ocean breeze kicked up. She'd picked the boardwalk near the pier for a reason. One, it was away from her home, and two, it was public. Although, in the month of March, the beach wasn't exactly bustling with tourists. Still, she could never be too careful. After all, she'd expected the man she'd talked to on the phone to be here meeting her today. Not some woman.

"Where's Mr. Richardson? I spoke to him on the phone."

Juliet nodded. "My co-worker is out in the field today. Besides, we thought you might be more comfortable meeting with a woman after what Mr. Richardson said he saw the other day at the bar. You apparently ran right into him while fleeing from a pair of gentlemen? I do hope everything is okay."

Melanie's stomach dropped. "That was him?"

"Indeed. I'm sorry to hear you were let go."

Melanie scuffed her shoe along the pavement. "Thanks." She hadn't expected to be fired, but apparently enough patrons had complained. The regulars had no love for her; she never flirted with them, she never let them touch her, she stayed in her own little safety bubble. Thus, she was expendable.

"So," said Juliet. "I hear your brother needs our help. How did you find out about us, if you don't mind me asking? We're not exactly listed in the Yellow Pages."

Melanie cleared her throat. "I heard a lot of things when I worked in the bar. One night I overheard a man talking to his buddy about his sister-in-law, or someone like that, acting strange. I heard him say the doctors diagnosed her with sudden onset schizophrenia. He was really upset, saying there were no warning signs, that it was impossible, but the doctors refused to listen. Then he came across this group and his sister was cured. When he gave his friend the contact info, I took notes too. You see, my brother was diagnosed with narcolepsy—"

"But you don't think your brother suffers from narcolepsy, do you?" Juliet cut in. She stopped walking to stare up at Melanie. Juliet couldn't have been older than Melanie's twenty-six years, but her eyes showed a woman hardened by experience. "You think your brother has something more, just like you think that man's sister had something more than schizophrenia. Am I correct?"

Melanie hesitated.

"You don't have to be afraid," Juliet soothed. "I'm quite aware of there being more to this world than what meets the eye."

"My brother doesn't have narcolepsy. He has visions."

Melanie waited a few seconds for it to sink in, but Juliet's expression never changed.

"My brother used to get visions of what was going to happen in the future," she continued. "You know, like who'd win a boxing match or a soccer game. Everything was fine in the beginning, but then he started getting visions of different people. People he didn't know, people in pain, people about to die. He thought he was going insane. Too many people in his head, he always said. It only got worse, so he tries to block them out completely."

"I understand. My organization has dealt with many individuals. Your brother's ability should be no problem."

"You mean you can get rid of it?"

Juliet smiled, but for some reason it had the opposite effect on Melanie. A shiver ran down her spine. "Trust me when I say that stripping powers is our specialty."

Stripping?

"Now, I must ask," Juliet said as they began walking again, "have *you* been experiencing any strange feelings? Specifically speaking, a tingle at the back of your neck?"

Melanie started. She chanced a quick glance out of the corner of her eye to see if the ringleader of this mysterious operation noticed. With how FBI-esque everyone seemed, she expected Juliet to catch every little detail, but her face remained impassive.

"No," Melanie managed to croak. "Nothing."

Juliet made a non-committal noise in the back of her throat. "And what about the man who was pursuing you the other night?"

"I thought you said that was Mr. Richardson."

"You ran into Mr. Richardson, but he says there were two other men in the alley that night. One of whom helped him with his … honey situation. Do you know this man he's talking about?"

Those midnight blue eyes locking with hers, her heart racing, her body throbbing. Oh yeah, she knew him.

"I've never met him before in my life," she told Juliet a little breathlessly.

Another thoughtful sound came from Juliet. "Does the name Joel Kegler ring any bells?"

Joel. Joel Kegler.

The name suited him.

"I've never heard of him."

Juliet studied her for a moment. "Very well. Let's get inside somewhere; we have much to discuss, including your form of payment."

Melanie followed after Juliet as she steered them toward a place to eat, glad for the distraction. She needed to push Joel from her thoughts. She'd never see him again. She didn't want to see him again.

Chapter 3

Joel didn't think he'd find himself back here for a long time.

He stared at the familiar wood for a few seconds more and then knocked.

Footsteps sounded behind the door before it pulled open. Merrick Haskell's stunned face greeted him. "Joel?"

He tried not to let his imagination run away with him. He ignored Merrick's rumpled black hair and clothes. This was Sydney's Mirror Mate—her other half. Joel was happy for her. Merrick was a good guy.

"Hey," said Joel. "I need your help."

Merrick couldn't have looked any more surprised if Joel had pulled out a top hat and started tap dancing.

"Who's there, Merrick?"

Joel flinched inward as Sydney appeared, winding her arm through Merrick's. She barely reached his shoulder. Her short height, coupled with her petite frame, made her look younger than her twenty-five years, but beneath that child-like exterior was a brilliant mind, one that pushed her through school faster than anyone thought possible. When her emerald eyes caught sight of Joel, her arm instantly dropped.

"Hey, Syd." She should be at the clinic. He forced himself to smile. It didn't seem as hard as it used to be. He clutched the plastic baggie in his pocket and a pair of crystal-blue eyes stared back at him in his mind's eye. "Do you mind if I borrow Merrick?"

Sydney's shock lasted about a second. "Uh, sure. I'll just leave you two alone." She disappeared behind the door and Merrick stepped back to let him in.

Joel was as familiar with Sydney's home as he was his own, but he waited near the door for Merrick to lead him into the kitchen where he took a seat at Sydney's round oak table. The one he knew she'd pleaded with her parents not to donate to Goodwill when they'd gotten a new one. He ran his finger over a chip in the wood that was his fault. He'd wanted to help Sydney clean up when she'd cooked for them on their fourth date so many years ago. He'd still been so nervous back then that he'd dropped the dish and taken part of the table with it. He'd felt awful, but Sydney believed chips and dents built character.

"Do you want anything to drink?" Merrick asked.

"Water is fine."

He heard Merrick open and close a cabinet, followed by opening and closing another one.

"Second cabinet from the fridge," Joel called absently.

The noise from the kitchen momentarily stopped, then he heard another cabinet *whoosh* open, followed by clinking glasses.

A few seconds later Merrick returned with two glasses of water.

"Still getting used to the place?" Joel asked as Merrick took the seat across from him.

Joel had meant the question to come across as idle chit-chat, but Merrick's face was carefully neutral, as if he didn't know whether or not Joel was trying to prove that he knew Sydney's home better than Merrick.

Whatever. It didn't matter what Merrick thought. Joel wasn't trying to win Sydney back and he wasn't here to show up Merrick either.

He pulled the plastic baggie from his pocket and pushed it across the table.

Merrick eyed the napkin inside. "What's this?"

Joel shifted in his seat. He felt like some kind of creepy stalker. After that night when Fern had disappeared, he'd gone back inside the bar and snatched up the napkin she'd put down for him. It had been an insurance measure, but now it was Joel's only lead. He'd scoured the Internet looking for anything on a woman named Fern who lived in Orange County. When he got no leads there, he broadened his search to all of Southern California. No such luck.

It had been six days since he'd seen her. He'd gone back to the bar only to find that she'd been fired. And her co-workers refused to give him any more information.

"I need you to read an impression off of that napkin," Joel told Merrick.

Merrick watched him steadily. "Vander?"

That one name brought on a whole hurricane of emotions. *Vander Donahughe.* The Guild of Aletheia's antithesis. Their archenemy. The man responsible for kidnapping Joel and breaking his arm nearly six months ago to conduct an experiment, the one who held Merrick prisoner for four months, the man who tried to take Cali, Felix's Mirror Mate, and forced Felix to fight nearly to the death in an underground cage match.

Joel pushed down the anger. He'd spent the last six months keeping tabs on the Kratos Corporation—the conglomerate Vander owned and did his dirty work through—in an attempt to find anything incriminating that would bring them down. But so far there was nothing. Not to mention they kept beefing up their security, which meant Joel had to continuously hack their systems when he wasn't busy doing his own IT work to make a living. A task that was getting harder by the day.

The only obvious change in the business was their steady financial decline. Vander was burning through their resources in an attempt to find his Mirror Mate. It kept Vander busy and out of their hair, but when the suited man from the alley began showing up at their usual haunts, too, their hackles instantly rose. Was Vander back in the game? Was this stranger a new goon looking for more supernaturals to steal and torment? If Fern was their next target, Joel owed it to her, as one supernatural to another, to get involved and keep her from Vander's clutches. Vander had hurt enough people, and Joel wouldn't be able to call himself a member of the Guild of Aletheia—the Guild of Truth— if he just sat by and let Vander harm more of their kind.

Plus there was his own underlying reason for seeking her out. He had to see if his drunken state had imagined the whole incident between them, that spark of awareness.

Could it be possible she was his Mirror Mate?

He'd always wanted one, always thought he'd rejoice the day he found her, but now, after Sydney, he didn't know.

"I'm not sure," he answered Merrick. "I take it you've heard about the suspicious men popping up?"

Merrick nodded then gestured to the napkin. "Did one of them touch that?"

Joel hesitated. "Not exactly." He glanced down the hall but found no trace of Sydney hiding out in the shadows. "I'm looking for a woman. She's the one who touched this napkin."

Merrick's ice-blue eyes widened fractionally.

"I met her nearly a week ago, but all I got was the name from her badge. It said 'Fern,' but when I searched for her on the Internet, I got no hits. None that were her anyway," Joel said dejectedly. "She ran into one of the men we've been seeing around lately, and I want to make sure they aren't after her."

A small part of him wished for her to be some foreign exchange student working night shifts at a bar to pay for school with no super powers to link her to Vander, because, dammit, no one deserved to get involved in their world if they could help it. Hell, no one should have to deal with him right now. He was a jumbled mess.

Without another word, Merrick reached across the table and took the plastic bag. He pulled out the napkin and held it between his hands. He closed his eyes.

God knows how long something like this was supposed to take. He'd seen Merrick glean information off of a security control panel in five seconds. But this time Joel was asking him to find anything he could. What if Fern's impression wasn't strong enough? Or what if it faded over time?

A few seconds passed. "I think I know why you couldn't find anything."

Joel sat up straighter. "Why?"

"Her name's not Fern," said Merrick. "It's Melanie. Melanie *Fern* Vyntra."

Joel whispered her name to himself, testing out the syllables. "Did you find anything else?"

Merrick nodded. "She spends a lot of her time at the community center. She attends yoga classes there every Monday, Wednesday, and Friday."

Joel leapt to his feet. "Today's Friday. Thanks, Merrick, I owe you one."

"Joel," Merrick called after him.

Joel turned. Merrick held out the napkin for him, but he didn't let go when Joel went to take it. Instead he said, "I felt the connection. I know what she is to you." Something close to dread settled in his chest. So it was true. Or at least Merrick thought so. That didn't mean it was fact. But why now? Couldn't fate have waited until he was less emotionally fucked up to shove a woman at him? No matter how much he lied to everyone else, he couldn't lie to himself: he wasn't ready. He didn't want this.

"I hope you find her." Merrick continued, clearly unaware of Joel's inner turmoil. "I won't tell Sydney if you don't want me to, but she'll be devastated to know you kept this from her. She wants you to be happy, too, Joel. She still cares about you."

Joel's fingers tightened around the napkin. "I know. I'll tell her in my own time. I just need to find Melanie first." Everyone wanted him to be happy. Poor broken, fucking Joel, with his shattered heart. What was taking him so long to pick up the pieces? Sydney had moved on, why hadn't he?

Well, now he had the perfect reason—only he didn't want it. He really hoped his mind had been fucking with him.

Merrick offered a small smile. "I understand. Good luck."

On the way to his car, Joel pulled out his phone and dialed.

"This had better be important," Felix's irritated voice answered a few seconds later.

"Her name is Melanie—that's why I couldn't find her," Joel said without preamble. "I had the wrong name. I'm heading to the community center to see her right now."

"Hang on there, Joel." The sound of movement came from the other end of the phone, followed by Cali's voice protesting in the background. "You don't want to scare her. You can't simply rush in there and proclaim she's your destined soul mate. If she was using a fake name at work, it's pretty safe to say she doesn't want to be found by someone she saw at the bar."

"Don't worry," Joel said as he got into his truck. "I won't freak her out."

"Joel." The sternness in Felix's voice gave him pause. "I'm serious. I know you mean well, but you can't walk up to her and expect to become a couple instantly." Joel's hands fisted. Little did Felix know that wasn't Joel's first concern. At one point in his life it would have been, but that felt like a long time ago. Now his first concern was protecting himself, and that included his heart.

"I'm not going to profess my undying love or anything," Joel bit out. "I'm going to check on her, make sure she's safe."

Felix remained quiet on the other end for a beat.

"In that case, you'll probably want to approach her cautiously. If she's anything like Cali was, she'll try and flee. You're going to have to gain her trust. Hell, she might not even know that powers exist. You have to move carefully. She could be freaking out about what she saw last Saturday. "

"I'll go slow. Any ideas on what I should say so she doesn't think I stalked her?"

"To be perfectly honest, you probably won't get that far. My money's on that she'll see you and run. Again."

"Great. Thanks."

Chapter 4

Joel's here.

It was just as Juliet predicted.

Melanie didn't like the idea of a man tracking her down. It triggered old memories of Alexander, her ex, the man who wouldn't take no for an answer. He'd stalked her, so she'd been there, done that, got the restraining order to prove it. But Juliet had informed Melanie about Joel's ability to Lock anything together and assured her that wasn't fatal. Melanie was safe. Or so Juliet said, anyhow. Juliet didn't know she had firsthand experience.

Melanie's first task was to see if Joel even sought her out.

And he has. Juliet was right. He'd found Melanie at the community center.

Melanie inhaled deeply to try to calm her racing heart. Joel was sitting in the main lobby like a little kid waiting in a doctor's office, holding an activity schedule upside down as he scanned the crowd. He wore a dark blue Superman shirt that brought out the color of his eyes. His shirt showcased his lean build—not too small but not overly bulky either. A swimmer's physique. He looked to be around twenty-eight, his mop of hair as messy as before, and Melanie got the strangest urge to walk over and run her fingers through it. Instead, the introductory computer class let out, and the people flooding the lobby provided Melanie the perfect cover. She pulled the hood of her jacket up over her hair. She wanted to observe him a little more before he saw her. She wanted to get closer to him, to gauge his response to being startled. Would he attack? Flee? Was Juliet wrong and she was in danger?

As the mass of people started to thin, Melanie pulled back her hood and approached him from the side.

In the event that Joel showed, which he had, Juliet wanted her to talk to him. But what was she supposed to say? Juliet hadn't exactly been clear about that. All Melanie knew was that if she helped Juliet gather intel about Joel and his guild, Juliet promised to help Nathan.

Joel was busy studying a group of girls at the far end of the lobby, his body leaning forward heavily.

Was he checking them out?

She cleared her throat loudly.

Joel jumped.

Serves him right. "Hi," she said when he turned to her. "I thought you looked familiar." Her voice hardened. "Why are you following me?"

Joel hastily got to his feet, hands out. "I'm not." He winced. "Well, I am … but it's not what you think. The thing is, I thought you might be scared—I mean, confused. You have nothing to fear from me though, I promise."

Melanie repressed a smile. It was hard to stay frosty with a guy who was so openly nervous. He clearly wasn't a threat; his reaction to her was proof enough. Still, she wasn't going to let her guard down. "How'd you know I'd be here?"

Joel instantly started looking around as if searching for potential eavesdroppers. The sudden change in his behavior made her stiffen.

"Is there somewhere we can talk privately?" he asked. "I'm sure you have plenty of questions about last Saturday."

Melanie quickly went on the defensive. She took a step away from him. "What do you want?"

"I only want to talk," Joel said. Those guileless, midnight-blue eyes stared steadily into hers, promising no harm.

Go with him, a small voice deep inside whispered.

Don't go with him. It could be some elaborate trap, the paranoid and usually sane part of her brain spoke up.

Suddenly, she was the nervous one, and Melanie didn't like it one bit. She licked her dry lips. Joel followed the movement, something flickering across his face. The hair on her arms rose. The air around them felt too heavy to breathe. She hastily took another step back. "Follow me," she rasped. "There shouldn't be anyone back at my yoga class for at least another half hour." Not bothering to check if he followed, she scurried back the way she'd come.

• • •

Joel watched as Melanie toyed with the leather band around her left wrist. They both sat across from each other on separate yoga mats, waiting. Joel didn't know where to start. He thought she'd have question after question for him, but as soon as he'd mentioned last Saturday, something in Melanie's expression closed off. Was she trying to pretend the whole thing hadn't happened?

"So," he drawled to fill the oppressive silence. "I should probably introduce myself, huh? I'm Joel Kegler. I also possess the power to Lock any object to anything else." Maybe if he shared about himself first, she'd feel a little more comfortable. Like those anonymous group meetings he saw on TV. 'Hi, I'm Joel and I'm a super-powered individual.'

"Melanie," she said crisply.

He waited for anything to follow. For her to mention her powers. For her to mention his powers.

Nothing.

Fan-fucking-tastic.

This was going to be harder than he thought.

He rubbed the back of his neck before coming to a decision. "All right, look, I'm just going to lay it all out here. I'm a part of a guild that uses our abilities for good, the Guild of Aletheia or Guild of Truth if you're like the rest of those bastards in our group who are too lazy to use our *real* name." He cleared his throat. "Like I've said, I Lock things. I'm a LockSmith. My buddy Felix can Erase anything, his future wife can manipulate sound, our friend Niella is a Dreamer and can see the future." Here a ripple of awareness crossed her face, but she quickly covered it.

"My girl—" Joel caught himself, but Melanie's brow furrowed, catching his slip-up. He plowed on. "My friend, Sydney, can negate power around her, and her boyfriend can read impressions from objects. Our newest member, Luke, has regenerative capabilities." He stopped, studied her. "You're not freaking out," he said after a few seconds. "Why aren't you freaking out?" Then it hit him. "You already know people with powers exist."

Melanie glanced away, playing with the leather band around her wrist again. It was clearly her nervous tell. She was hesitant to tell him something, and that bothered him more than he liked to admit. His chest ached and his fingers itched to reach out and touch her.

Dressed as she was in tight yoga crop pants that showcased her legs and a hoodie that was unzipped enough to give him a teasing glimpse of her ample breasts, Joel had a hell of a time keeping himself in check. She wasn't short like Sydney. Joel would put Melanie at around five eight with a lithe frame that came from years of yoga.

His groin tightened. Fuck. Finally Melanie sighed, her hands dropping into her lap. "I know people with powers exist because my brother is one of them. He's like your friend, Niella. What did you call her? A Dreamer?"

That was the last thing Joel expected. "That's amazing, but what do you mean your brother is one of them? You're one of us too."

Melanie shot to her feet. "I'm not!"

Okay, so she was in denial. *Tread carefully; remember Felix's advice. Go slow.* Joel carefully started to stand. "Yes, you are. I was there. I witnessed it. You absorbed my power. You accidentally Locked that man's arm to his chest."

"No. It was a fluke."

He scoffed. "It was not a fluke."

Her eyes narrowed. "Don't come any closer," she warned.

Joel stopped his advance. She was only a few feet away. One lunge really. So close he could smell her, white chocolate and strawberries.

His throat went dry as desire flared.

There was an answering flare deep within Melanie's gaze. She gasped and quickly grabbed the back of her neck. "No."

"Yes," Joel whispered. She'd felt something between them, something strong enough to send her emotions on the fritz. And when emotions were going haywire, powers reared their ugly heads. He knew that better than anyone. Why else would she grab her neck if it weren't to stop the tingling? Joel had done it countless times when he'd first gotten his powers. He took a gamble and closed the distance between them. "You feel it, don't you? That sensation means your powers are activated."

Her crystal-blue eyes widened. "No." She turned to run. Joel grabbed her, felt the spark of her skin meeting his. His cock stirred. A few seconds later his hand started to go numb.

She must've felt something because she tried to pull away. He held on.

"See?" he said and held up their conjoined hands. The prickling sensation started to travel up his forearm. "You're accessing your powers, and that's not a bad thing. There's nothing to be scared of. You're borrowing my power; there's no harm in it."

She tugged again and this time he released her. She backed up. One foot, two …

Joel heaved a sigh. "Would you stop already? Or do I have to Lock you to the floor?" He was only half joking.

Melanie froze.

Joel grinned, an idea coming to him. "You know, now that I think of it, teaching you to Lock would probably be a good first step." Before she could react, he dropped to the floor and covered the top of her sneaker with his hand.

Melanie yelped and kicked out.

And the craziest part was that her foot actually came off the floor. Joel had a split second for *what the hell?* before pain exploded in his jaw.

He went reeling. "Fuckin' hell."

Tentative hands touched his shoulders. He was flat on his back. "I'm sorry. You startled me. Are you okay?"

"I'm fine." He started to sit up but found he couldn't move his shoulder blades off the floor. "What the—?"

Melanie instantly released him and drew back. "What's wrong?"

"Well, this is embarrassing. You Locked *me* to the floor, but not to worry, this'll only take a second." Joel put his hands on his shoulders and waited for the tingle at the back of his neck.

"You're still on the floor," Melanie said after a few moments.

He shot her a quelling look. He closed his eyes and concentrated, but the only thing he felt were the pins and needles in the hand he'd grabbed Melanie with.

His eyes shot open, instantly seeking Melanie. "You." He tried to get up. Failed. Damn, this was frustrating as hell. Was this what people felt like when he Locked them? "You took my power."

Melanie crossed her arms over her chest. "Isn't that what you wanted? You're the one who pounced on my foot."

"Yes, but—" He tried again to rise. No luck. Dammit. "Would you hurry up and Unlock me?"

Melanie widened her stance, as if settling in for the long haul, arms still firmly crossed. "No," she said plainly. "I rather like it this way, and while you're just lying there, why don't you tell me why you sought me out. I don't like it when people try to track me down. More specifically, I don't like it when men try to track me down."

Joel stopped struggling. Was someone else looking for her? Like the man outside the bar?

"Is someone after you?"

His concern caught her off guard. That much he could tell.

He renewed his struggle with her Lock. "I'll protect you," he vowed. Especially if it was that bastard, Vander, who was sniffing around.

When next he glanced up, her arms were hanging by her sides. Their eyes locked. Joel felt the air sucked from his lungs. *Fucking hell, she was gorgeous.* Silver-blonde hair framed her face, cut in one of those trendy fashions Joel could never remember the name of. A-line? B-line?

"Why?"

He barely heard her. "What?"

"Why would you do that?"

"Why would I do what?"

"Protect me."

Joel opened his mouth but nothing came out. He didn't know. *Liar.*

Deep down a part of him suspected why, but he refused to listen.

Attraction. That was all this was. He'd been celibate long enough to be in the running as the next saint.

She started to make her way toward him, as if drawn to him against her will. She stopped a foot away from his shoulder and crouched down. "Why do I have this weird … feeling inside me?" She placed her hand over her heart.

Joel's body went tight with wanting. He couldn't drag enough air into his lungs. He couldn't think past what her mouth would taste like against his own. What she'd feel like naked beneath him.

"Unlock me." The words slid from his lips, roughened with need.

Melanie swallowed. Her body was trembling as she leaned over him. She hadn't Locked his arms, and it would have been so easy to simply grab her and kiss her, but Joel held himself back. He'd wait until Melanie closed the gap between them.

And she was so close.

Her breath tickled his cheek, his chin, his lips.

"CPR is in the next room over," a bored voice spoke up from the doorway.

Melanie fell backward with a yelp, giving Joel a view of the young girl who'd interrupted them. She looked to be around thirteen, with her arms crossed, and half of her hair in her face.

He narrowed his eyes at the teen and growled, "Get out."

The girl scurried away. But where she had been standing, another figure stepped out from the shadows into the foreground.

Joel's blood froze.

Chapter 5

Mr. Richardson, Juliet's right-hand man she'd run into at her bar—literally.

Melanie scrambled to her feet.

"Wait." Strong fingers wrapped around her bare ankle. Heat bloomed low in her abdomen. Joel stared up at her from the floor. "There's nothing to be afraid of. I'll protect you."

Nothing to be afraid of?

There was plenty, including this unwanted—unneeded—deep yearning she had for him. But she couldn't concern herself with that now. She had to leave. How long had Mr. Richardson been there? Had he seen her use her powers? She didn't want anyone to know about them; she didn't even want them. Juliet's group might treat her differently, they might change their mind about helping Nathan.

She needed to clear her head. And she couldn't think straight with Joel's hand on her. The warmth from his skin seeped all the way into her bones and made her blood pound and her breasts ache. She'd very nearly kissed him.

I still want to kiss him.

She wanted much more than that and she had no idea why.

"I need to leave." She wrenched her ankle from Joel's grasp and rushed to the back exit of her yoga class.

"Wait." She heard Joel struggle behind her. "Motherfucker. Wait, Melanie."

Her name from his lips sent a shiver straight down her spine. She continued out the door without looking back, before her nerves failed her.

She needed to reach another exit, maybe the woman's locker room. The locker room led out onto the pool deck and from there she could slip out the side gate—

A firm hand clasped her upper arm and dragged her sideways. "Your presence is requested."

Melanie stared up into the cold, hard eyes of Mr. Richardson. *Shit.*

Her stomach turned to lead. She experimentally tugged on her arm, but his fingers were like a vise.

"This way." Mr. Richardson led her to the east end of the community center where they slipped out one of the side exits. A sleek BMW sat idling by the curb, and she was roughly steered into the backseat.

She didn't scream; she didn't struggle. She needed to stay calm. Nathan needed her. She still didn't know if Mr. Richardson had seen anything. And if he did and they asked her about it, she could always play dumb blonde. It was the only good thing about having stereotypical large breasts and silver-blonde hair.

As the car pulled away from the curb, Melanie rubbed her aching chest. She turned around in her seat to survey the community center and saw Joel burst out of the doors. Her heart constricted. He was looking around frantically.

He's looking for me.

She wrapped her arms around herself for comfort and hunched over so he wouldn't catch sight of her.

Why? Why would he want to look for me? Why did he promise to protect me? And why ... why do I want him to be the one to protect me?

A few minutes later, the car came to an abrupt stop. The driver and Mr. Richardson made no move to get out, and Melanie let out a surprised yelp when her car door opened.

Juliet appeared and smiled at Melanie. "Come with me, Miss Vyntra." She walked away, leaving Melanie the option of following or staying in a car with the two men, who remained unmoving.

Melanie hastened from the car. They were pulled over on the side of a street with office buildings on either side. Juliet was already making her way toward one of them and Melanie quickened her steps to catch up to her. Juliet didn't speak until they were inside a small office in one of the buildings that had a For Lease sign out front. The space was sparsely furnished with nothing but a table and two chairs. Juliet gestured for Melanie to take one.

"It appears that you haven't been completely honest with me," Juliet said when they were both seated.

"You were spying on me!" Melanie shot at her.

Juliet held up her finger. "Correction. We were spying on *him*."

Him. Joel.

"What kind of person would I be if I let you go out into the field without backup? You're essentially working for us now, Melanie, and I take care of my employees. But as it turns out, you haven't been telling me the whole truth, have you?"

Moment of truth. Did she admit to her powers or lie? She could already taste the lie on her lips, but twenty-six years of having honesty pounded into her by her mother made it difficult.

Don't lie to them, Lanie. A voice sounding eerily like Nathan's spoke inside her head. *What if they find out you're lying and ditch me? Who'll help me then?*

But what if they found out she had powers and kicked her and him to the curb anyway?

Her brother's cryptic voice didn't answer.

She pictured Nathan before everything got so messed up. His tawny hair rustling in the wind as they rode horseback on their ranch, before it was scammed from their parents; his blue eyes sparkling with laughter, the dimple in his cheek flashing.

She owed this to him. She couldn't risk the lie.

"No," she answered Juliet. "I haven't been honest with you. But you have to believe me when I say that I was protecting myself. I didn't know enough about you and your company." She still didn't, but that was beside the point now. "I have powers, too. I can—" How was she supposed to describe her powers? She barely understood them, barely understood anything in this crazy world that she thought only her brother belonged to. She'd been naïve to think only a select few would have abilities. There must be hundreds of them—thousands—and she'd gone from being a sibling to someone with powers, to a comic book character herself. How would she describe what she could do? "I can take another person's abilities." She stared down at her hands. "Temporarily."

When Juliet didn't speak right away, Melanie glanced up and found her leaning back in her chair, her hands steepled under her chin in thought. "And how long have you had this power?"

Melanie fiddled with her leather bracelet. "I didn't find out until that night I ran into Mr. Richardson," she confessed.

"Well, that explains why you didn't want to say anything."

"Are you still going to help my brother?" Melanie dreaded the answer. What if they said no?

That shark's smile was back on Juliet's face. She leaned forward and gently touched Melanie's forearm. "Most definitely, only now, you've become much more valuable to us."

Melanie pulled her arm away from Juliet's touch. "What do you mean I've become more valuable?"

"So," Juliet completely ignored the question, "did Joel tell you what he wanted? Why he was searching you out?"

"He didn't exactly say." Melanie remembered the fierce look in his eyes. "He kept saying he'd keep me safe and protect me, but I don't understand why. He mentioned teaching me to Lock too, whatever that means."

"Hmm." Juliet steepled her hands once more, making Melanie feel like a schoolgirl sitting in the principal's office. "I think that is a good idea. I want you to continue getting closer to him. Let him teach you to use your abilities. It'll come in handy later."

"Come in handy?" Melanie echoed.

Juliet got to her feet. "I think it's time for you to understand first." She left the room. Simply walked out without a word.

"What the heck is going on?" Melanie mumbled to herself. She followed after Juliet and found her waiting in the hall by an open door.

"In here," she said.

Melanie craned her head to see into the room. She wasn't about to be led so easily into a trap if that's what this was. But the room wasn't a cage or any sort of containment cell—it was a computer room. The blinds were shut, the lights dimmed, the whirl of the computers' fans filling the silence.

"Have a seat." Juliet closed the door behind them and instantly the air conditioning turned on.

Melanie shivered as frigid air flowed through the vents. "Why are we in here?"

Juliet pulled out a chair and woke up the nearest computer. "There's something I want to show you. You need to understand what my organization stands for, what our mission is."

"And who is your organization again?" she asked while lowering herself into a nearby chair.

Juliet's fingers flew across the keyboard. "We don't have a name; it's too easy to track down that way. We want to remain anonymous. I take it you can understand this?" She paused from her work and looked at her.

Melanie nodded. Message received. If she breathed a word of this to anyone, she would most likely end up at the bottom of the ocean. And after running into Mr. Richardson at the community center, she knew it'd be easy for them to keep tabs on her.

"Excellent. Now, there's something here I'd like you to see." She turned the monitor. The screen was filled with news clipping after news clipping of tragic stories, disasters, murders—

"What is all this?" Melanie scooted closer.

"This," said Juliet, "is the destructive force of those who possess supernatural powers."

Melanie reared back, but Juliet held up a hand before she could say anything.

"I'm not saying you are destructive, Melanie. I'm only here to show you this in the hope that you'll help us. You see, all around us are those using their powers for personal gain, or those wasting away because they wish they didn't have powers at all. Here." She double-clicked on a link. "Last summer, a corporation known as Kratos was holding underground fighting tournaments to earn extra money. The main owner was a supernatural who bullied those weaker than him to do his bidding, and many people died. This woman," she pointed to a different article, "killed a man who cut her off on the freeway by mentally shoving his vehicle off the road. And this is an article about a sixteen-year-old girl in an asylum because she claims she can hear people talking blocks away. She's like your brother: no one to help her, no hope to have a normal life, imprisoned for life because no one will believe her."

Melanie found herself leaning forward to see the monitor better. "How do you know these were all instances involving someone with powers?" A corrupt business owner wasn't something unheard of. A car swerving off the freeway? It was sad, but it happened. And unfortunately there were plenty of people, teenagers included, who thought they heard voices in their heads. Nothing Juliet was telling her was new.

"You don't believe they're supernatural occurrences? What if I told you I've met some of them? The young girl could indeed hear a conversation going on two blocks away; we proved she could do what she claimed. And the woman who shoved the man's car off the freeway? We observed her in the comfort of her own home and watched her pull the remote from the table right into her hand." Juliet swiveled back around to the computer and pulled up a video feed. "I'll prove it to you," she said before playing the clip.

Melanie watched in stunned silence as a grainy camera zoomed into a small home window. A woman no older than forty sat on her couch, a tub of ice cream cradled in her arm. Melanie watched as the woman shoveled the dessert into her mouth before she stuck the spoon in the tub and held her hand out. The camera tried to follow her hand, but the window didn't permit for them to see what she was reaching for. It wouldn't have mattered. A few seconds later, a remote flew into her hand as if pulled there by a magnet.

Juliet stopped the video. "She killed a man and doesn't feel the least bit responsible."

Melanie didn't speak.

Juliet must've realized she had Melanie on the fence because she pressed on. "The point I'm trying to make is that powers ruin lives." There was something both bitter and painful in her voice as she said those words. What had happened to Juliet to make her feel that way so passionately? The woman wouldn't have been in this line of work if she didn't believe with every ounce of her being what she was saying.

But Juliet didn't have to tell her that powers ruined lives—she knew firsthand.

"The world is better off without these abilities giving others an unfair advantage, or in some cases disadvantages, and you are an invaluable asset to help make that happen."

Melanie jerked her head to the side to stare straight into Juliet's blazing blue eyes. "How?"

"Your power. We've collected—*helped* people all across the country. We discovered your kind of ability nearly a year ago. And we found it's the key to our success."

Melanie frowned.

"Think about it: you take others' powers."

"But that's only temporarily." Wasn't it? Suddenly, Melanie wasn't sure of anything anymore.

"Help us," Juliet avoided the question again, "help you. And help your brother."

"Are you telling me that I could *cure* my brother?"

Juliet shook her head. "Not you specifically—that'll take time—but we have others who can heal Nathan so his visions won't bother him any longer. And all I ask in return is for you to get close to Joel Kegler, let him teach you how to use your abilities; he's much better suited at it than I."

Joel's name was like a punch to the gut. "Why him?" Give her anyone else in the world, anyone except the man who made her heart hammer in her chest for no good reason. She glanced at the computer screen. Was there something about Joel and that … guild he was talking about, buried in all those articles?

But he'd said they'd only used their powers for good.

Good is in the eye of the beholder.

Still, she couldn't help but ask, "Have Joel and his guild done anything … ?"

"He told you about his guild?"

Melanie shrugged. "Only bits and pieces really."

Juliet tapped her chin in thought. "That's good. Get close to him, get close to the guild," she instructed.

"What has their guild done?"

Juliet's stare was flat. Finally, Melanie's brain caught up and it all fell into place. "You want to take their powers."

"Don't sound so horrified. You've seen the pain and suffering powers cause. Tell me, wouldn't you want to be normal again? Don't you want your brother to be normal again?"

Melanie dropped her head. She did want to be normal. She didn't want to worry about a strange tingling in the back of her neck, or fear touching random strangers by accident and absorbing some new ability she couldn't control. She wanted a normal family again. She wanted to look at her mother's face and see the lines of worry erased.

I can give that to her.

So what was holding her back? All the proof she could ever want, showcasing the evil of supernatural abilities, was right in front of her. It was a curse, a curse she could help purge from her life and family.

"Fine," she conceded. "I'll do it."

Chapter 6

"He was there? At the community center?" Felix sat with one arm wrapped protectively around Cali.

"Yeah." Joel continued to walk in circles. He'd driven to Sydney's veterinary clinic, the guild's unofficial headquarters, to meet with everyone after he'd called Felix and explained what had happened.

"I still don't understand how Melanie got away from you. I mean, didn't you run after her right away?" Felix continued.

Joel had strategically left out the part about Melanie Locking him to the floor.

He glanced around the small lobby where six pairs of eyes waited for his answer. "That's not important," he brushed off the question. "What's important is Melanie and finding her." His gaze instantly sought Niella, their guild's Dreamer. He knew she couldn't control her Dreams, but sometimes, if she thought about a certain person long enough, she could steer her Dreams in a certain direction.

Niella's hazel eyes narrowed. She threw up her hands, sending her wheelchair rocking. "I'm not everyone's goddamn missing persons finder, okay?" she exploded. "I have enough on my plate. We have someone else now to help lessen that particular load." She flung her hands in Merrick's direction. "Ask him. He's the one who can take information off an object, not to mention he's a fucking PI. Can't I go one day without needing to Dream?"

Joel stared in stunned silence.

Merrick eyed Niella worriedly.

Niella closed her eyes and rubbed her temples. She looked tired, on edge, and Joel had no idea why. She'd been getting worse, that much he knew. He'd heard through the grapevine that Niella was snapping at Sydney's patients more and more, until Luke had to replace her at the reception desk. And when Niella wasn't busy tidying up, she was frantically writing in a small notebook she kept in her purse.

It was the notebook that scared Joel. Last fall the guild had searched for a notebook belonging to another Dreamer. It had contained valuable information about Vander's Mirror Mate that needed to be hidden, but Joel had also learned that the notebook was a way Dreamers kept themselves sane. With too many Dreams bombarding their minds, some Dreamers lost the sense of what was real and what wasn't.

Was that happening to Niella now?

She'd always been snappish but never like this. It had been a gradual change over time and now Joel stared at her with fresh eyes.

Her face was more drawn, her cheekbones more pronounced, and dark circles stood out under her eyes. Her pixie cut lay flat against her head, as if she hadn't had the energy to do her hair that morning.

And he felt like a real asshole for even asking her to use her powers for him.

"I'm sorry," he said instantly. "I shouldn't have assumed you could do that. I shouldn't have even thought it. I'm sorry, Ell." He adopted Felix's nickname for her.

Niella opened her mouth as if to say something but shut it again. She waved him off, still rubbing her temples. Luke left the lobby and returned a few seconds later with a mini water bottle to offer her.

Niella stiffened. Everyone knew from experience that she hated to be coddled. Though Joel didn't really think a bottle of water would constitute being coddled. But Luke was new. They'd rescued the twenty-year-old with Merrick in the fall and he'd instantly won the guild over with his quiet gentleness. Niella especially.

Instead of tearing Luke's head off, she took the bottle from his hand and went back to massaging her temples.

The rest of the group let out a collective sigh of relief. Disaster averted.

"So," Cali broke the silence. "How are you going to find your Mirror Mate?"

Sydney, sitting next to Merrick, jerked back in surprise.

Shit. Thanks a lot, Cali.

He'd only told Sydney that Melanie was a girl from the bar where he and Felix drank. And when they saw the same man from the bar poking around the clinic, they instantly thought she might be in danger. Hell, that's the only story he wanted to stick with. He wasn't even sure she was his Mirror Mate. Melanie was the first woman he'd been attracted to since Sydney. Not to mention he hadn't had sex in more than six months. Nine if he was to be exact. Sydney had stopped sleeping with him the moment she saw Merrick locked in a cell. That made for a lot of pent up energy on Joel's part. He was overdue when it came to urges. Wants. Needs. He didn't need to add a label to Melanie; she was just someone he wanted. His gaze hesitantly rose to meet Sydney's emerald one. Hurt stared back at him.

"This woman's your Mirror Mate?" she asked in a small voice. "Why didn't you tell me?"

Despite Joel's assurances that they were still friends, things changed when they broke up. He couldn't drive to her house after a long day at work to tell her about exciting new projects or drag her along to midnight video game release parties—she had Merrick to do those kinds of things with now.

She'd kept the knowledge of her Mirror Mate from him for three months, secretly pining for another while she was dating him. That knowledge still left a nasty taste in his mouth. He'd say he was entitled to keep his Mirror Mate, if Melanie was even that, from her for a few weeks … hell, not even that. "I wanted to tell you in my own time."

"And when would that have been? After everyone else knew?" She turned to Merrick. "Did you know?"

"Syd." Joel tried to get her attention; he didn't want her to be angry at Merrick. It was him she should be mad at.

But it was too late. There must've been something in Merrick's eyes that gave him away. She pulled her hand from his. "I see," was all she said as she stared down at her lap.

Joel shot Cali a dark look.

The last thing the guild needed to witness was Joel and Sydney still trying to smooth out their relationship.

My bad. Cali's voice echoed in the recesses of his mind, meaning he was the only one she was directing her voice to. *I didn't mean to cause any trouble.*

He wanted to rub his own temples in agitation but refrained. "Whatever," he mumbled instead, knowing she'd hear him.

"So back onto the subject," said Felix. "We need to know if our new goon works for Vander and if he took Melanie, right?"

Joel was glad to be back on topic. "Right." He hoped Melanie had been able to get away. As soon as she left, his powers had returned and he'd Unlocked himself from the ground, but by the time he reached the front of the community center, there was no one in sight. He'd lost Melanie and the man in the suit. His hands fisted. He tried his best to ignore the ache pulsing in his chest. *It means nothing, only that you're worried about someone who might be in danger.*

"Have there been any sightings of the men in black around here today?" Cali asked.

"Not that I've seen," Luke spoke up. "Why?"

"Because if there was one creeping around, we could snatch him and question him."

Sydney sighed. "I'll get a clean cage prepped, just in case."

"Meanwhile, you should return to the community center," Felix said to Joel. "See if Melanie returns and if not … " His expression turned sympathetic and Joel's stomach cramped.

If she didn't return, then they'd know she'd been taken.

He clenched his teeth and resumed his pacing, needing to burn off his nervous energy.

"If you still have that napkin, I'll keep searching for a home address," Merrick offered.

Joel nodded in thanks. "I'll go to the Internet and see if I get any hits on her real name."

And just like that the meeting was adjourned.

Joel headed to the door. There was no need to stick around. Sydney was upset with him, Niella was a ticking time bomb that refused help, Merrick would be busy dealing with Sydney, and Felix and Cali only reminded him of the empty feeling in his chest.

"Joel?"

He turned. Luke stood a few feet behind him.

Joel forced a smile to his face. "What's up, Skywalker?" He'd dubbed Luke with the nickname months ago. With his mousy brown hair, blue eyes, and the small cleft in his chin, everyone agreed there was a similarity between the young Rejuvenator and the Star Wars character.

Luke didn't even bat an eye at the nickname anymore. "Everyone is going home for the night, and I was wondering if you needed any help or anything."

Joel didn't need any help when it came to computer tracking. He opened his mouth to thank Luke for the offer, but the hopeful expression on his face stopped Joel cold. He knew Luke didn't have any family. He'd been in the foster care system before Vander kidnapped him, and once he'd been rescued he had no desire to return home.

It must've been hard for the kid to return every night to an empty apartment.

And lonely.

Joel knew what that was like. "Go grab your stuff. I'll wait for you out front."

Luke beamed and scampered off to the back room to retrieve his belongings.

Joel rubbed his chest while he waited outside the clinic. It'd be nice to have someone else in the house besides himself. Briefly he wondered what it'd be like to have Melanie in his home, in his bed. Her cheeks flushed, her lips parted, her legs open—

His cock hardened painfully and he stifled a groan.

Patience, young Padawan.

Joel inhaled the cool, salty air in an attempt to snuff out his lust. Lust did not equal a soul mate. Love didn't even equal a soul mate. He'd been in love before and that had ended in heartache. He needed to make sure Melanie was okay, needed to explore whatever this sexual attraction was between them. And if there was any more proof of who she was to him, he'd deal with that when he got to it. First, he needed to teach her how to survive in their world. He needed to earn her trust, and he'd be an idiot if he expected her to welcome him with open arms.

And once you earned her trust?

Did he dare explore this attraction?

It didn't matter. He needed to gain her trust and he needed to go slow.

Chapter 7

Melanie clutched the straps of her backpack as she rushed off the bus and into the community center. She was never late to yoga class, but Ma had needed help around the house, and even though she hadn't asked for it, Melanie put down her things to collect all the dirty dishes around the house and wash them.

The sun was starting to set and the wind kicked up to blow her jaw-length hair straight into her face. She hastily tucked the loose strands behind her ear and tried to ignore the slight tremble in her hand.

She was nervous. No, she was beyond nervous; she was downright anxious. The weekend had passed in a hazy blur. She'd even gotten a new job working at a frozen yogurt shop, but damned if she could recall the name of it. Her mind was focused around one thing. One person.

Joel.

She inhaled deeply but the tightness in her chest remained.

It'd been two days since she'd seen him.

I'm only anxious to see him because that's what Juliet wants me to do.

She wished that was all it was, but deep down she knew it was more, and that terrified her. She craved it. Her body tingled with it. She felt like a high school teenager again, hoping to catch sight of her crush somewhere on campus.

Was Joel at the community center? Was he even looking for her anymore?

What if he's not here?

How was she supposed to get close to him if she couldn't find him?

She snuck into her yoga class a half hour late after doing a quick scan of the lobby and side hallways. She remained in the back and easily transitioned into the appropriate positions, her eyes scanning through the open doors for any sign of dark mahogany hair and midnight eyes. But there was no sign of him.

When class was over, she hung her head and exited with everyone else. Two steps out the door she paused. The pressure in her chest eased. She looked up.

Across the hall in a dark jacket and Green Lantern tee, Joel watched her.

Melanie's stomach clenched, her heart tripping over itself.

Someone jostled her from behind and she stumbled to the side. She instantly lost track of Joel and when she looked back, he was gone.

Had she imagined him?

No. She could have sworn he was right there.

"Looking for someone?" A voice spoke up from her far right.

Melanie whirled. Usually the sight of a man so close to her made her back up cautiously, but this was different. She didn't want to back away. She wanted the exact opposite, and that in itself was a cause for alarm. Could it be possible Joel had more than one power? Was he making her feel this insatiable attraction to him?

The idea kept her focused.

She had an assignment to do. Juliet wanted her to get close to him, get tutoring for her powers. Melanie was not to get emotionally involved. She needed to keep her distance.

"I'm glad to see you're okay," Joel said when the last members of her yoga class were out of hearing range. "I was worried last week when you ran off."

Worried.

The word threw her for a loop and she tried to force down the emotions.

"Did anything … happen?" His eyes flashed dangerously, as if promising pain to anyone who'd dare lay a hand on her.

"Nothing happened. I was just spooked. Usually when I see a guy from work outside of work ... " She shrugged. It wasn't a complete lie.

"Do you know who suit guy is?"

Melanie forced herself to keep eye contact. "I don't." That was a lie.

"Have you seen him since?"

She shook her head and felt a little better that she was able to be completely honest. She hadn't seen Mr. Richardson since last Friday. In fact, Juliet's whole organization had been keeping their distance, and it made her nervous. Of course, Juliet said Melanie could call her if she ever felt the need.

Joel's posture relaxed. He shifted his weight from one foot to the other.

"So." He broke the silence that fell over them. "How was yoga?"

Melanie blinked. Surely someone this nervous and awkward couldn't have done something awful. A smile tugged at her lips. "Do you want to sit down somewhere?" It was time to get to know Joel a little better.

• • •

Joel blinked at Melanie from across the small table they'd found in the community center. "Wait a second, I'm confused." Joel held up his hand. "Did you just suggest we hang out?"

Melanie's shrug was all nonchalance. "Yeah."

You've been out of the game for a while, Kegler.

Still, it couldn't be *this* easy. He'd been expecting hesitation, resistance—something! It was almost anti-climactic. Almost. The burning need inside him didn't give a damn who asked who out, as long as it meant he'd get to spend more time with her. The past two days without seeing her had been torture. He was still no closer to finding out who those new suited men were. Cali had volunteered to contact Jente, a man in Vander's employment who had helped her out once, to see if he would divulge any information. Felix had been completely against the plan, but it was all they had to go on. They couldn't leave this potential new threat alone to grow stronger.

He wheeled in his stray thoughts. He could plan heroics later. Right now he needed to figure out the puzzle in front of him.

As much as Joel would like to think that Melanie returned the sexual attraction between them and wanted to explore it, it wasn't true. Felix had been right—if she'd worn a fake nametag when she'd worked at that bar, she didn't want to be found. She admitted as much when he'd first tracked her down. So then why the hell was she seeking his company?

Did she finally come to terms with the fact that she had powers? Did she want him to teach her?

The idea of being her mentor made him sit up a little straighter. He could teach; he was a great teacher—teaching led to camaraderie, a way to get to know her without having this big cloud of expectation looming over his head.

He eyed her hand resting on the table and itched to reach out and take hold of it. He'd always been self-conscious of his hands around Sydney. She used to wince at his scars, as if she could feel the pain of how he'd acquired them. But with Melanie he got no such vibe. In fact, twice already he'd found her staring at his scars in fascination, as if she wondered what they'd feel like under her fingertips. The image of her soft skin tracing over his hands heated his blood and stiffened his cock.

He cleared his throat and shifted in his seat. "I still don't understand. You said before that you don't like men looking for you outside work, so why the sudden interest in spending time with me? What changed?"

Melanie's hand went for the leather bracelet around her wrist, but she seemed to catch herself. "Well, you mentioned something about teaching me ... ?"

Joel's chest puffed up. He grinned. "Of course. We can start tonight if you want." He tapped his finger on the table. "Though we'd need to find somewhere private to do it."

"What about with the rest of your guild?"

Any and all images of potential romantic one-on-one time with Melanie were snuffed out. He'd never get a moment alone with her that way.

"I think it'd be best if we left that till later. They can be a little … much. But I promise to introduce you to them eventually."

Something flashed across her face, but with her head bent away from him, he couldn't make out what it was.

"We can always rent out a room here," he offered. It wasn't what he had in mind, but he'd do what he had to, to keep her comfortable.

She shook her head and glanced at the clock mounted on the wall. "I can't tonight. I have to start my shift at my new job in"—her eyes widened—"fifteen minutes!" She cursed under her breath.

Joel jumped to his feet before she could flee from him again. Keeping Melanie in one place was turning out to be harder than beating Diablo 3 on the highest level of Torment.

"Hang on there." He reached for her and nearly groaned aloud when his fingers rested against her bare forearm.

Heat surged between them. Desire flared white-hot and Joel clamped his jaw shut against the sudden onslaught.

Melanie stared up into his face, her eyes burning with unconcealed emotion. "What is this?" she whispered. He knew she meant the connection between them. "Do you have more than one power?"

She thought *he* was making her feel this way?

Joel repressed a grin. "I have only the one power, and you've seen it."

"Then why … ?" She stared down at where his hand touched her skin. She licked her lips.

Joel's gaze followed the movement of her tongue and he couldn't help but remember when she'd been about to kiss him. How her smell had intoxicated him, her nearness firing every nerve ending in his body.

He wanted to know what she tasted like, what her body would feel like flush against his.

You're my destined soul mate. The answer to her question rested on the tip of his tongue, but he swallowed it down. He didn't dare break the intimate moment with something he didn't even know for fact. He couldn't risk it. He wanted to feel Melanie. Craved to taste her.

He found himself leaning into her, or perhaps she was leaning into him. They shared the same breath and it was invigorating. He wanted to grab her and kiss her, but he also wanted to drag it out. He enjoyed watching the way her eyes tracked his lips, the way her pupils dilated when he drew closer still.

He could feel the brush of her lips on his. Hers were oh so soft, and that was when his control snapped. He pressed his lips firmly to hers, waiting—expecting her to pull back, but she didn't. She pushed into him, a full-body tilt as if she'd lost her balance and didn't care if she fell. But Joel would never let her fall. He caught her around the waist and her hands grasped his biceps, hanging on for dear life as she molded her mouth to his. Hungry. Greedy.

Joel groaned with the heat and pleasure of it. His tongue dipped into her mouth, and she took him in as much as possible, sucking him long and hard. His cock throbbed with need.

When they finally pulled apart, they were both breathing heavily. Melanie's face was flushed, her eyes glazed, her focus on Joel's mouth like she wanted another sample. It slayed him. He wanted to pull her into him again and never let go, but he had to be the bigger man here. And he hated every second of it.

"We have to leave now if you want to make it to your job on time." He voice came out lower than he intended. He cleared his throat. "I can drive you, if you want."

Melanie blinked as if surfacing from a dream. "Hmm?"

He mentally groaned. Slayed him!

He traced his fingers down her forearm, marveling at the goose bumps he raised before letting his hand drop away completely.

Fuck, he wanted her.

"I offered to give you a ride to your new job." He motioned to the clock where they'd already wasted six minutes.

Melanie snapped to attention. "Shit." She slung her bag over her shoulder.

Joel waved to get her attention. "I can take you," he repeated.

Melanie hesitated. After a moment's contemplation, she nodded once. "Thank you."

It took all of Joel's self-control not to lead her out with his hand on the small of her back. He was hyperaware of her every move, and once she was safely tucked into his truck, he took his time walking around to the driver's side. He needed a breather, not to mention he needed to readjust his pants, but the small respite he granted himself was pointless when he opened the car door. The smell of white chocolate and strawberries hit him like a punch to the gut.

He started the truck and instantly blasted the air conditioning.

"What are you doing?" Melanie held her bag to her chest, but not before Joel caught sight of her hardened nipples.

He tore his eyes away and instantly cranked the dial to heat. "Sorry. Where do you work?"

She gave him directions and he turned on his stereo as he pulled out of the community center. Ten seconds into his CD, Melanie reached over and switched it to radio.

"Hey," he protested. "I was listening to that."

Melanie stared at him incredulously. "It was a commercial."

"It was not a commercial, it was Daft Punk."

"They were talking. I thought it was a commercial."

"That's how *Giorgio by Moroder* starts. What the hell is this?" Joel cringed as country music blared from his speakers.

"It's Sugarland."

"Is that like an expansion set for Candyland?"

She shot him a look.

Joel groaned and let his head fall back when they came to a red light. This was all the proof he needed. What he felt for Melanie had to be only attraction. Fate would never pair him with a Mirror Mate who liked country music. Sydney had at least liked hip-hop. Joel didn't know if he could take *Honky Tonk Badonka* whatever.

It turned out he only had to endure it for seven minutes.

"Thank you for driving me," Melanie said when he pulled up in front of the frozen yogurt shop. She was out the door before he even finished putting his truck in park.

"Hey," he called before she shut the door. "When can I see you again?"

Color rushed to her cheeks. "Tomorrow?"

"Community center, five o' clock?"

She nodded and hurried off through the front doors of the yogurt shop.

Joel exhaled and peeled his white-knuckled hands from the steering wheel. It was the only way he could think to stop from reaching over and touching her throughout the car ride.

"This is going to be torture," he said to himself. To be in Melanie's presence without being able to run his hands over her body …

He swallowed thickly.

He could still feel her lips on his, taste her flavor there. Her scent still lingered in the cabin of his truck and he drove the rest of the way home with the windows down.

He was so screwed.

Chapter 8

The next day Melanie was busy in the back room of the yogurt shop, tidying up so she could finish her shift, when Daphne strolled in.

"Hey, Fern. Some guy who came in wanted me to give this to you." Daphne held out a neatly folded piece of paper.

Melanie stared down at it. Her heart started to pick up speed. Was it from Joel? Her lips tingled just thinking about him.

There was no name on the paper, and Melanie frowned. Joel wouldn't have left the note blank, which meant it wasn't from him.

Her gut sank. What if it was from Mr. Richardson, delivering a note from Juliet? She didn't know if she was cut out for this covert ops kind of stuff. On her first night, she'd already kissed the man she was supposed to be gathering intel on. What kind of special agent was she if she couldn't even keep her emotions in control?

A moment of weakness, that's all it was.

She took the paper. "Thanks. Hey, Daphne?" Melanie called to her.

Daphne turned and cocked a hip as she waited by the door.

"What did this guy look like?"

Daphne's head tilted to the side as she recalled. She held up her arm well above her head. "He was this tall with long, dark hair, really intense eyes, and oh yeah, he had a scar." She touched her chin. "Right here."

Melanie's blood turned to ice.

Daphne dropped her arm. "Are you okay? You look like you're about to hurl. Do I need to get a bucket or something?"

Melanie reached out to steady herself. "I'm fine." She forced a smile.

Daphne didn't look convinced, but after a few seconds she shrugged and went back to help what few customers they had.

Melanie quickly scanned the room, half expecting to find a camera watching her. She huddled into a corner and unfolded the note.

> You insist that it is I who follow you. But then why do you appear to me when I least expect you? Fate wants us to be together and as you know, I'm not one to go against Fate. I'll see you soon. I promise.

There was no name, but there didn't need to be. She knew exactly who left this note for her.

Alexander.

Phantom fingers tightened around her wrists and forearms, and she could all but feel the bruises that had long since faded. She could still smell the scent of Alexander's breath when he used to pull her close and threaten her. Onions and weed.

Melanie's limbs started to shake, and she crumpled the paper in her hand and threw it for all she was worth.

See you soon.

The words haunted her. She knew he'd search her out. She'd been naïve to think that the restraining order would keep him away. Okay, it had. For three weeks. It was the longest period of time she'd ever gone without seeing him. She'd actually believed that he'd forgotten about her, that maybe, just maybe he'd moved on and she wouldn't have to look over her shoulder. She should have known better.

She curled her fingers into her palms to stop the trembling in her hands. She forced herself to finish her chores and clocked out.

• • •

"Is everything all right?"

Joel's brow was wrinkled in concern. He was wearing another graphic tee, this one with "bow ties are cool" plastered across the front. She could feel his eyes assessing every last inch of her as they sat across from each other in a classroom at the community center, reading the stress in her shoulders and neck.

She almost couldn't stand it. She rubbed at her temples. She was supposed to be gathering information for Juliet, learning about her annoying abilities, but all her thoughts could do was circle around Alexander and how his stupid-ass note was going to ruin her mission and she'd let Nathan down.

Joel, Nathan, Alexander. Three men in her life. Three men too many.

She pushed harder against her temples and closed her eyes. "I'm fine," she lied to Joel.

Warm fingers encompassed her wrists. Melanie's eyes snapped open. Joel watched her carefully, gently tugging her hands away from her face. A few seconds later he released his hold and reached for her. Melanie had no idea what to expect, but when his strong fingers pressed against the sides of her head she nearly moaned. He rotated his fingers in a circular motion and she felt her eyes sliding shut.

"Tell me what's wrong," Joel's voice slid over her like silk.

His massage was lulling her into a daze, and she opened her mouth without thought. "It's—" She stopped as her mind caught up to what she was about to say. "It's nothing."

Joel's fingers froze.

Melanie bemoaned the loss of his massage. She didn't want him to stop. She hated how he was the only thing that eased the pressure in her chest. The only thing that eased the tension in her body, made her feel safe, secure, and every other girly tendency she shouldn't be feeling in his presence.

"Why don't you confide in me?" he asked in a hushed voice.

There really wasn't any need to whisper, but Melanie found herself doing it too, as if she couldn't draw in enough breath to speak louder. "I don't even know you."

Joel studied her. One of his hands fell away, but the other trailed down the side of her face. Slowly. So slowly.

Her heart stuttered in her chest. Her stomach clenched in anticipation.

His fingertip was so hot against her cheek it practically seared her skin and made her want things she hadn't wanted in quite some time.

He traced down to her chin then lazily made his way back up. He took a detour at the level of her mouth. His finger brushed the edge of her lips and recklessly Melanie opened her mouth. Her tongue darted out and laved the tip of his finger, coaxing it to come closer.

Joel inhaled sharply. The dark blue in his eyes churned with raw emotion.

Melanie's breasts ached and heat pooled low in her abdomen. She drew Joel's finger further into her mouth.

His gaze never left her, and she'd never felt a stronger connection with someone. She should feel embarrassed by her actions, but she wasn't. She enjoyed the animalistic desire staring back at her, the way Joel's Adam's apple bobbed and the muscles in his neck bunched. She was driving him nuts and she loved it.

She ran her tongue over a callus and bit down just behind his nail bed.

"Fuck." He hastily glanced to the front of the room where two people were working on laptops, with their headphones on. Neither one even looked up at the sound.

With one final suck she released his finger. His hand dropped to the table like a lead weight. Joel didn't even seem to notice.

What are you doing, Melanie? her inner voice of reason spoke up.

She didn't know. She didn't know anything anymore.

"I don't even know you," she repeated. Maybe if she spoke the words aloud, her brain would stop what her body seemed to be doing all on its own.

Joel's knee brushed hers under the table as he slid closer. "Sometimes you only need to know what you already know, and fate will take care of the rest."

Melanie reared back from him. His words were like a slap in her face.

Fate. That damned goddess Alexander worshiped.

Could it be possible that Joel was as deluded as Alexander? Had she read Joel wrong? That she was falling for the same kind of guy all over again ate at her.

Wait … falling?

She cursed herself mentally. It was true. His charming, nervous boy routine was lowering her defenses. He was just so damn caring. Even now his face held nothing but worry.

"What's wrong?" He reached for her, but she pulled her hand away. The muscles in his jaw bunched at her retreat. "And don't tell me it's nothing," he added before she could open her mouth and say it. "Something made you shut down. What is it? You look frazzled. You can't hold it all in. Eventually you'll need an outlet."

"And you volunteer to be that outlet?" she snapped at him. She should have known this was bound to come back to sex. It always did when it came to men. God, she'd been an idiot, and here a few seconds ago she'd almost admitted to falling for the guy.

But Joel surprised her. "I'll always be here for you," he said without a hint of anything more attached to the statement. "Everyone needs someone to talk to, someone to listen to them. But if you don't want me around, I'll leave. I won't force my company on you."

Heat flooded Melanie's cheeks. What was wrong with her? She was sending mixed signals left and right and couldn't seem to stop herself. She was out of control and she didn't like it.

Focus.

Yes, she had a lot on her plate, but she could deal, she always did.

When Joel started to rise from his seat, she was the one to reach out. Her heart quivered when her fingers touched the back of his hand, and she started to trace the scars beneath her fingertips.

And just like that, desire flared between them again. It filled the room until it was a wonder the two people at the front couldn't feel the weight of it.

"How did you get them?" she asked.

Joel stared down, studying her. Whatever he saw made him sit back down. "Cars," he said simply. "My dad used to own a '73 Pontiac Firebird, red," he said with a grin, like the color meant everything. "I used to help him work on it. My mother hated it, hated how cut up I used to get because I never paid any attention to the danger. I never wore the gloves she got me, either. She used to get so mad at Dad for not enforcing the covered hands rule. I just liked taking things apart with my hands and putting them back together again." He shrugged. "But Dad knew the importance of getting your hands dirty. I used to have oil and grease in my fingernails for weeks." He stared down at his nail beds, as if imagining the grime there again.

She withdrew her hands and folded them into her lap, tracing the carvings in the wood tabletop with her eyes to keep them from drifting to Joel. "I received a note earlier today," she said when she built up the nerve. Joel was silent, and she wanted so badly to look up and see the expression his face held, but she plowed on.

"It was from my ex." She heard a knuckle pop. Still, she kept her eyes down. "I put a restraining order on him weeks ago, and I really thought he'd stay away this time, but apparently my new job is somewhere he frequents. So, of course, he thinks this is a sign from Fate—that bitch goddess he seems to love so much." She gave a snort. "I don't even know if Fate is a real goddess or not, but either way he thinks we're meant to be together." She shook her head and finally lifted her head. "It's not, though—a sign, I mean. There's no such thing as destiny. Fate doesn't decide who we love. We do. Free will. I thought I loved him, but love doesn't hurt you intentionally." She realized too late that she'd slipped. Let go of something she didn't intend to. "Not that kind of hurt anyway," she whispered.

Joel's eyes widened at the word *hurt*. His face darkened with rage. Trepidation crept up Melanie's spine, but Joel's anger wasn't directed at her.

"He never hit me," she explained, though she had no idea why she was defending Alexander. "He used to leave lots of bruises on my arms. He liked to grab me, especially when we'd get into arguments, as if he could force his opinion into me with nothing but the pressure of his fingers on my skin." *Never again.* "He's also the reason why I carry this around." She pulled out her key chain and showed him the bright pink can of pepper spray.

"So that is why you pulled away from me earlier when I mentioned fate?" Joel asked carefully.

She nodded. "There's no such thing. It's just an excuse. A reason someone can keep pursuing another when clearly the interest is only one-sided."

Joel's shoulders slumped and something passed through his eyes too quickly for Melanie to identify. She felt as if she'd let him down.

"What's this guy's name?"

"Alexander." She didn't offer his last name.

She didn't trust the dangerous and protective glint in his eye.

"If he ever shows up at your work, you call me." He pulled a business card from his wallet and handed it to her. "Call me whenever you need anything. And I mean that. *Anything.*"

Again, if she'd received that line from any other man, she'd have taken it sexually, but maybe that wasn't the case with Joel.

Maybe he cared about her and she'd been too caught up in her own problems to probe deeper into why that was.

What was so special about her?

Besides the obvious supernatural ability she held.

It was a mystery she was determined to unravel, but the moment had passed.

Already Joel was shifting into mentor mode. He let his arm fall across the table, his palm open to the ceiling. "Okay," he told her, "training starts now. Try and take my ability. I want you to Lock my arm to the table as well as my index and middle finger together."

Chapter 9

She didn't believe in fate. She didn't believe in destiny. And Joel knew Melanie sure as hell wouldn't believe in Mirror Mates.

Maybe that was a blessing in disguise.

He drove home in silence, his mind replaying his conversation with Melanie. His fingers tightened around his steering wheel at the idea of that bastard Alexander leaving bruises on her. He ground his teeth and pulled into his driveway. He shoved his truck into park perhaps a bit too forcefully and slammed the door as he took his front stairs in one big leap.

There was a message waiting for him on his cell when he pulled it out. Sydney. The last person he wanted to hear from right now. Ignoring the voicemail, he pitched his cell into the living room as he headed to the kitchen.

He fixed himself something to eat before calling Felix. He needed a distraction from Melanie. While things were taking a step in the right direction, he had no idea how he was going to breach the topic of Mirror Mates, or even if he should.

"Please tell me you have something to report on these new suit guys?" Joel asked as soon as Felix picked up.

"Sorry, man, nothing. The only new information we have is that these guys aren't working for Vander. Cali got ahold of Jente. We ruled out that it's not them. Cali asked Jente to let her know if he comes across anything else." Joel could hear the repressed anger in Felix's voice. Nearly a year ago Vander Donahughe had abducted Cali, and it still rubbed Felix the wrong way that Jente and not he had been the one to save her from that horror house.

"I guess if anyone can gather information on these suit guys, it's that kid," Joel said. Jente was a Veiler, so he had the ability to turn invisible, which made him such a great commodity. The only problem was that he worked for Vander. He couldn't be trusted, but what choice did they have at this point? Joel was coming up with nothing electronically. And now they knew these goons didn't work for Vander. Joel didn't like how this was playing out one bit. New meat sniffing around was not what he needed. It stacked the odds against them, and now that Melanie had shown up in his life, he had one more person to worry about.

"Did you listen to the message Sydney left you yet?" Felix asked, breaking Joel from his thoughts.

He should have known Sydney would ask Felix to do her dirty work. Sydney and Felix had been best friends for years, well before the Guild of Aletheia was ever formed. "Not yet. Want to give me the Cliffs Notes version?"

"Niella called in sick today at the clinic," Felix said.

And this was concerning, how?

"She's never called in sick before," Felix explained. "She's not sick either; she just didn't want to come in, which isn't like her."

"Maybe she wants a vacation."

Felix sighed. "I don't think that's it. Sydney's worried, Merrick's worried ... shit, we're all worried." Joel could all but see Felix running his hand through his hair, a habit he did whenever he was stressed out.

"Did anyone go check on her?" Joel was technically the closest and he could drive over if they needed him to.

"Luke and Cali drove over there earlier, but Niella didn't open the door. She talked to them through it."

Joel frowned. That didn't sound like Niella. She might close the door in your face, but she'd at least open it. Why didn't she want anyone to see her?

"We don't know what's wrong with her," Felix said. "Do you think you could search the web for anything?"

Joel was already on his way to his office. "I'm on it." He booted up his computer.

"How'd your date go with Melanie?"

Joel dropped down into his computer chair. "Not so good. I mean the lesson went great, but she … " He drifted off as he remembered her tongue along his finger, the wet heat of her mouth as she sucked on him. His blood quickened.

"If you dozing off is any indication, than I don't think it went that bad." Felix's voice held a smile.

Joel wished that was all that happened. Well, if he were honest, he'd wished more than her mouth on his finger had happened. "She doesn't believe in fate," he confided to Felix. "Or destiny or anything like that, where a higher power is in control of who she loves."

Felix was quiet for a moment. "That could be a problem."

"Maybe not. I mean, I'm only here to keep her safe."

Silence. Then finally, "Joel, she's your Mirror Mate."

"We don't know that."

"Why are you denying this?" Felix asked.

"Because I'm not ready for it," he confessed.

Felix laughed without humor. "What a bunch we make, huh? Our whole guild knows about Mirror Mates, and what do we do when we find them? Hop on the denial train. Cali denied it, Sydney did, Merrick too. Now you. You'd think we'd know better by now, but I guess it's human nature or something."

"Or something," Joel mumbled.

Was he being unreasonable? To deny something he'd dreamed of simply because he wasn't ready?

Was this fate's way of saying, "So you had a bad breakup. Life goes on. Now start living"?

"So she's not your Mirror Mate," Felix said with an air that made it obvious he thought Joel was an idiot. "Where did this disbelief in fate come from?"

"It turns out that her last boyfriend would get a little violent with her, and he believed fate wanted them to be together."

"Well, shit."

"In a nutshell. Things were going great between us and then she mentioned something about not knowing me and I stupidly opened my mouth, telling her that she knew enough and that fate would take care of the rest or some bullshit. It completely freaked her out."

"Why'd you bring up fate in the first place if you didn't think she was your Mirror Mate?" Felix said with annoying rationale.

Angry silence was Joel's answer.

"Look, I know right now you think Melanie isn't your Mirror Mate, but *if* she is, trust me when I say that everything you're going through now will be worth it in the end. The feeling you get when the bond is complete is simply indescribable."

Joel could only imagine. He felt the spark between himself and Melanie, couldn't imagine a stronger chemistry with anyone. He'd been so content with Sydney that he didn't think there was anything more out there. How wrong he'd been. What he felt for Melanie was intoxicating. He wanted to hear her voice, touch her skin, and breathe in her scent. He wanted to be able to put a sparkle in her eye and a flush on her cheeks.

You're in over your head, Kegler.

Maybe.

Maybe he was an idiot for ignoring what appeared to be right in front of him, but he didn't care. He was going to be there for Melanie. As much as he'd love to knock that bastard Alexander's teeth in, he wasn't a fighter like Felix was. If by chance Joel ever learned that fucker's last name, perhaps he'd ruin his credit scores and destroy his whole electronic identity.

The thought made him smile.

"You still there?"

He'd forgotten he was even on the phone. He chatted a little more with Felix before hanging up and searching for anything on Niella's condition.

The task was a good distraction from Melanie and Mirror Mates.

• • •

Melanie blinked, certain she wasn't seeing properly. Nope, nothing wrong with her eyes. Joel was sitting on a yoga mat on the far left side of her class, waving her over. He was in black basketball shorts and another graphic tee. This time it was Batman.

"What are you doing here?" she whispered as she rolled her mat out beside him.

A couple of people shot her dirty looks for making noise during their warm up stretches, but she ignored them. Joel didn't even seem to notice them.

He spread his arms wide. "I signed up for yoga with you," he said brightly. Then he proceeded to try to get his fingers to touch behind his back in that age-old test kids had been doing since grade school. "Think it'll help me with this?"

Melanie failed to repress her smile. "You do realize there's no talking during yoga, right?"

More angry glares and Melanie jerked her head in their direction.

Joel dropped his arms to his side. "I thought that was only for certain kinds."

She covered her laugh with a cough.

"Well, this was pointless," Joel mumbled, but it was too late to help him slip out. The instructor came in and started the session.

Melanie was oddly pleased at Joel's surprise appearance. It'd been a long time since she'd gotten this kind of male attention—healthy male attention. He wasn't a barfly ogling her, he wasn't stalking her out of some sick obsession, he was genuinely interested in spending time with her. She also had to admit that she didn't mind the view either. As the instructor took them through the poses, her gaze kept drifting over to Joel and the black material of his shirt stretched taut over his back, showcasing all that lean muscle hidden underneath.

She wasn't the only one taking in the lone male in the class either. Three young women had set up shop behind Joel. Melanie narrowed her eyes every time she caught them staring. Especially when they giggled at Joel's lack of flexibility. Melanie had to bite her cheek a couple of times when he nearly fell over doing tree pose and warrior pose. He was a trouper though, never getting frustrated, just persisting.

He caught her staring a couple of times and gave her one of those grins. She was tremendously grateful she hadn't signed up for a hot yoga class. She would have died from heat stroke.

Off-limits, Melanie.

She knew she couldn't get involved, but that didn't mean she couldn't look.

Once the class was finished, Joel rolled up his mat and flopped it over his shoulder. "Want to grab a cold drink?"

"Yes." Her answer was immediate. She needed something to cool her off, and quickly.

It wasn't until they were standing in line for a smoothie that she realized this was their first time hanging out outside the community center.

This was almost like a real date.

She tried not to think on that too long. It made her objective sit like a stone in her gut. It was time to play detective for Juliet.

Melanie grabbed one of the tall, bar-style chairs set up at the front of the smoothie bar, looking out at the people walking by on the sidewalk. Joel took the seat next to her and she propped herself on her elbow, all nonchalant. "So," she took a sip of smoothie, "ever been to jail?"

Joel choked on his drink. "Where the hell did that come from?" he said, once his coughing subsided.

Way to blow it.

She shrugged one shoulder and tried to think of a believable lie. "It beat asking you what your favorite color was."

She could tell he didn't buy it. He watched her as he took a long pull on his smoothie, and she forced her eyes to stay on his.

"Can't say that I have, and blue."

"What?"

He put down his drink and reached for her. "You asked if I've ever been to jail, can't say that I have. As for my favorite color," he touched his thumb to the side of her eye, "it's blue."

Her pulse kick-started; she wanted to tell him blue was her favorite color too. Midnight blue. Heat pooled low in her belly and her breasts ached for him.

His hand dropped away. He went back to drinking his smoothie. "So tell me, have you ever been to the big house?"

She'd walked right into that one.

She should have expected him to turn the question back on her. It was only fair she reciprocate, but she wasn't very proud of her past. Nathan hadn't kept the best company in high school, and she'd hung out with the same crowd. She'd even dated one of her brother's friends who she'd thought was different than the rest, but it only sucked her further down the rabbit hole. It wasn't until he'd tried to force himself on her when they were both baked that she flipped her life around.

"I have a juvie record," she admitted after a big gulp of her smoothie.

"Seriously?"

She stared miserably into the top of her drink. "It wasn't my finest hour."

"High school isn't anyone's finest hour, trust me."

Something in his voice made her look up. She couldn't imagine the man in front of her having any difficulty in high school.

Stunning good looks, a rockin' bod, and brains to boot. What was hard for him?

He must've read her thoughts. He gave a short laugh. "I didn't look like this in high school, if that's what you're thinking. Cut my weight in half, slap on a ton of acne and a worse fashion sense. Oh, and add in my extracurricular activity of Magic: The Gathering and you got yourself a one-way ticket to Bully Bait, USA."

"I like your fashion," she said absently.

He stared down at the Batman symbol on his shirt and then swung his attention back up to her. He clearly couldn't believe it. "I think that's the nicest thing anyone has ever said to me. Can I have that in writing so I can show it to Niella?"

Melanie laughed and gave him a playful shove.

He rolled with the movement, graceful as could be.

"You've certainly filled out now. Who used to bully you?" She couldn't wrap her mind around the idea of someone picking on a younger version of Joel. He was probably the sweetest kid.

He shrugged one shoulder. "Jocks. They loved to pick on me around prom time 'cause they knew I'd never have a date. Then one year the principal's assistant asked me to be hers … the kiss of death."

"I take it she wasn't pretty?"

"She was fifty."

Melanie cringed.

"It wasn't my finest hour, to quote you from earlier. But I wouldn't change it for the world. My two younger brothers were the party animals. I got to live vicariously through them, which meant I got to pick their drunk asses up when they were sick from alcohol and needed a quick getaway car when the cops showed up to the parties they were at."

"I didn't know you had two younger brothers."

Another shrug. "Got one older one too." He took a long sip of his drink. "What about you? You mentioned a brother. Just the one?"

"Yeah, Nathan. We're only a year apart so we're pretty close. He's older, but that didn't matter. I used to hang out with him all the time in high school. He didn't have the best of friends, meaning they liked to pass needles and drink booze a lot. I steered clear of the needles, but I got into pot. I was caught with possession. My brother bailed me out and forged all the documents that needed to be filled out by my parents. He used to watch out for me all the time."

She didn't know what else to say after that. Nathan had been everything to her when she was growing up. They'd been made fun of in elementary school because their parents had strange accents and didn't follow American customs. Her father was from the Czech Republic and her mother from Greece. It wasn't until high school that they really branched out and made friends.

Nathan had been her rock for so many years. Now she was making her own path, trying her best to look after Nathan. She owed it to him.

"Hey," Joel's soft voice broke her thoughts. "Where'd you drift off to?"

She stared at Joel for a beat. It was easy to believe he knew all the answers. Joel didn't show an ounce of fear when it came to his powers. He knew his course, and that drew her to him, made him the perfect companion for this chapter of her life. She, too, wanted to know her course.

"Melanie?"

She blinked. "I'm sorry, got lost in thought."

"About your brother?" he hedged.

She wanted to lie. It was on the tip of her tongue. But again those eyes drew her in and she found herself sighing. "Yeah."

"How's he doing? You said he was a Dreamer, right?"

She reached for the leather band on her wrist and absently twisted it around and around. "Yeah, he's ... not doing the best."

Joel reached out and intertwined their fingers. "Niella, the Dreamer for our guild, she's not doing so great either. Sometimes I'm grateful for the powers I was given."

"Do you ever wish you were normal?" she whispered.

He was silent a moment. "I used to. I think it happens to all of us. I don't care who you are, when your powers first manifest, it's the worst thing in the world to deal with. No one likes to be out of control."

"Got that right," she muttered. She hated never knowing when her powers would activate, or what she'd do with them. What happened if she touched a regular person when her powers were activated? Could she harm someone without even knowing it? Their last lesson hadn't worked out so well. She hadn't been able to make her neck tingle. She'd sat there like an idiot, trying and failing to get her neck to do something—anything. She hoped it was a fluke, that she really wasn't cursed with some ability she'd have to hide for the rest of her life.

Joel squeezed her fingers. "It'll get better," he promised. "That's why I'm here. Every great superhero needs a mentor." He waggled his eyebrows.

She rolled her eyes, but she was smiling. "Aren't you supposed to have a long, gray beard or something?"

He grinned. "I can grow one out for you if you'd like."

She chuckled.

"What?"

She shook her head. "I just pictured you decked out like a Jedi with a gray beard. Somehow it doesn't seem that weird."

His gaze softened and his grin turned into something much warmer, more affectionate, and Melanie became intimately aware of their joined hands.

"How do you understand me so well?" he asked in wonder.

Because Nathan's life, and happiness, depended on it.

Chapter 10

Melanie stared, unseeing, out the bus window as she made her way home. She couldn't recall a night she'd had such a good time. She hadn't wanted the evening to end—they hadn't even had time to practice her powers—but suddenly it was late and she needed to get to bed.

She kept circling back to the way he looked at her, like she was a tall glass of water and he hadn't had a drink in months. It made her warm all over, and she found a dopey smile shining back at her in the reflection of the pane.

She turned from the image.

What was she doing?

This wasn't what Juliet meant when she said to get close to Joel.

She'd meant to learn all she could of her abilities from him. And Melanie's own agenda seemed to be backfiring as Joel got more information out of her than she did of him. Not to mention it appeared that he hadn't done anything criminal in his entire life.

She was grateful for that. She didn't want Joel to be one of those power-hungry monsters she'd read about in Juliet's database. He was just like her—an unfortunate cursed with an ability. But she'd return the favor—he was helping her and in return she'd make sure Juliet helped him.

She rested her head against the cool glass and watched the streetlights blur past. At home she slipped silently into her room and dressed for bed. She fluffed up her pillow and glanced at Nathan. His eyelashes fanned his cheeks and she stood over him, heart heavy in her chest.

She was his only hope.

She brushed the hair from his forehead and his blue eyes fluttered open. "Lanie?"

Melanie's breath caught. Was he caught in the throes of a vision, or was he really seeing her?

She rested her hand on his shoulder. "I'm here, Nathan."

His eyes swiveled around the room, as if he didn't know where he was.

She pressed firmer against his shoulder. "You're safe."

He relaxed into the bed. "Still watching out for me?"

"Always."

He suddenly squeezed his eyes shut, his whole body going tense.

"Nathan?" Her heart skipped a beat. Was he having some kind of panic attack? Withdrawal? Vision?

Her neck started to tingle in answer.

She gasped and slapped the hand over the back of her neck. But it was too late. The hand on Nathan's shoulder was the only connection her powers needed.

She stumbled back from Nathan as images assaulted her. She was in a home, but she couldn't make out the surroundings. It was as if the edges of her vision were blurred and she could only focus on the short-haired woman sitting in a wheelchair in the middle of the living room. An episode of *The Bachelor* played on TV; the finalists waited for their roses. The woman shook her head, clutched the notebook that rested in her lap, then suddenly wheeled herself from the room as if trying to escape whatever was bothering her. Her wheelchair hit against the table and her notebook flew from her lap. The woman kept going, up the ramp that led to her front door and out into the night. It was foggy, the marine layer coming off the ocean and into the streets; Melanie could smell the salt. The woman kept going, one of her hands intermittently coming up to her head, as if she could stop whatever went on in there. Her wheelchair dipped down a ramp at the corner of a street. The woman's head swiveled as a car with no headlights came out of nowhere …

Melanie blinked furiously, her whole body trembling. She was in her room again, flat on her back. Nathan held her in his arms, muttering soothing words and rocking her. She stared up into his eyes and found them the clearest she'd ever seen.

She reached one shaky hand up to cup his cheek. "You're up," she said inanely.

Nathan's smile was strained. "And you're down. Lanie, what did you do?"

She massaged her temple, her heart still pounding furiously in her chest. Trepidation racked her body. Who had that woman been? Her stomach lurched as she remembered seeing the car hit her.

Melanie wanted to curl up into a ball and cry. It was clear the woman had been in some kind of mental distress. She'd been watching TV but not been paying it much attention. And that was when Melanie focused on what she was shown of the episode. Her aunt liked to watch *The Bachelor*, but there were way more contestants still on the show than what Melanie saw on that woman's TV.

Icy cold fingers circled her heart.

She'd seen the future.

This woman, whoever she was, only had a couple more weeks to live. If that.

Melanie pressed the back of her hand into her mouth to keep herself from losing her dinner. "Oh God," she whispered.

Nathan gripped her chin and forced her gaze to his. He searched her face. "Lanie! Talk to me. What just happened?"

She couldn't open her mouth for fear of vomiting. She shook her head, tears pooling in her eyes.

Nathan's eyes softened in sympathy. "You had a vision," he said it matter-of-factly.

She could do nothing but nod.

Nathan swore under his breath. "You took my vision. I could feel it coming on, it was right there, and then suddenly it was gone." It was his turn to shake his head. "How the hell is that possible?" He looked down at her with such fierce protection. "Somehow they transferred to you. I can feel it, they're gone. I … I haven't felt like this in so long. I'm so sorry, Lanie." He pulled her close and rested his chin against her head.

She didn't know how long she stayed like that. Until the tremors stopped, that much she knew.

"It won't last." She spoke into her brother's neck when she could.

He leaned back. "What?"

"Your powers, they'll come back. It won't last." Her heart tore when she saw the look in her brother's eye.

"I knew it was too good to be true," he mumbled. Then louder, "How did you take them in the first place?"

Melanie extracted herself from his embrace and together they got up and sat on their respective beds. It reminded her of when they were younger and used to talk all the time. She hadn't realized how much she'd missed it until that moment. She felt sick all over again at the thought that this might be one of the last times she'd be able to do this with her brother. Her throat clogged with unshed tears.

"Lanie?"

She cleared her throat and wiped furiously at her eyes. "Sorry. It appears you weren't the only one in the family that got some kind of power."

"Son of a bitch," Nathan swore.

"I can … " She took a deep breath and told herself it would get easier the more she said it. "I can take another person's powers, temporarily."

Nathan swore again, his hands balled into fists. "I'm so sorry, Lanie." They were both silent for a few seconds. "I guess when it came to the talent part of our genetics, we got the shit end of it, huh?"

A small chuckle bubbled up from somewhere deep within her. "Yeah, it looks like the curse on the Vyntra family continues."

Nathan stared down at his white knuckles. "This is so fucking unfair. We never wanted these. We never asked for them."

"I know." Melanie tried to console him.

He turned on her. "No, Lanie. You don't know, and that was the whole point. You shouldn't know. You should never have to go through what I do. You think I haven't been aware of what my condition is doing to this family? I can see how tired you are, the circles under your eyes, the dust building on the college applications you keep under your bed. You've put everything on hold to help the family because my life decided to take a shit on me. You put your career of becoming a community center coordinator on hold because of these damned powers. And now it's sucking you in too." He threw the closest object near him, which thankfully turned out to be a pillow. It bounced off the wall harmlessly. "When does it end? Huh?" His eyes burned into hers, but she knew he didn't expect an answer. The harsh lines of his face softened with his voice. "Are we to go insane together, Lanie? Is that our fate?"

She bristled at the mention of fate. "No," she said fiercely. "I found people who can help us. Seriously help us," she clarified when she saw his dubious expression.

Nathan wasn't fooled for a second. "What do they get out of it?"

"Me."

Nathan shot to his feet.

Melanie held out her hands. "It's not like that," she said hastily. "They know of my ability and they want to use me to get close to some other people with powers." She sighed and rubbed her tired eyes. "It's one big complicated mess that I still haven't wrapped my head around yet."

"Do you trust these people?"

"For now."

He sat back down, was quiet for a moment as he glanced around the room. "Do we have any alcohol in here?"

"Nathan ... "

"I know," he cut in. "But I can't help it, you said the respite wasn't going to last." His gaze latched on to hers. "I'm afraid, Lanie. I'm sick of seeing the faces, I'm sick of all the death and destruction. I want it to stop, and this is the only way until I get that help you mentioned. I know what I'm doing is weak, and I hate it. But ... please."

• • •

Joel sat with his laptop in the middle of Syd's clinic. He was busy answering emails, trying to keep his mind off Melanie and how he wouldn't see her for another day, while Syd and Luke cleaned up. Cali and Niella were at the reception desk computer, looking through wedding stuff while they waited for Merrick and Felix to arrive.

"What do you think of these flowers? Normally I don't go for flowers, but I think this would look sexy in the front pocket of Felix's suit or pinned to the front. Whichever."

Joel shuddered.

Cali noticed. Her dark head of hair popped up over the computer and her onyx eyes narrowed at him. "You can't even see the flowers from over there, so shut it."

"I didn't say anything," he protested, then mumbled under his breath, "Bridezilla."

A dog biscuit hurled through the air and smacked him in the side of the face. A big dog biscuit.

"Hey!"

Cali's face was the perfect expression of innocence.

Joel rubbed the side of his face but refrained from mumbling under his breath. With a Silencer it was useless. Cali would able to hear everything; it was part of her gift to heighten her own ears and manipulate how others perceived sound. "When's Felix getting here?" he asked instead. "All this estrogen is choking me."

This time he was prepared for the flying biscuit. He ducked and it sailed harmlessly over his head.

"He'll be here soon," said Cali. "But don't think just because he gets here the wedding talk will stop. He has to weigh in on the flowers, too, you know."

Joel groaned. "Niella, please tell me you're not letting Cali pick ridiculous flowers for us to wear in her wedding party."

"I've got Niella in the romantic mood," Cali boasted. "I even caught her watching *The Bachelor* the other day."

He perked up at this revelation. "No way." The idea was unheard of, but it had to be true because Niella shrank down into her wheelchair like a turtle trying to hide.

"Not a word, both of you. I just so happen to think the guy is hot. That's it," she said.

Cali tossed her hair over one shoulder. "Well, if you're into those blond, green-eyed types, you should just hang out at the pizza place a few doors over. Don't either of you repeat this to Felix, but Tom's quite the looker."

Niella shifted uncomfortably in her seat. Joel was about to comment on her unease when another voice spoke up.

"So the truth comes out."

Cali jumped at the sound of Felix's voice. She swore under her breath but quickly plastered a smile on her face. "Felix!"

Felix's blue green eyes sparkled with humor. "Don't you 'Felix' me, I heard what you said. Tom lover. You and Syd should start a club."

"Sydney likes Tom?" Joel asked. She'd never mentioned that before.

Felix grinned. "Oh yeah, big time. Like the biggest crush I'd ever seen when she was younger."

"I never knew that," Joel said absently. *More secrets she kept from me.* But a small twinge in his chest was the only reaction he got.

"I didn't know either," a new voice came from the far end of the room where Merrick must have slipped in through the back door.

So Syd kept things even from her Mirror Mate. Merrick's confession made Joel feel a little bit better.

Sydney came up behind him. "Didn't know what either?"

Felix and Joel shared a look, hiding their smiles in their hands.

Merrick caught the look that passed between them and gave them the smallest hint of a smile before his face turned to stone. "That you have feelings for Tom Larkin, the pizza man a few shops down."

As if there was any other pizza maker in the Costa Mesa/ Newport area with that name.

Sydney's smiled faltered. Felix didn't even try to hide his grin anymore. "That was ages ago. Who said I still had feelings for him?"

"The blush on your cheeks," Cali supplied helpfully.

Sydney's hands flew to her face. Merrick chuckled. When Sydney turned her heated eyes on him, he tried to turn it into a cough.

"You don't even care, do you?" Sydney's face was completely red now. "You just wanted to give me a hard time." She pointed a finger at Felix. "This was all your doing."

Felix shrugged without a care in the world. "Hey, I'm just as outraged as you."

As if, Joel thought, but continued to enjoy the spectacle before him. He watched as the couples bickered and teased, noted the differences in personality and how they each made it work. Could he and Melanie make it work? Could he make more out of the attraction they had, build more out of their chemistry, like a lasting relationship?

Did he want to?

Chapter 11

Joel was in the exact same spot as when Melanie first saw him in yoga class.

"I thought you weren't coming back once you found out you can't talk during the sessions," Melanie said by way of greeting.

"I already paid for the class, might as well get my money's worth, right? Plus, the view isn't so bad." He winked at her, but his playful manner didn't cover the sense of wariness she got off of him.

"Is everything all right?" She ignored the angry scowls women warming up sent her way.

He rolled his shoulders as if trying to ease some tension. His chest strained his tee and Melanie found herself entranced by the image of Darth Vader and "I give free throat hugs" written underneath. "Just a rough day yesterday," he said.

Melanie made a noise in the back of her throat. "I know the feeling."

"What's wrong?" He reached out and captured her hand in his. The warmth of his skin seeped into her body. The contact made her nipples hard and the ache in her chest ease.

She wrenched her hand from his.

The last forty-eight hours hadn't been all sunshine and rainbows. Her short moments with lucid Nathan had ended with her trying to keep him sober. She'd attempted to talk to him, keep him distracted—anything to stay away from the alcohol, but she'd been exhausted. She'd tried to stay up as long as she could, but eventually she'd succumbed to sleep and woke the next day to find Nathan passed out on his bed, an empty bottle of vodka on the nightstand. It tore at her heart when she thought of how vulnerable and weak he'd sounded. She should have tried harder to stay awake all night with him.

And on top of that haunting memory was the horrifying vision she'd had when she'd taken Nathan's powers. She couldn't shake it. Every time she closed her eyes she saw that woman's face, the vehicle hitting her wheelchair, and a snapshot of *The Bachelor*—the countdown to how much time the woman had left. Yesterday Melanie had sought out her aunt and asked how the show was going, how many weeks would it get down to the final two. The episode was less than three weeks away, and the thought made Melanie sick to her stomach.

She'd tried to contact Juliet, wanted to get answers. If this was what Nathan had to deal with, she wanted him fixed immediately. When Juliet's contact info went to voicemail, Melanie left a very terse response, asking where the hell they were and when were they going to do anything?

And then because her life just kept getting better, she'd seen Alexander before work yesterday, across the street, standing there watching her. She'd seen him for only a moment before a moving van blocked her view. When the van left, Alexander was gone. She'd spent her whole shift tense and sweating. Was he planning something? Should she file a police report again? She didn't know what to do and waiting was weighing heavily on her mental well-being.

She was emotionally exhausted and felt like a coward when she breathed a sigh of relief as the instructor came in to start their yoga.

She wouldn't have to talk to Joel, not yet anyway. She had till the end of class to figure out what she wanted to tell him, because they both knew he'd question her until he got some kind of answer.

When the hour was up, Melanie took her time getting her things together. It was a stall tactic that backfired when the room emptied, leaving her and Joel alone. He came up behind her, the heat of his body seeping into her back. He smelled like sweat, man, and, funny enough, electronics.

She sighed. "I don't feel like talking right now."

"That's fine." His breath ruffled her hair. "We don't have to talk."

She jumped when his arms came around her waist. She dropped her yoga mat but didn't dare reach for it. Her body was frozen—not in fear, oh no. Desire held her prisoner. All her soft curves were flush with the hard planes of his body. She wanted to arch further into him, but she didn't dare react. She wanted him to make the first move, wanted to know that she wasn't the only one trapped in this crazy sexual tension. And move he did. His hands inched up the sides of her body, tracing her rib cage, up, up, until they brushed the underside of her breasts. She drew in a ragged breath, silently willing his hands to move further up, to push harder. She wanted more friction; she wanted his hands all over her. She was a burning ball of need.

His breath tickled her neck. "Do you know how much it pains me to see you in these tight outfits but not be able to touch you?" His low voice slid over her, making goose bumps erupt along her arms.

He dragged his hands down her abdomen and back up again; this time when he reached her breasts he cupped one in each hand.

Melanie sighed, her head falling back in response to his touch. She was throbbing all over, moisture collecting between her legs. For the first time in forty-eight hours she wasn't thinking about anything—except Joel. She wanted to see him naked. She wanted to taste his salty sweet skin and explore his entire body with her hands, her tongue, until he was nothing but a puddle of desire.

One of his hands ventured south again, his palm lazily sliding down her stomach, over to her hipbone and then … further.

She swallowed thickly when he didn't go back up like she'd expected. Instead, his hand crept slowly toward her center, where she ached fiercely. His fingers danced over her most sensitive flesh, and when he slid his hand in between her legs to cup her, she moaned.

"Are you wet?"

She could feel an impressive erection pushing into her backside, and she melted into him, eliciting a growl from deep in his throat. The sound made her wild. Or maybe that was from Joel torturously gliding his fingers back and forth over her sex.

Her legs wanted to give out and she had a mental image of the two of them getting down and dirty right there on her yoga mat. She entertained the idea more than she should have.

When she spoke her voice came out shaky. "We can't do anything, Joel. What if someone comes in?"

His arms tightened around her like a boa constrictor, bringing her that much closer to all that lean muscle. "I could Lock the door," he suggested in her ear.

No one would be able to come into the classroom then. They'd be alone for however long Joel wanted them to be. She shivered. The idea appealed to her way too much.

But what if they break down the door?

She couldn't see the community center being that desperate for a room.

"Cameras," she spoke aloud, not sure why she was looking for excuses to get out of this situation.

Joel's hot mouth pressed an open kiss below her ear. "I don't see any in here, do you?"

She quickly scanned the ceiling and found nothing. Joel sucked her ear lobe between his lips and her eyes slid shut.

He disappeared from behind her, taking all that glorious body heat with him. She heard a faint *clink* and Joel was back. Her pulse spiked as she realized he'd actually Locked them in.

Anticipation made her whole body quiver.

She didn't dare turn around when she felt him return. She waited; there was a faint *whoosh* and then the sound of something soft hitting the floor.

He's laying out his yoga mat.

Her heart tripped over itself. Her nerves were on overdrive.

"Afraid to turn around?" he whispered huskily.

She licked her lips. "Yes." There was no need to lie. But she wasn't afraid of Joel; she was afraid of what she might do. That feeling of being out of control was back and she didn't like it—or she liked it too much. Either option frightened her.

As if he understood her unspoken thoughts, he chuckled. "No need to be afraid, Melanie. I'm right here."

I'll always be here.

The statement hung in the air unspoken. And for once Melanie let herself believe it.

She turned to face him. He was breathing just as unsteadily as she. His eyes swirled with desire, roaming over her body, and she felt their touch like a physical caress.

She reached out to touch his chest. She could feel his heart beneath her palm, and for a moment she let herself marvel in the strength of its beating.

She stepped into him and his arms went around her like it was second nature. It felt right. It felt good. But not as good as when his lips came down on hers.

They stole the breath from her lungs and lit her nerve endings on fire. She pushed closer against him and twined her arms around his neck. Her breasts pressed against his chest; one of his hands moved from around her waist to cup her bottom, drawing her hips flush with his.

They both groaned at the contact.

His erection pressed hard into her hip and she untwined one arm from around him to stroke him through his shorts.

He cursed under his breath and took hold of her wrist to bring her arm back around his neck. "I'm not going to last if you keep touching me like that."

She nipped his bottom lip. "Maybe I don't want you to last."

Joel closed his eyes as if trying to draw strength from within. "Jesus, Melanie," was all he said. "You slay me."

His words made her feel powerful and sexy, and she loved every minute of it. "You make me feel more alive than I've felt in a very long time," she confessed.

Those midnight eyes opened and fixed on her. He cupped her cheek and brushed his thumb across her skin. "I know the feeling."

This time his kiss was painfully slow, creating a gentle warmth in the pit of her stomach that radiated out. Joel was a man who could make a woman melt. She was halfway gone when the handle on the door jiggled.

They both looked up.

The door shook, but Joel's Lock stayed intact. Muttered cursing came from the other side and Melanie grinned. Joel mirrored her grin. His eyes glittered with mischief, like a little kid getting away with a prank, and she wanted to kiss him all the more.

"What do you say? Want to stick around and see how far they go to get the door open or blow this Popsicle stand?"

Melanie arched a brow as a wicked idea came to her. "Want to see how far they'd go if we pretended to be locked inside and freaking out?"

Joel laughed. "You're a little rebel, aren't you?"

She looked meaningfully at his Darth Vader shirt. "Just call me Princess Leia."

She grabbed his ass.

Chapter 12

Joel couldn't get the image of Melanie in a Princess Leia slave costume out of his head. All that creamy skin exposed, her silver-blonde hair shining, those crystal-blue eyes flaring with heat.

They'd driven down to the beach after making a break from the community center. Melanie had cracked. She didn't want the community center staff to break anything unnecessarily and she didn't want to get banned from the establishment for any reason, so they'd Unlocked the door and made a run for it.

They stood on the boardwalk, Melanie slipping her shoes off to walk in the sand. They'd just missed the sunset, but the lingering light still hung in the air. The wind carried the salty scent of the ocean, and Joel breathed it in deeply. He'd never tire of that smell.

He followed Melanie as she made her way to the water.

They passed an empty, boarded lifeguard tower and Joel nudged her. "Hey, want to sit up there?"

"Sure."

They situated themselves on the tower, legs dangling over the edge. Joel glanced at Melanie out of the corner of his eye. She seemed better than when he'd first seen her walk into yoga that evening. There had been something in the air around her, a sadness that had pulled at Joel, but the class had started before he could get any information out of her.

He could make out the lingering sadness coming back. It was in every step she took, the slight hunch to her shoulders, and lack of bounce in her step.

He bumped his shoulder against hers. "Want to tell me what's bothering you?"

She tightened her jacket as the wind kicked up.

He wrapped his arm around her, expecting her to stiffen. Instead, she snuggled into him and rested her head on his shoulder.

He was finally doing something right.

"Can I ask you something?" she said.

"Sure." He didn't point out that she was avoiding his question.

"How does your friend, the Dreamer, keep herself … ?" She sighed and started over. "How does she deal with all her visions?"

So that's what's bothering her.

She was worried about her brother.

Joel tried not to dwell on Niella's dwindling mental health. That was not the comforting information Melanie sought.

He stared out at the waves. "She writes stuff down. I think it helps her keep her Dreams and the real world separate. Acts like a barrier, I guess. If she writes them down right away, she can put them out of her mind and try to forget about them. They're out of her head, you know?"

She moved off his shoulder. "It's that simple for her?"

He shrugged. "I don't know about simple, but I think it eases the burden. She has this notebook she carries around all the time." Melanie's body stiffened at the mention of a notebook, but he hesitantly continued. "I don't know what she writes in it, I've never looked, but maybe it's therapeutic and can help your brother."

She was quiet for a moment. "Maybe. So there's no … cure?"

It was the perfect opening for Joel to mention Mirror Mates. Did he dare?

He didn't want to scare her off. Hell, he didn't want to have to answer her if she asked him outright if they were Mirror Mates.

As they sat together watching the vast ocean, the waves crashing rhythmically into the sand, he came to a decision. He wouldn't keep her in the dark any longer. She needed to learn about Mirror Mates eventually, and he wanted her to hear it from him first. If she met the guild then it would only be a matter of time until Cali or Sydney mentioned Melanie's possible connection to Joel.

"There is one way," he said.

Her head snapped around so fast he could all but feel the whiplash. "There is?"

Was that fear in her eyes?

"Niella will able to control her Dreams if and when she becomes full-forced." He'd keep the conversation all about Niella. He'd let Melanie come to her own conclusions about them.

"Full-forced?"

He puffed out his chest. "It's a term I came up with." Felix would have his neck if he knew Joel was cutting him out of the credit. "It signifies when an individual with powers experiences an added boost to their ability and gains complete control over them."

He waited for the next question.

"How does someone become 'full-forced'?"

He kept his expression as neutral as possible, channeling his inner Jedi, while holding his breath at the same time. "They find and bond with their soul mate."

He dropped his arm from around her as she nearly jumped out of her skin. "Soul mate?"

Think Jedi, think Jedi, think Jedi.

"Yes, Melanie, soul mates," he said as calmly as possible. "Out there somewhere is a person's other half, and when people like us find it, we experience this instant connection, this yearning inside that draws us together. And once those two people bond, each person's powers are amplified—they become stronger and more controllable. Felix knew a Dreamer who could control what he saw and when. If the Dreamer can just withstand their journey leading up to that point, then they're free."

She'd scooted a few inches away from him on the lifeguard tower. Her hair flew around her head as she stared unseeing at the sand, eyes darting from side to side.

Shit. Had he overloaded her with too much information?

"Melanie?" he asked hesitantly. Should he reach out and touch her, or would that spook her?

"That's impossible," she said finally. "Soul mates don't exist. How do you know you're not being lied to?"

"Because there are four members in my guild, two couples, who are bonded with their Mirror Mates."

"Mirror Mate?" she asked incredulously.

"Another term I came up with."

"Why Mirrors?"

He rubbed the back of his neck. "It seemed like a good idea at the time. Have you ever been outside and the sun reflects off of a window or a mirror in a car and seems like it's so much more potent?"

She nodded.

"Well, when a person bonds with their Mirror Mate, their power is reflected back at them—stronger. Some of my guild members like to say that souls who truly reflect one another are destined to find one another." He waited for her recoil at the mention of destiny, but Melanie remained seated, digesting all he had to say.

"And you said there are people in your guild who are full-forced?"

He nodded. "My best friend, Felix, and his fiancé, Cali, as well as my friends Sydney and Merrick."

"But they still have their powers. If my brother became full-forced, he'd still have his powers?"

Joel nodded. "There's no way to get rid of someone's powers. They're a part of us."

"So you don't know of any other way someone could be cured?"

He frowned. "Not that I know of, but it's not like powers are a sickness, if that's what you're implying."

She grew silent, lost in thought as she stared at the white caps out in the distance. Joel had a strange lump in his gut and he couldn't place his finger on what it was. He only knew that Melanie's odd behavior worried him.

Full darkness fell and with it came a colder wind that went right through Joel's clothes. Melanie had to be freezing. "Let's get out of here."

She shook from the cold but managed a quick bob of her head in agreement.

They made their way back to his vehicle, but he held an arm out in front of Melanie to keep her from getting any closer.

A shadow moved in the dark, suspiciously close to his truck. "Hey!" he yelled.

The stranger froze and then made a run for it down a side alley.

"Son of a bitch." Joel sprinted over to his truck, Melanie right behind him.

"Did he take anything?"

The outside of the vehicle didn't look like anything had been taken. He pushed his face into the driver's side window to check that the radio was still there. It was.

"Huh," he said, a chill running down his spine.

"Maybe it was just someone looking for any visible cash in the car," Melanie said.

Joel turned in the direction the person had taken off, debating whether he should pursue them in his truck and figure out what the hell they'd been doing so close to his property. Ever since Vander came into their guild's lives he'd adopted a healthy dose of paranoia. And the idea of someone messing around with his truck didn't sit well with him.

He crouched down and checked the underside, looking for anything suspicious.

Melanie's face came into view on the other side. "What are we looking for down here?"

He wanted to tell her that he'd take care of it, that she could wait in the truck with the heater on so she wouldn't freeze her cute little ass off. But what if whoever that was had planted a bomb?

Okay, the idea was ridiculous, but he also knew Vander has made his dislike for the Guild of Truth very obvious. They'd been there every step of the way to keep Vander from the one thing he wanted: his Mirror Mate. For all Joel knew, Vander was keeping a low profile so he could pick off each member of the guild with a bomb, one by one. He was just the right amount of crazy super villain to do it, too.

"Look for anything that doesn't seem like it belongs," he told Melanie. "If you see anything blinking ... "

"Run?"

"Yeah, but don't forget to tell me first so I don't get blown to smithereens."

She shook her head at him, but she dutifully started to check the undercarriage of his truck. "I'm curious—who do you think would want to blow you up?"

"Wackos?" He didn't dare tell her about Vander, not right now, not when he'd already told her enough to saturate her brain. The last thing he wanted her to know was how potentially dangerous it was to hang out with him. It might scare her off, and at this point he couldn't stand the thought of losing her.

She seemed content with his answer and didn't ask further questions as she continued to search for any suspicious objects.

"Clear on this side," she said after a few moments.

Joel finished his fourth check, debating a fifth check when he gave up. "Same here." He hung his arms over the bed of his truck.

Melanie mimicked his moves on the opposite side, watching him. "You okay? You look confused that you didn't find anything. The guy was probably homeless, looking for something in the bed of your truck to pawn."

Joel couldn't shake the feeling that it wasn't some bum off the street who'd been near his vehicle. "Yeah, maybe."

He unlocked the doors and gave the interior of his truck a quick once over. Nothing looked touched. He sniffed the air, but there was no trace of gas or any other chemical he could detect.

Melanie was already buckled in and ready, her eyes taking in his every move, one brow arched as he sampled the air.

Heat rushed to his face— he probably looked like a freak. He cleared his throat and shoved his key into the ignition.

He needed to get over his paranoia. Everything was fine. He just needed to get Melanie home safe and sound.

Chapter 13

Melanie sat in the passenger seat as Joel took them up Newport Boulevard. Her head whirled with so many thoughts that she didn't know which ones to focus on.

Did she dare believe that Juliet could cure Nathan without this so called Mirror Mate? Should Melanie confide in Joel? Was Joel her Mirror Mate? She couldn't deny the instant attraction she felt the first time she'd laid eyes on him. Or the way her heart always seemed to flip in her chest when she saw him or even thought about meeting him. Then there was the fact that she felt a physical ache when he wasn't around, like her body craved—no, *needed*—him around. And it was only in his presence that the ache left her. Was she really buying into the whole soul mate concept? She couldn't believe she was even entertaining the idea. Alexander was the kind of guy who believed in things like fate. Joel … Joel was normal, the first normal guy she'd met in so long. She wasn't afraid of him. She enjoyed his company, and she loved the way he made her feel, as if she were a rare treasure and he was the luckiest guy in the world.

Soul mates.

Did she dare believe in some all-powerful being that decided who she should love?

What happened to free will? If she ended up with Joel, she wanted it to be because it was something *she* wanted, not because it was something destined for her.

If destiny really existed, that meant there was nothing she could do about anything in her life; she would live through every event knowing she had no power to change or alter it.

It's not true. It can't be.

There was that Dream she'd had when she'd taken Nathan's powers. That woman. Melanie had the power to change those events. Free will was all around her, shaping what the future could and couldn't be.

So, maybe she had to accept that certain things were fixed. Like whom she would love. Perhaps it was easier this way, to not have to worry about settling down with the wrong guy. There were worse things in the world than being stuck with someone like Joel. And if she really did believe what Joel was telling her, that would mean she would be guaranteed this one thing in life.

But did she dare believe it?

Around and around her thoughts went. She felt overwhelmed and rolled down her window an inch to let in some of the cool air, hoping it'd help clear her thoughts.

They started up the bridge that led over the bay. She wanted to remove her seat belt. It felt too tight, too constricting. She tugged at it, hoping to give herself more breathing room. It wouldn't budge. She frowned and tugged harder. When nothing happened she pushed the release so that she could re-buckle.

It didn't release.

Unease trickled down her neck. She turned in her seat and felt where the fabric dispenser connected near the passenger side door. Her fingers brushed over a small, metallic lump.

Frowning, she pulled at the object until it came loose. In the dim light of Joel's truck, she brought it up to her face to examine it more closely.

Her blood turned to ice as she stared at the small tracking chip. Or at least that's what she thought it was. Maybe it was a listening bug? She hadn't gotten a good look at the person who'd fled Joel's truck, and both she and Joel had checked the exterior for anything suspicious, but only Joel checked his side when he'd gotten inside.

Melanie's mouth went dry. She'd screwed up. Big time.

"What's wrong?" Joel turned to glance at her momentarily. His eyes snagged on the chip in her hand. "What the hell is that?"

Melanie's response was cut off as a tremendous force hit them from the left.

Melanie screamed as Joel's truck spun into the side of the bridge, hit the concrete wall, and tipped over.

She heard Joel grunt in pain as his truck hit the water. She could hear tires squealing and people yelling from the bridge, and then she heard something worse.

Rushing water.

Her eyes snapped open. They locked on Joel's and for the first time she realized that they were upside down and water was flooding in through the window she'd opened.

"It's okay," Joel said to her. He reached out and grasped her hand. "I'm going to get us out of this."

She wanted to ask how, but her heart was beating too frantically, her breath coming in too short gasps to speak. She nodded.

His truck groaned. Melanie whimpered.

Her traitorous mind decided at that moment to flash an image of her drowning. Panic seized her.

"Breathe, Melanie," Joel's soothing voice broke through her panic. She tried to focus on him and not the foot of water that was getting her hair wet or the fact that it was getting darker in the car as they sank further into the bay.

"Oh god." She squeezed her eyes shut.

"Breathe," Joel repeated. "I'm going to release my seat belt and then I'm going to get you out of yours, okay?"

She heard a *click* followed by a curse and a splash as Joel fell into the water and probably banged his head on the way down.

"Joel?" she squeaked, afraid he might have knocked himself unconscious. "Joel!"

Her eyes popped open to see Joel surface and shake his head. She was sprinkled with water, but the sight of him made her breathe easier.

"I'm right here." He shuffled over to her and pushed the release on her seat belt.

She braced for the fall that didn't happen. Her seat belt didn't open.

Joel's brows drew together as he pushed again.

Melanie shivered in her seat. "It won't open. I already tried earlier; that's how I found that bug. I'm trapped."

"No you're not," Joel said vehemently. He grasped her head in his hands and made her stare him in the eye. "I'm going to get you out of this."

The water was touching the top of her head now and she was trying really hard not to panic. Blood was rushing to her head too from being trapped upside down, the seatbelt holding her in place as the water filled the top of the vehicle.

Joel started looking through the cabin of his truck, talking aloud, no doubt to try and keep her calm. "There were lots of people out, someone had to have seen us. It's not that late. A rescue team will be on their way. I'm not leaving you, Melanie, even if I have to stay here and breathe for you with a straw until help arrives." He held an old straw in his hand that had fallen from his middle console when he'd opened it. A whole bunch of little tools had fallen out, too, and he quickly went diving for them.

He came up with needle-nosed pliers and tried to jimmy the seat belt. "If I can just get the damn thing open, I can take it apart and free you."

His hair was slicked back from his face as he worked. His shirt clung to his lean frame like a second skin, and Melanie focused her attention on following all the hard planes and ridges. It was a welcome distraction to the fact that water was now flirting with her eyebrows. Soon she wouldn't be able to keep her eyes open at all.

There was another groan from the truck and Joel's door was wrenched open. "What the—?"

Water flooded the cabin. Melanie slammed her eyes shut and suddenly she felt Joel's hands, the ones that had been grasping the belt and touching her hip, being torn away from her.

"No!" she screamed. Water flooded her mouth and she coughed, choked.

"Melanie!" She heard Joel's voice right before water took her hearing.

She reached out blindly to find him, but all she encountered was cold water. Her heart rate tripled. She was going to die. Joel was being rescued and she was going to be left behind. There was so much she hadn't said to him. So much she hadn't done with him. Tears clogged her throat. Her lungs started to burn and she felt herself losing consciousness.

Her heart cried out for him.

Joel!

In her oxygen-deprived mind she could have sworn she heard Joel's voice.

Melanie!

Everything went white.

Chapter 14

Melanie floated back to consciousness in intervals. She heard doctors and nurses and nothing. At one point, she woke to her throat and eyes burning … and then nothing. She had been cold and then hot.

When she woke for what she assumed was the fourth time, she felt like something the tide had dragged in. It was an accurate description, as she could feel her damp hair around her face and she felt raw all over, as if she'd been dragged through the sand a couple times. She surveyed her arms and found no abrasions, so that meant the pain was on the inside.

"I think she's coming to." A voice spoke from the corner.

Melanie's gaze darted to the far left side of her room where she was shocked to find her family.

"Ma, Pa, Aunt Bernie?" Her voice sounded like sandpaper. She winced and grasped the paper cup filled with water next to her bed. She took a hesitant sip.

"Oh, Melanie!" Her mother rushed to her side and knelt. Her graying hair was thrown haphazardly into a ponytail. Her father's face was drawn with concern as he stood behind her mother. Aunt Bernie stayed at the foot of her bed, a relieved smile on her face.

There was no sign of Joel. Yet somehow Melanie could tell that he was near.

She rested her hand over her heart where a deep, comforting warmth radiated. "Where's Joel?" she asked.

"Joel?" her mother echoed.

Her father placed his hand on her mother's shoulder. "The man in the accident with her. He was the one driving, I believe."

"Pa," Melanie warned. "The accident wasn't Joel's fault. Someone hit us."

Her father didn't look convinced. His face hardened into stone where it had been creased with worry only moments ago. "Who is this man? How long have you known him? What were you doing in a car with him? I thought you were taking time off from men after what happened with Alexander. This one clearly isn't any better; he nearly got you killed."

Melanie wanted to throw her hands in the air. Actually, what she really wanted to do was throw these blankets off and go look for Joel. Her father wouldn't listen to a word she had to say. She could praise Joel till the cows came home and her father would still think he was the scum of the universe.

"Who's watching Nathan?" she asked instead, wanting to take some of the attention off her and Joel.

"Paul is looking after him," Aunt Bernie answered.

Paul was Aunt Bernie's boyfriend, and while Melanie didn't always see eye to eye with him, she did trust him with Nathan. She breathed a little easier.

She started to get up, only to have her mother and aunt race to push her shoulders back down.

"You need your rest, Melanie," her mother said gently.

"Ma, I'm fine," she said through gritted teeth. She didn't like hospitals; she'd spent enough time with Nathan in them and they hadn't worked out so well for him.

Another thought hit her and she checked her arms again, this time looking for any puncture marks that would signal a blood draw. What if the hospital took a sample of her blood and it came back different than a normal human being's? She tried to recall all the times she'd come to the hospital with Nathan after he'd started having his headaches, all the times they'd gone to the ER after he'd had a vision, thinking at the time he'd swallowed some kind of toxin that was acting like a hallucinogenic. They'd drawn his blood then, hadn't they? And nothing had come up strange.

"Melanie, are you alright?" Aunt Bernie asked.

"Did they take any blood from me?"

Her mother took a step back at her aggressive tone. "Well, I'm not sure, Melanie, but why does it matter? Are you sure you're okay? Did you hit your head?"

Her father stared down at her, disapproving. "Were you taking illegal substances?"

Melanie barely refrained from rolling her eyes. Of course, her father's train of thought would lead there.

Her mother stifled a gasp. "Oh, Melanie."

"That's not it at all." Rage simmered under the surface. "I just want to get out of here." Who knew how long she'd been here. If it'd been for any length of time and the hospital took her blood, they'd know by now if anything was abnormal. Clearly no one had alerted her parents, and that had to count for something.

"Your release papers haven't come yet," her father's voice rumbled.

She pushed the blankets off and noticed for the first time that she was in a hospital gown. "Where are my clothes?"

She spotted her personal items in a bag, the clothes inside sopping wet. She groaned. Maybe the gift shop would have some sweats she could buy.

Aunt Bernie went over to one of the chairs and pulled out some fresh clothes from a duffle. "I thought you might need these." She held up a pair of hideous peach sweats. It wasn't the most attractive clothing, looking to have come from the back of Aunt Bernie's closet, but they were dry and warm.

Melanie smiled gratefully and took them. She quickly pulled the curtain around her bed, effectively forcing her family to take a few steps back and give her some space.

"Honestly, Melanie," her mother huffed. "I don't see what the big rush is. You were in a major accident; you need to remain here. Nathan is being taken care of, so I don't understand what the hurry is all about."

Her mother might not understand, but her father certainly did. "You aren't going to find that Joel character," he said in a stern voice.

Melanie heard her mother's sharp inhalation. "You're going to seek him out? Why? Who is this young man?"

There was no point lying now. "I want to make sure he's okay." She was getting antsy sitting here. She had to see him. She wanted to touch him, make sure he didn't have any scrapes or bruises. She wanted to breathe him in and feel his arms around her. She wanted it with a burning passion. Maybe she *had* hit her head on something, what else could be the cause of wanting to see him so badly?

She recalled the accident … thinking she was going to die, calling out to him, hearing him respond—but that wasn't right. It couldn't be. He'd been pulled from the car, so how could she have heard him as clearly as she'd thought?

"He nearly got you killed," her father's voice boomed, interrupting her thoughts. "And you want to make sure he's all right? You need to find him to get his insurance and lawyer information. You need to press charges for reckless driving. I want a restraining order on this man."

Once she was dressed in her aunt's peach-colored sweat suit, she shoved the curtain aside and shot her father a dark look. "For fuck's sake, Pa, would you listen to me when I tell you it wasn't his fault?"

Her parents stared at her as if she'd sprouted another head. "What did you just say to your father?" Ma asked in a small voice.

Heat rushed to Melanie's cheeks, but she vowed not to let them cow her. She was done being coddled. They were so worried something bad would happen to her after Nathan's addiction, they'd done everything they could to keep her safe and protected. Then Alexander had happened and her parents had tightened that vise of protection. She hadn't realized until that moment how suffocating it was.

"I'm sorry." She apologized for her temper, but she wasn't going to stay in the hospital room any longer. "But I know what happened, and having you guys put the blame on the wrong person is aggravating me, especially someone as nice as Joel. Now if you could wait here for my release papers while I get out of this stifling room, I'd really appreciate it."

She turned from their startled faces and left before they could recover from their shock.

Now where did she even begin to look for Joel?

The hallway was filled with nurses, doctors, and families spilling out of patient rooms. A staff member gazed at her patient ID bracelet and gave her a long look, Melanie tried her best to appear like she wasn't trying to flee.

Pretend you're going to stretch your legs, or better yet, use the bathroom.

Her bathroom ploy was wrecked when she came upon the restroom but still hadn't seen any sign of Joel. She continued down the hall, her heart picking up speed as she neared the end.

Had he left? Was he released well before she even woke up and didn't want to stick around?

No.

He promised he wouldn't leave, and she'd seen that determined glint in his eye. He was around. She could feel it.

But doubt niggled in the back of her mind. What if this heat in her chest was just some side effect from a drug they'd given her and she needed to get back to her room before she dropped dead?

A hand on her shoulder stopped her cold.

"Looking for someone?" That delicious voice traveled down her spine.

Melanie spun around.

Joel's smiling face greeted her and instantly her hands went to her mouth.

"What happened to your face?"

Joel tenderly touched the black eye that was starting to spread along his cheekbone. "I punched the guy who pulled me from the car and in return got coldcocked. Apparently I was 'hysterical' when the Good Samaritan was trying to save me from the wreck."

"So he punched you?"

Joel shrugged. "I guess I was causing more harm than good conscious, so he took me out." He mimicked getting hit in the face.

Sympathy swelled in her chest, and at that moment she was so happy to see him she didn't care that they were in the middle of the ER, or that her family was right down the hall, or that they had an audience. She pulled Joel to her and kissed him for everything she was worth.

The flame in her chest sparked, sending tendrils of heat down her entire body. Her nipples perked, her stomach flipped, and her sex clenched.

She came alive when his lips were on hers.

What intentionally started out as an I'm-so-glad-you're-all-right kiss quickly turned into an I-want-you-now kiss as Joel pulled her flush to his hot body. His tongue ravaged her mouth.

Someone cleared their throat.

They broke apart and Melanie found her father staring at them, his eyes dark with disapproval. Her mother was peeking around him, eyes wide. There was no sign of Aunt Bernie, who must've volunteered to stay behind for the release papers. Behind her parents, farther down the hallway but still in viewing range, were four men who looked suspiciously like Joel and a woman with lighter hair but the same midnight eyes.

Melanie blushed to the roots of her hair and quickly pushed away from Joel, who did nothing but grin down at her, not a care in the world that they'd pretty much made out in front of their families.

"The doctor wants to see you before you are released," her father growled. He cast Joel a murderous look. Joel swallowed.

Melanie pushed her parents in front of her, trying to get them into her hospital room as quickly as possible. A few nurses and doctors caught her eye; some shook their heads at her public display of affection while others gave her blatant winks and knowing smiles.

"I'll be out in a second," she told Joel before shoving her parents completely into her room and shutting the door. She heard Joel chuckle, followed by a different muffled voice asking who she was and why Joel kept scoring all the blondes.

Chapter 15

It had taken all of Melanie's finesse and patience to get away from her parents once she was released from the hospital and questioned by the police about the accident.

It was now nearly four o'clock in the morning and Melanie's eyes were burning from lack of sleep. She sat in the passenger's seat of a small sedan with Joel behind the wheel again. Apparently, his mother had left him their extra car. Joel bemoaned the loss of his truck as he started the rusted piece of metal. The car shook violently when they idled at red lights, and the heater seemed to emit a strange smell, but Joel conceded it was better than nothing, and would get them from point A to point B safely.

Melanie questioned the safety part but figured Mrs. Kegler wouldn't lend him a piece of crap after he'd just been in a car accident.

As for their destination, Melanie hadn't thought that far ahead or what going home with Joel might imply. All she knew was that she didn't want to go home with her family. She couldn't deal with any more nagging about her poor choices in men. She could live without the angry stares and the head shakes of disappointment for at least a few hours.

"We're here." Joel's voice jolted Melanie. The car was stopped and they were on the side of the road in a residential area.

She must've dozed off.

She rubbed her eyes and unbuckled her seat belt, glad that it actually released when it was supposed to. She stepped out and took in the small community of townhouses.

Joel was already heading up the steps of the one they'd parked in front of. Melanie followed after him. She would never have guessed that Joel lived somewhere like this. It was so … quaint.

The homes alternated in color schemes from pale blue to green to orange then yellow. Joel lucked out with a blue one. She wondered if that was on purpose. She stepped into the small entryway, where there was a little closet on the right and a few stairs leading to the first floor landing, which consisted of a living room and kitchen.

She couldn't help the grin that spread across her face when she ascended the stairs and got her first good look at Joel's living room. An old Star Wars Episode IV poster was framed and hung on the wall, right next to a Tron Legacy poster. The TV was the biggest she'd ever seen and the entertainment cabinet was filled with every video game console she could think of. Next to the TV were two media shelves, one filled with DVDs, another with video games. Equipment for the game 'Rock Band' was shoved in a nearby corner.

On the coffee table was an upside down laptop, its guts looking as if they'd exploded all over the place.

Joel left her to bypass the living room and head to the kitchen. "You want anything?"

"Water, please," she said over her shoulder as she marveled at the Samurai sword Joel had propped up in the corner with all the Rock Band guitars and drums.

"Here you are."

She jumped. She hadn't even heard him come up behind her. She took the water. "Thanks." She nudged the Rock Band equipment. "I haven't played this in years."

Joel's eyes widened. "You play?"

Melanie sipped her water and smiled at him. "Only the country edition, but yeah."

Joel laughed. "I should have known. Country." He gave a full body shake while making a disgusted sound in the back of his throat.

Melanie rolled her eyes and made her way over to the media shelf holding his video games. "Haven't played this in a while either." She took one of the games— this came with fond memories.

"Whoa, whoa, whoa." Joel came around her, snatching the game and shaking his head in disbelief. "There's no way you played and *liked* CoD."

"Cod?"

"Call of Duty," Joel supplied helpfully, holding up the video game next to his face.

Melanie placed the hand not holding her water on her hip. "Why do you think I wouldn't like it?"

Joel looked at her as if the answer were simple. "Because you like country. Country and shooting things don't go together … "

Melanie snatched the video game right back from him. "I'll have you know, when my family and I used to live in Phelan we shot things almost every weekend. I was pretty good at it, too, for your information. I used to play this all the time with Nathan and his buddies."

Joel stared.

Melanie dropped his gaze; suddenly uncomfortable, she busied herself with putting the DVD back in its proper place.

Her gaze snagged on a game about bridges.

The bridge … that chip.

Melanie had almost forgotten about it because of the accident.

Suddenly she wasn't so sure it was an accident anymore.

Could it be possible she was wrong about Joel? Could he have done something so horrible that someone wanted him dead?

She put her glass of water down. She spun around, arms crossed, and narrowed her eyes at him. "Who's trying to kill you?"

• • •

Joel hadn't expected the question. One second he was staring at Melanie in awe and the next her whole demeanor shifted to nothing but business. There was no denying it any longer. Melanie was his Mirror Mate. He'd tried to push it from his thoughts as best he could, but what happened on that bridge lined up with everything Felix and Sydney had told them about the bonding process. The problem now was that he hadn't even been willing to admit she was his Mirror Mate and suddenly they were bonded. That was like going from zero to sixty in the blink of an eye. He didn't know what to do with a Mirror Mate—not to mention a fully bonded Mirror Mate.

How the hell his life got so complicated, he'd never know.

But he had something more important than sorting out what to do about their bonded relationship status without involving an emotional investment, because right now Melanie's expression was no longer open. Her eyes were closed off, her stance hostile as she demanded to know who'd attacked them.

He tried to buy himself more time. "What?"

She raised her brows in expectation. "Our accident wasn't an accident. At least I don't think it was. Who's after you? And why? What'd you do?"

"What makes you think I did anything?" he asked in mock outrage. He didn't like where this questioning was leading, specifically because it was leading him away from the conversation he knew they really needed to be having. The one about how they'd bonded during the accident and Melanie needed to understand that whatever was happening between them aside, her powers were no longer what they were before.

He also didn't want to alarm her with the fact that the man who had shown up at her work that first night they'd met and who had shown up again at the community center had been at the wreck. Melanie had enough to worry about with one stalker ex-boyfriend—she didn't need the added stress of knowing Man in the Suit, as Joel was starting to refer to him now, was following her.

Or, more likely, following him.

It was possible they weren't after Melanie at all. What if they were just after Joel and the guild? At every instance when *he'd* seen the man, Melanie was present, sure, but Man in the Suit was also there when she wasn't. Like the time the guild had spotted him outside Syd's clinic. Merrick had called a halt to the group's plan to follow him, calling the situation "fishy." "No one stands there waiting to be captured," Merrick had said. "This feels like a set up."

Set up or not, the man hadn't waited around long, and with one final smirk in their direction he'd sauntered off, as if his only mission was to let the guild know that he was watching them. If Joel had to fathom a guess, he'd say that Man in the Suit had been toying with them, getting them riled up so that their nerves would eventually fray from being on end too long.

Joel's mind went back a few hours to the accident and the man who'd pulled him from the car. He could have sworn it was the same guy, minus the suit.

That had also been partially why Joel had punched him.

"Are you all right?" She reached out and cupped his face.

He winced despite Melanie's care with his eye. She released him instantly. "I'm going to get you some ice for that."

He stared at her peach sweat suit body as she moved into the kitchen, unsure how the hell he'd avoided that whole conversation without even trying.

And Mom told me spacing out on conversations with women would never get me anywhere.

He gave himself a firm shake and took a seat at the small table in the kitchen.

"Was it safe for you to have been driving?" Melanie asked as she took one of his ice packs and wrapped it in a towel.

"I was fine to drive." He took the compress and held it to his eye. "I didn't have a concussion or anything. It was a punch to the face, and I've had lots of those."

Melanie frowned.

"I'm not really looking forward to tomorrow though, I'm probably going to have severe whiplash." With his free hand he felt the back of his neck; it was a little tight, but it'd be a million times worse after he slept.

Melanie cautiously reached up and felt her own neck.

"How's it feeling?" he asked.

"A little sore."

He smiled. "That's not what I meant." Then in a more serious voice, "I meant did you have any problems at the hospital, you know, any flare ups?"

Understanding dawned. "I was fine," she said curtly.

Joel gently put down his ice pack. "Melanie, we need to talk about what happened between us in that bay."

Her expression grew weary. "I don't really feel like talking about it."

He drew back in surprise. "Then why did you come home with me? I thought you would want to discuss everything that's happened, all the changes."

He could see her cheeks begin to flush in the profile view. "I wanted to get away from my family. I—"

He walked up to her and gingerly turned her to face him. He had to tread carefully; he could sense the flight or fight response warring within her. He knew she wanted to be here, but if he pushed too hard, she'd leave, and there was no way he was going to let that happen.

"You … ?" he prompted.

She tilted her head up to look him right in the eye and his breath caught. The burning inside his chest intensified and his whole body tensed with want.

"I wanted to be near you," she said softly.

He reached out and tucked her hair behind her ear, letting his fingers linger near the side of her face, teasing her skin. Did she already suspect what had happened between them on the bridge?

She shivered visibly, and through the heavy material of the sweatshirt he could make out her stiffened nipples.

She wasn't wearing a bra.

Joel swallowed thickly as that need within him grew to nearly uncontrollable proportions.

"Then stay." His voice came out low and gravelly.

Her gaze heated and she licked her lips.

He wanted to groan at the sight. His pants were suddenly too tight, his cock straining against the material. Blood roared in his veins.

Melanie lifted her fingers to trace the side of his face that wasn't bruised and said thoughtfully, "I don't want to think about what happened tonight or what it might mean. For right now I only want you."

That did it.

Joel crushed her against his body, fusing his mouth to hers. She met him with equal fervor, like a damn busting open. She melted against him, lips parting, tongue tangling with his. Her fingers delved into his hair and she ground her hips erotically into his.

Holy shit.

He wasn't going to last two minutes if she kept this up.

Melanie pulled back and grasped the hem of his shirt to pull it over his head, nearly frantic in her movements. Her eyes blazed with uncontrolled desire, and when she stared up at him with that mischievous grin …

His head dropped back.

Yup, not going to last two minutes.

She pulled him to her, her lips back on his, ravaging him. He dropped his grip from her waist to cup her ass. Taking the initiative, Melanie jumped, wrapping her legs around his waist, as if she couldn't get close enough.

Joel hadn't been expecting the move and he stumbled with the added weight. His back hit the wall, something crashed to the floor, but Joel didn't pay it any attention. With one hand holding Melanie firmly against him, he let the other explore underneath the oversized top she had on.

He traced his fingertips up her spine, marveling at how smooth her skin felt and how she arched her back and seemed to purr from his caresses.

He pushed off the wall and quickly switched their positions, so that Melanie's back was now against the wall. He tore the peach sweatshirt from her body and his heart thumped erratically in his chest as the sight of her breasts. Her chest rose and fell with her heavy breathing, hypnotizing him. He dropped his head and started a trail of kisses along her collarbone. He could taste the sea salt that was still on her body, but underneath he could detect the faint trace of her white chocolate and strawberry scent. It drove him crazy and he thrust his hips against hers in need.

She moaned, her hands pulling his head closer to her chest, urging him downward. He knew where she wanted him to be, and he wanted to be there, too, but first he wanted to make her beg.

Keeping one hand firmly beneath her, he moved to cup her breast. He trailed his tongue down the center of her chest and slowly over to the nipple where he circled the peak, once, twice. She squirmed. He placed feather light kisses all around and then moved to the next breast, repeating the same torture.

"Joel," she begged.

It was music to his ears. Taking pity on her, he gave her what she wanted—what his mouth watered to do. He took one nipple into his mouth and suckled it.

He heard a thump as Melanie's head dropped back to hit the wall. From his position at chest level he could barely make out her eyes shut in ecstasy. Her hips were already moving into his with an erotic rhythm.

He tore his gaze away, afraid her wild sensuality was going to push him over the edge before he even got out of the gate.

Fuck, he needed to be inside her. Now.

He stepped back from the wall and released the hold on her bottom so that she started to slide down his body, her legs reflexively moving from around his waist to the ground, where he'd be better able to tear those hideous sweats from her sweet legs.

As if surfacing from a dream, she righted her head and blinked up at him. "What're you doing?"

He grinned at her, slid a finger into the waistband of her pants, and gave a playful tug. "Liberating you from this fashion atrocity."

The flush already on her cheeks darkened. "They're my aunt's," she said defensively.

"I don't care who's they are as long as you're no longer wearing them."

He tugged again and Melanie's breath caught as he lowered himself with her pants, exposing all that beautiful flesh one inch at a time. When the sweats were nothing but a puddle at her ankles, he looked up at her with a predatory smile.

He could have sworn her legs wobbled.

He ran his hands up the backs of her calves, silently telling her that he'd catch her if she fell. He leaned in and pressed an open-mouthed kiss on the inside of her knee. First one leg, then the other. He moved up and pressed another set of kisses on the inside of her thighs. She quivered beneath his lips. He dragged out the torture, skimming his mouth up, up to her hipbone, then back down to slowly blow on her exposed flesh.

Her hands dove into his hair again, trying to drive him to her wet center, but he resisted. "Not yet." He chuckled and moved to her other hipbone. "I want to learn every last curve of you. I want to taste every last inch."

Melanie whimpered. "Joel, please."

Her fingers tightened in his hair, urging him—no, begging him—to take mercy on her.

He followed the pull of her hands to between her legs. At the first lick she swore, her body going tense, nails digging into his scalp. He pushed her legs further apart and didn't cease his pursuit. Her taste was intoxicating, and he slid a finger deep inside her wet heat. He slowly thrust with his finger, sucking her clit between his lips until her body bucked, the muscles around his finger tensing. She cried out in the throes of her climax, and Joel devoured the sight of her. He continued to thrust his finger in and out until she came down from her high.

When she finally peeled her eyes open he stood before her. A satisfied grin pulled at his mouth. He waited till her eyes locked on his before he took the finger he'd pleasured her with and sucked it clean.

Chapter 16

She was in big trouble.

She was done.

Addicted.

Joel had made her come so effortlessly, so explosively that she still shook from the aftershocks. And the way he'd licked his finger like he couldn't wait for seconds?

Her sex clenched in anticipation.

He simply stood in front of her, male satisfaction rolling off him in palpable waves. His midnight eyes sparkled, his hair in complete disarray. He looked sexy beyond all reason.

And she wanted more.

So much more.

His pants were strained at the zipper.

She hadn't realized he was still partly dressed. She snaked a finger through one of the front belt loops and tugged him closer. Close enough that her breasts brushed his chest. When that friction wasn't enough, she leaned into him further and wantonly moved her chest against his.

His eyes flashed with hunger and she smiled up at him while her hands quickly made work of the button and zipper on his pants. She pushed them down along with his boxers in one quick move, careful of the impressive erection he was sporting.

Clearly the guys who used to bully him in high school never got a look at him in the locker room. There was nothing to tease about in *that* department.

Wanting to deliver the same kind of torment, she placed her hands on the back of his ankles and dragged her fingernails up his calves with just the smallest amount of pressure. When she got to the back of his knees she stuck her butt in the air and rose into a half bent position.

She could feel the muscles of his legs, coiled tight, as if fighting for control. All that restrained strength. Mmm …

Her face was level with his crotch, and she called up to him in a husky voice, "Do you taste as good as you look?"

"Hell."

She smiled.

She slipped one of her hands between his legs to cup his balls as she took him in her mouth. His body jerked, sliding his cock another inch deeper into her mouth. She moaned and sucked him long and hard.

She closed her eyes, finding her rhythm.

She didn't get very far.

In a blink her back was against the wall again, his warm body pressing into hers in all the right places. She had no idea how it happened. Her legs instinctively wrapped around his waist.

He paused. "I can grab a condom from upstairs."

She shook her head. "I'm on the pill and I'm clean."

"Same. I mean, I'm not on the pill, but I'm clean."

She kissed him.

And then he was inside her.

She cried out as he filled her completely.

He paused momentarily. "Are you okay?"

She felt herself flush. So she was a little vocal in the bedroom. She couldn't help it. "I'm good."

He arched a brow. "Yeah?" He pulled out and thrust back in. "How good?"

She bit her lip to keep from moaning, but it escaped her anyway. "So good." She clutched his shoulders and ground down on him.

He growled low in his throat before increasing the speed and intensity of his thrusts. He pounded into her over and over again. She was consumed by the sensations. Pleasure overrode everything else, the tension in her body building. Joel continued his relentless attack and she arched against him until she came apart with a shout.

She was still wrapped around him like a boa constrictor when he found his own release. He called her name, his body quaking.

His hot breath fanned her neck for a few seconds before he got himself back under control. He leaned back, giving her room to drop to her feet and stand on her own two wobbly legs.

He pushed off the wall but one palm still rested against it, as if he wouldn't be able to stand otherwise.

"Still good?" he asked with a smirk.

She pushed her sweaty hair out of her face and smiled coyly up at him. "Beyond good," she told him honestly. She stretched like a cat after a long nap, feeling all that delicious tension leave her body. She was abuzz with endorphins.

She was ready to take on the world.

She turned to Joel, who'd stepped back to give her room to stretch. He smiled lazily at her, eyes half lidded. He looked sated and ready to sleep.

"You look sleepy." She ran her hands through his hair like she'd always wanted.

"You're not?"

She shook her head. As well as being a vocal bedmate, she was also one of those people who got a boost of energy after sex.

Joel seemed to put that all together as he studied her, one brow arched in disbelief. "You're really deflating my ego right now with the fact that I can't keep up."

She laughed. "You had a long day, and I slept in the car. I'd say you're entitled to being tired right about now. Your sexual prowess is still very much intact, but next time you better bring your stamina." She winked.

"Next time, huh?"

She could see him growing hard again.

"Come on." He held his hand out to her. "Let's head upstairs and I'll show you the bedroom. I'm sure there's something we could find in there to keep that energized body of yours entertained."

• • •

Joel woke to the vicious vibrating of his phone on the hardwood nightstand. He threw one of his arms over his eyes, as if that would make the sound go away.

It didn't work.

Beside him Melanie started shifting. Cursing under his breath, Joel snatched the phone and went into his bathroom so as not to wake her.

"What?" he hissed into his cell.

There was a shocked paused on the other side followed by Felix's tempered voice. "I get a text message from my fiancé that you were in the ER last night after a car wreck and when I call to check on you, all I get is an annoyed, 'what?'"—a brief pause—"and not only that, you texted *Cali* about your accident but not me?"

Joel grimaced. He'd done it on purpose, of course, texting Cali and not Felix. He'd sent the message once they were released from the ER, and Joel knew with Felix's schedule as a baker he would have been awake that early. Cali, on the other hand, didn't like to wake up before ten o'clock, giving Joel time for some much needed sleep as well as peace and quiet before having to deal with the guild's questions and concerns.

He glanced at the clock on his phone: 11:45 a.m. Bless Cali's heart, she'd slept in much later than Joel could have anticipated.

"I'm sorry," he said to Felix. "I needed to rest. I wasn't up to meeting the guild and rehashing what had happened."

"Joel, that's not why I'm giving you a hard time. I'm your best friend. Why didn't you call me right away? I would have been there in a second to give you a ride, to bring you donuts, anything."

Joel felt like a real jackass. Of course Felix only wanted to be there for him as a friend; this had nothing to do with guild business. Felix would have wanted a call if Joel had stubbed his toe and been admitted to the ER.

Joel rubbed the back of his neck. "Shit, I'm sorry, man. My whole family was there, it was so crowded already I didn't even think … "

Felix sighed through the line. "It's all good, but next time call, all right?"

"Sure."

There was another sigh and Joel could picture Felix running his hand through his hair. "You need me to pick you up?"

"No need. My mom loaned me her extra wheels."

"That rusted piece of shit?"

Joel grinned. "Yeah."

"It's no problem for me to swing by and get you, you know."

Joel peeked out of the bathroom. Melanie was still sleeping. She'd already invaded his territory on the bed, lying smack in the middle, arms splayed wide. His chest swelled with emotion. "I appreciate it, Felix, but there's no need. I'll be by Syd's after closing to debrief you guys."

"Debrief?"

Joel's free hand fisted. "Yeah, it appears our men in black are getting bolder when it comes to approaching us."

Felix swore. "They're the ones that hit you?" He cursed some more.

Joel hesitated. Did he tell Felix the rest?

He was still debating if he would tell the guild about him and Melanie. Their bonding still felt so new, he didn't want to share it with anyone. Hell, he'd been denying it all to Felix. Felix would probably gloat until the end of time. But after he left Felix in the dark about being in the ER, Joel owed it to him.

"That's not the only thing." He interrupted Felix's colorful language tirade.

Felix's voice cut off instantly.

After a tense moment, he said, "What else happened?"

"Melanie was with me when they attacked. That's how I know they're behind it; the guy we saw loitering outside Syd's clinic pulled me from my car when we went over the bridge."

"Fuck, you went over a bridge? What bridge?"

Joel waved his comment away even though he couldn't see over the phone. "Newport Boulevard. We landed in the bay. Melanie's seat belt wouldn't release ... "

Joel drifted off as his rested mind started to put the puzzle pieces together. The man outside his car. Melanie's seat belt. Getting hit into the bay.

They'd planned everything. But down to pulling him from his truck? Effectively leaving Melanie?

It didn't make sense. Why would they want Joel but leave Melanie to die? Why orchestrate that whole fiasco?

"Joel? You there, dude?"

"Yeah," he said, distracted. "I'm here." He told Felix the whole story, ending with how he and Melanie had bonded. Then he waited.

It didn't take Felix long.

He let out a low whistle. "And who was the one who thought Melanie wasn't his Mirror Mate?"

Joel pinched the bridge of his nose. If he didn't answer, Felix would only continue to bug the shit out of him. "I was," he conceded.

"I'm sorry, I think my phone broke up there for a second. What was that?"

Joel could hear the shit-eating grin in Felix's voice.

"I said go to hell."

Felix laughed. "Fine, fine. I'll take what I can get. Congrats, man, not on the accident, of course, but on bonding. How do you feel?"

Joel rubbed his chest. "I feel fine."

"Fine? Just fine?"

Joel leaned against his doorway, double-checking on Melanie again. "You don't understand," he said in a hushed tone. "Our time was rushed. Melanie didn't reach out for me—or whatever you want to call it—because she wanted me, she did it because she was scared. It was almost like it was forced upon us, and that's not exactly how I'd envisioned bonding with my Mirror Mate."

Felix made a sympathetic sound on the other side. "I hear you, but you have to remember that no one can force you to bond, so something had to be there in the first place. It might have been a bit rushed, like you said, but think of it as a shotgun wedding. You got the major part over with faster than most of us and now you only have to smooth out all the bumps and grooves. And, you know, hope Melanie's not some secret psycho that you're accidently bonded to for life."

Joel grinned despite himself. "Thanks, man."

He hung up but stayed where he was in the doorway of his bathroom, watching Melanie. His mind whirled, trying to piece together everything that had happened. He somehow felt he was missing something, something big, and he hated every second of it.

What if it was right in front of his face?

He stared at Melanie, unseeing, as he tried to force his tired mind to work everything out, to go over every detail.

What was he missing?

He sighed and rubbed his face. All he could do was wait for this mysterious new group to make their next move.

Chapter 17

"What do you mean I've changed?" Melanie stuffed another forkful of scrambled eggs into her mouth. She'd awakened nearly an hour ago only to find that it was almost time for her shift at work. She'd showered and changed back into her aunt's horrible sweats before finding Joel in the kitchen, making her food. She expected idle chit-chat, maybe some awkward morning-after sex silence that sometimes happened, but nope. Joel had launched right into business. Starting with a topic she rather not think about: soul mates.

According to Joel, when they'd called out for each other, that was a major sign they were Mirror Mates and had completed some kind of bond.

Melanie was still wrapping her head around the whole bonding process. She'd concede there was something there between them, but that didn't mean they were some perfect match to go riding out into the sunset. This just meant they were stuck with each other a little more than she would have liked.

Right?

"When we bonded, your powers ... they amplified. I don't know what that means for you, I'm not an expert, and the encyclopedia Felix and I are creating doesn't have every power known to man, yet. So we have no idea what this means for you, but we can figure it out together."

She shoved another forkful of egg into her mouth, her mind tumbling over the idea of her powers changing. She didn't know how to feel about that. She did know she was more relaxed than she'd been in a while, her powers the furthest thing from her mind. In fact, she'd been hoping for a mid-afternoon romp. She eyed the broken picture on the floor near the trashcan. The glass looked to have been swept up already. Melanie felt a pang of guilt for breaking one of Joel's possessions during their lovemaking. She'd pay him back. She would be happy to pay him back with sex.

"You should practice on me," he was saying, his hand held out to her, palm up on his table, urging her to take it and thus his powers.

She eyed it warily as she chewed her food. The thought of using her powers still made her stomach churn. "Can't we do this another time?" she asked once she'd swallowed.

Joel shook his head firmly. "I don't want to scare you, but the people who caused our accident yesterday might strike again. It's good to know your abilities and limits."

The way his face softened pulled at her heartstrings. No man had ever looked at her like that. Add in the fact that his face was even more swollen from the hit he took yesterday, and how could she say no?

She let out a puff of air. "Fine, but I want to know something first." She took his hand and felt that electric shock that always happened when she touched Joel. It traveled up her arm and all down her body, heating her blood. "Who would be after you and why?"

He hesitated.

Melanie tightened the grip she had on his hand. "You avoided the question yesterday and I let it slide. Not today."

His gaze dropped to the table. "His name is Vander Donahughe. He's kind of the archenemy to the Guild of Truth."

Melanie sat back and listened as Joel described the power-hungry CEO, his horrendous powers, and the horrible things he'd done to Joel and his friends.

"Why didn't you tell me before?"

"Because I didn't want to scare you off. I didn't know if anything would become of us. It's risky to know me."

"Risky to my social standing, maybe." She tried to lighten the mood.

His lips twitched. "I won't tell anyone you're a closet nerd who likes Call of Duty. Your secret is safe with me."

Or at least until he learned what her real secret was.

Should she bring this information to Juliet? Juliet's company already had the Kratos Corporation in their sights, so maybe it was possible for them to join forces with Joel's guild and put a stop to them permanently.

One thing at a time. She wasn't a superhero, not yet anyway. She didn't go looking for trouble. She needed to dig herself out of the hole she was already in, or in this case get Nathan the help he needed and get out from under Juliet's thumb as quick as possible.

She squeezed Joel's fingers. "So, what am I supposed to be doing now?" She motioned to their conjoined hands.

Joel snapped into mentor mode.

"Try to activate your powers."

She nudged her empty plate and closed her eyes. She concentrated on what he asked of her and pushed away as much of her fear as possible. Activating her powers was usually the hardest part—she didn't know if it was because she was in Joel's presence or because she was touching him, but her neck instantly began to tingle.

She inhaled deeply, trying to keep her heart calm. If Joel was right, she had no idea what she was capable of anymore, and the last thing she wanted to do was hurt him.

Why had she agreed to do this with him?

She would never forgive herself if she hurt him or anyone for that matter.

"I think they're, uh, active." She opened her eyes. She was stiff as a rod, afraid the slightest movement would do something horrible.

As if sensing her unease, he smiled warmly and squeezed her hand. "That's good. Now imagine slowly pulling my powers into you. Slowly," he stressed.

She licked her dry lips and did as he said.

She concentrated on pulling from his fingertips, letting his powers trickle into her hand, like water dripping from a faucet. Her hand started to grow warm, but she couldn't tell if it was from her powers or the heat from Joel's body.

"You're doing great," he encouraged her. "I can feel the pins and needles in my fingers and palm but it's gradual, so keep it up."

The heat was traveling up her arm now and she wanted to let go. She wanted to stop. How long did she have to do this? Wasn't the first display of control enough?

From the living room her phone *dinged* in her purse.

Melanie pounced on the distraction and broke contact. "That's my phone. What if it's work?"

His level stare spoke volumes. "You can get it in a second. Try and use my powers now. Remember, your ability is kind of a two-parter. Take the powers; use them yourself."

She nodded, knowing it was no use trying to get away from him now. "Right." She might not have liked the part where she took from someone else, but she had to admit there was a small thrill when using Joel's powers. She often forgot that he could freeze someone to the ground, literally, with nothing but a touch.

She eyed the tabletop—she'd start small. She grasped the napkin holder and relaxed her shoulders, letting the tingle in the back of her neck flare up again before it completely disappeared.

After a few seconds she released the napkin holder. "Well?" She gestured nervously for Joel to lift it.

He tried to shift it. It didn't move. He tried to lift it. It didn't budge.

Melanie felt herself mirroring his smile. She'd done it.

"See how easy that was?" Joel said. "You don't have to be afraid of your powers."

Her smile wavered.

The idea of not fearing her powers seemed an impossible dream. She'd always have to be mindful of them; she'd never know the life she had before. Already the time she'd spent with Joel was proof enough that there were risks to having supernatural abilities.

"I should check my phone."

The text was from Juliet. No apology about leaving Melanie in the dark for so many days or for not answering her phone calls. It was a simple command.

Contact me as soon as possible.

Melanie wanted to ignore it out of spite but she couldn't. She had to help Nathan.

She glanced over her shoulder. Joel piled a few dishes into the sink, and her heart gave a little flutter in her chest.

What if she could find Nathan's soul mate?

She had no idea what Juliet had in store for her brother. She hadn't mentioned anything about soul mates, and Melanie seriously doubted that was her organization's mission. Juliet's company wasn't a matchmaking business. Melanie had to trust that Juliet had another method that would at least give Nathan a temporary reprieve. And if it wasn't a permanent fix, Melanie vowed right here and now that she'd help him find his—what had Joel called them?—Mirror Mate.

"Was it work?" Joel asked.

Melanie fumbled her phone. "No, my parents," she lied and instantly felt horrible about it.

Joel made a noncommittal noise. No doubt her answer didn't need further questioning, given her family's reaction last night at the ER.

Once finished in the kitchen he came over to her, keys in hand. "I can drive you home to grab some clothes and take you to work. That way you won't be late."

He glanced meaningfully at the clock and she followed his lead. Dammit, she'd done it again—she had just over a half hour to get to work.

There was no time to feel timid or embarrassed about where she lived. Melanie simply gave Joel directions and rushed from the car to get changed once they arrived.

The house was empty, which was just as well since Melanie didn't want to run into anyone at the moment and she didn't want anyone running into Joel. He might figure out she lied about the text message.

She left the front door open for him as she sprinted for her room. Nathan lay on the bed, drugged to sleep if the empty Nyquil bottle was any indication.

Her chest constricted and she hastily threw her aunt's clothes into the hamper and dug around for black slacks and a white top. She was pulling her top on when she heard Joel come in.

"I didn't miss you changing yet, did I?" He was pretending to shield his eyes, a huge gap between his middle and ring finger. He wore a playful smile that instantly dropped off at the sight of her brother.

She knew how horrible everything must look to him. The cramped living spaces, furniture and belongings scattered everywhere. Clothing and sleeping bags in the TV room, a kitchen overflowing with boxes of mac and cheese, instant noodles, and dirty dishes in the sink. And the cherry on top: her brother drugged out on his bed.

She felt like splaying her arms and welcoming Joel to her glamorous life.

That attitude will get you nowhere. This was the hand life had dealt her and she was making the best of it. She stiffened her spine, bracing for any jokes Joel might have, but he wasn't even looking at her. He made his way over to Nathan, his face as serious as she'd ever seen it.

He gently sat next to Nathan, studying him as if looking for a way to fix him. When there were no obvious cure-all buttons lying around, he placed his hand on Nathan's shoulder. "We're going to help you." He picked up the Nyquil bottle and threw it in the garbage can that was already stuffed with beer bottles and over-the-counter medications.

She'd have to take it out soon, before the room started to smell.

Wordlessly, Joel got up and picked up the stray bottles on the floor and placed them within. Then he took the bag out and held it up. "Where should I put this?"

Emotion clogged her throat. She couldn't speak. Nathan and Joel probably would have gotten along famously.

And they will.

Once Juliet helped Nathan.

She almost let it slip that Nathan was getting help, but Juliet had stressed the importance of secrecy. Melanie was in a different world now, and she definitely didn't want to step on Juliet's toes. Especially when those toes had men like Mr. Richardson working for them. The man was built like a linebacker, and powers or no powers, she didn't want to get on his bad side.

"There's a large dumpster outside," she said and led Joel out the front.

With nothing left to do but leave Nathan to his hopefully dreamless sleep, Melanie climbed back into Joel's mom's car.

They arrived at the yogurt shop with a few minutes to spare.

"Thank you so much." She leaned over and kissed Joel.

His warm hand cupped the back of her head, keeping her close longer than was decent. When he released her she was flushed and breathing heavily. There was no judgment in his eyes, no pity, only affection. Her body ached for him, and from the bulge in his jeans, she bet he ached for her, too.

"See you tomorrow at yoga?" She hoped her voice didn't sound as needy as it did to her own ears.

Joel grinned. "And miss seeing you in those tight yoga pants?" He shook his head. "Never."

She kissed him one more time.

"You better go before I make you really late for work," he said when she regretfully pulled back.

She went to shove him playfully when her eyes caught on a figure in the distance, standing near one of the trees by the bus stop. Her blood turned to ice and her arm froze halfway to Joel's chest.

Joel immediately went on high alert. "What?" He followed her line of sight and his body tensed. "Is that who I think it is?"

"Yeah." Her voice came out breathless and she cleared her throat, shaking herself. "That's Alexander," she said in a stronger voice.

"Son of a bitch." Joel reached for the door handle.

"No, don't." The last thing she needed was Joel to get all macho and try to intimidate her ex-boyfriend.

Joel halted. "I won't hurt him. I was going to give him a little scare. You know, Lock his arms to his side and let him freak out for a bit. Or better yet, Lock him in place so you can call the police. You said there's a restraining order on him, right?"

She drew back. "You can do all that?"

Would that be all it took to get rid of Alexander for good?

He rubbed his hand up and down her arm. "We have to solve this problem, and you're calling the shots. Including leaving that rat bastard alone if that's what you want. All I'm saying, though, is that if the police aren't enough to scare him, maybe it's time to go beyond the police. Supernaturally, of course."

Something sparked in the back of her mind, like the Grinch when he got a wonderful, awful idea.

All the times she'd been frightened to leave her house, get on the bus, go to and from the community center and now to work.

There was nowhere safe from Alexander. Maybe what she needed to do was scare him, like Joel said. Stand up to him.

"I'll think on it," she finally conceded, already getting a game plan ready in her mind.

Chapter 18

Joel parked his mother's piece of junk car outside Syd's clinic as the sun was dipping below the horizon. The buildings were cast in bright orange and yellow light.

Joel raised his hand in greeting to Tom staring out of the pizzeria window, smiling to himself at the look of horror Tom would no doubt wear if he ever found out he had a fan club two stores down. Joel still couldn't believe that through all the years he'd dated Sydney, she never once mentioned the crush she'd had on the pizza man.

He gave a careless shrug to the night air—the thought didn't hold as much power over him as it usually did.

He certainly felt lighter than he had in ages.

With an extra bounce in his step, he headed for the clinic, and for once found everyone already waiting for him when he entered.

Sydney's hands instantly went to her mouth. "Oh no, Joel, your eye." It looked like she wanted to rush to him and inspect it herself, but she refrained, for which he was grateful.

He might concede that he was getting over her romantically, but even a friendship still needed the trust she'd wrecked. And distance. Lots and lots of healthy distance.

"It looks a lot worse than it really is," he told her.

Felix came close and stared at the bruise. "Let me guess, handiwork of Man in the Suit?"

"You got it."

"These guys are getting more aggressive," Cali said. "It might be good if we started taking some precautions here."

Feeling Cali was right, Joel leaned back until he could touch the front door and Locked it.

"Now no one can get inside," he said.

"Unless they're already inside." A new voice spoke up from the far side of the room.

Everyone jumped, except for Felix. He growled low in his throat. "Jente."

The young Veiler gave a mock bow. Jente possessed the ability to go invisible, which made it possible for him to be there one second and gone the next. Or, in this case, lying in wait until he wanted to show himself.

Hostility radiated from Felix. Cali stood at his side, hand on his chest, as if to keep him from doing anything rash.

Jente eyed Felix with outright amusement, something that did nothing to calm Felix.

Joel got his first real look at Jente and was shocked to see how young he appeared. He looked barely older than Luke, with jet-black hair that could have been styled by a Final Fantasy fanatic. He wore jeans and a hoodie with the sleeves pushed up his forearms, revealing tan skin despite the cool weather, which hinted at some kind of mixed heritage. But it was his eyes, one gray, one green, that caught Joel's attention. They scanned the room, assessing everyone—for signs of violence? Joel didn't know what the kid was looking for, but he seemed to deem it safe for himself when he stepped further into the room, away from the window.

"You could really work on your security around here," he said conversationally, shooting a meaningful look at Joel.

Joel cracked his knuckles, and suddenly one of Cali's hands pressed against his chest, too.

"What are you doing here?" Cali asked.

She was the only one who didn't look upset at his appearance. And given her history with Jente, Joel guessed that it was warranted. Jente had saved her from Vander, which earned him a little bit of leeway. But not much. Anyone working in Vander's employment was on his permanent shit list.

"I thought you'd like to know that the men you told me about have been poking their noses in places they shouldn't be," Jente said. "Also, some of my co-workers have gone missing."

Everyone immediately perked up.

"You mean like they're on vacation missing or … ?" Sydney left the sentence hanging.

Jente sucked in a lungful of air in an exaggerated manner that spoke volumes about what he thought of Sydney and her comment. "If their idea of a vacation is a cell with metal bars, then yes, they're on vacation."

Sydney ignored his sarcastic response and gulped nervously. She wound her arm through Merrick's.

"Do you know where they were taken?" Merrick asked.

"Not a clue," Jente deadpanned.

Did this douchebag even care where his co-workers were? It sure didn't look like it.

Gee, what a team player.

A long silence followed.

"Anything else you'd like to report, Jente?" Cali prodded.

Those mismatched eyes locked on hers and didn't leave. "Vander is missing."

To say a ripple of shock went through the group was an understatement. More like a bomb explosion of surprise.

Jente didn't go into any more detail. "Have you heard anything?"

Cali shook her head. "These guys are slippery. I'd say I'm sorry but I'm not."

Jente nodded.

"Why do you stay with him?" Joel asked, his curiosity getting the better of him. Of all the people to align with, what did Jente see in Vander? Similar moral codes? If that were true, Jente wouldn't have helped Cali out when he had.

"His resources," Merrick spoke up.

Jente's gaze swung to him.

Merrick stared him down. "I was inside Jente's mind in the fall— not for long, but I did see that."

Jente's eyes narrowed.

"We have resources," Cali said.

Joel noted the way Felix stiffened at the unspoken invitation.

Jente smirked. "I should be going. I'll be in touch."

Joel Unlocked the door and held it open for him.

Jente silently left the vet clinic.

Once the door was shut and re-Locked, Luke spoke up from his seat next to Niella. "Did anyone else get the creeps off that guy?"

They all collectively raised their hands.

"I don't like this." Felix ran a hand through his hair. "Someone is picking off people with powers—someone *not* working for Vander."

"And now they *have* Vander," said Merrick.

"Who knows what that could mean for the rest of us?" Joel rubbed the back of his neck to relieve some tension.

Cali dropped her hands from both Felix and Joel. "Do you think that's how this new group found out about us? Vander could have sold us out for some kind of deal. It's the only thing that makes sense. It's not like we're waving our hands in the air or shouting from rooftops about our gifts."

"There has to be a link," Merrick said. "Vander is a very reasonable explanation, but we shouldn't stop there. Somewhere we messed up and alerted whoever these people are to our whereabouts."

"Then we should find them before anything else happens to us." Sydney motioned to Joel and his black eye.

There was a murmured agreement before further talk of what could be done ensued. Joel was only half listening as his mind kept going back to what Jente had told them. They weren't the only ones being targeted. Could it be that the Guild of Kratos and the Guild of Truth had a common enemy? If Merrick was right and it wasn't Vander who'd sold them out, who was hunting them down? Around and around his mind went, trying to find the piece that connected them all together.

• • •

Juliet Arden stood with a bright smile on her face. Her long, brown hair cascaded down past her shoulders in large, smooth waves. She looked confident, radiant, and Melanie wanted to punch her in the face all the more for it.

"Two days?" she said when she was within hearing distance from Juliet. "You tell me to contact you immediately and then you make me wait for two full days?"

Juliet's smile disappeared, but she didn't look contrite. "Trust me when I tell you that it was necessary for us to get certain things in order."

"What things?" Melanie snapped at her.

Juliet crossed her arms. "How about curing your brother?"

Melanie's mouth hung open, no comeback ready. She hadn't expected that. After the silence, she had almost given up on Juliet, writing her off as another scam like the ones her parents had lost their house to. But Juliet hadn't asked for money.

No, she asked for my help.

Again, that only added more questions.

"What is this cure?" she questioned Juliet. "Because I've spent a lot of time around Joel, and he says the only way Nathan can be cured is if he finds his soul mate, which I doubt you did in the span of a couple weeks. Also, I don't know why you wanted me to get close to Joel. At first I thought it was because he had some kind of skeleton in his closet. But he's clean. He's done nothing like those people you showed me on the computer. In fact, those people are the ones after Joel, which I think means you are on the same side."

"We're not concerned with Joel at the moment anymore." Juliet waved her comment away. "And for your information, Joel doesn't know everything about people with powers. We've found another way, one we hope you'll help us with now that you've grown into your full power."

Melanie drew back. "How did you know I … I … "

"Became full forced?" Juliet threw out Joel's terminology like she knew him. She shrugged her shoulders. "Call it a hunch. We watch out for you, Melanie, and we know about your car crash. We also know that sometimes following traumatic events, powers can change."

"They have," she admitted, "but I don't know what I can and can't do yet."

A smile slowly bloomed to life on Juliet's face. "That's quite all right—we know what you can do. We'll take care of everything."

"Yeah?" she asked suspiciously. "You keep mentioning needing my help, that's your price, but what exactly am I going to be doing with my power?"

"Why, helping others, of course. People like your brother. You're going to make a huge difference in the world, Melanie, trust me."

At that moment Melanie's phone went off.

She pulled it from her pocket. Ma.

"I'm sorry. I have to take this."

Juliet didn't look bothered at all. Her smile broadened.

Melanie turned her back and answered.

"Oh my God, Melanie! It's a miracle. Nathan. I've never seen him like this before. My God, our prayers have been answered."

"Ma, slow down." Melanie could hardly keep up. Her mother was speaking too quickly and her voice was full of tears. "What happened? Is Nathan okay?"

"Oh, Melanie, you have to come home, quick. You have to see. It's a miracle. My boy, oh my dear boy." She broke into sobs.

Melanie couldn't make out any more after that. She told her mom she'd be there as soon as possible and hung up.

"Need a lift?" Juliet asked.

"What did you do?" Melanie asked as she turned around to face her.

"Exactly what you wanted from the beginning. I'm sorry it took so long." She appeared genuine and Melanie didn't know what to think.

If what Juliet was implying was true …

Nathan was cured.

He was cured.

Hope flared in her chest, but she tamped it down. No. She wouldn't let herself believe it until she saw it. She didn't want to have to deal with the disappointment if it wasn't as good as it seemed.

She stared at Juliet a moment longer. "How?" was all she managed.

Juliet's blue eyes softened. "All in due time. For now, I'm sure you want to see your brother."

The drive went by in a blur.

Melanie hesitated outside the front door, afraid to go inside. Afraid of what she might find.

"I don't know if I'm ready for this," Melanie confessed.

There was nothing behind Juliet's smile this time, only pure understanding. Juliet patted her arm comfortingly. "It'll be fine. Nathan will be a little disoriented for a while, I'm sure, especially if he has any lingering medications in his system. But in a few days you'll have your brother back. Enjoy the moment."

"If he really is cured like you say, then thank you. I don't know how I can ever repay you."

Her smile took on a greedy tinge. "I didn't want to discuss payment yet, but since you brought it up … we have an assignment, a sort of training assignment for you. If you would be so kind as to accompany me on Saturday, we can start your payment."

"Training?"

Juliet nodded. "You're going to help a lot of people, and in return, when you've paid us in full, we'll help you."

Her mother chose that moment to open the door. Juliet gave a quick nod before she slipped away, not giving Melanie any time to ask her question.

Help me with what?

"Oh, Melanie." Her mother dragged her into the house, her face streaked with tears, but she was wearing the biggest smile Melanie had ever seen.

Her meeting with Juliet forgotten, Melanie quickly followed her mom, hope growing in her chest like a balloon.

Her father was at the end of the hall, standing in the doorway to her and Nathan's room. His face wet too. When he caught sight of Melanie he picked her up in a bear hug. "You did it," he told her. "Whoever those people were that you found … they did it. You did it."

It was almost too much to handle. Melanie extracted herself from her father's burly embrace. He wrapped an arm around his wife and together they motioned for her to enter her room.

Butterflies erupted in his stomach. She held her breath and stepped across the threshold. The bed was empty. Clothes and other miscellaneous items still littered the floor. Where—?

The adjoining bathroom door opened and Nathan stepped out. He was wearing jeans and a white shirt that clung to his skin. He had a towel in one hand and was drying his damp hair. He stopped dead in his tracks when he noticed her.

"Lanie?"

Something between a sob and a laugh escaped her.

His eyes were clear. No glaze, no drugged out dazed look to them, just … clear blue, like she was looking in a mirror.

He flashed her a dimple and that was all it took. She threw herself at him. "Nathan, is it really you?" She hung onto his shoulder but pulled back to take him in. "Are you okay? How are you feeling?"

He chuckled and playfully brushed her hands off his shoulders. "Easy, Lanie, I'm fine. Mom and Dad already grilled me. I'm sure Aunt Bertie will have questions too, and Paul. I don't need it from you, too." He made a disgruntled noise then considered her for a moment. "Maybe you could help a brother out and bust me out of here before any more questions come up?" he asked in a hushed voice.

Her father's response rumbled through the room. "I don't think so, young man. You're on permanent lockdown until we see fit. In case you forgot, you were unconscious for a few hours."

Nathan winced and Melanie squeezed his arm in sympathy.

He was back. Her brother was back. She wanted to pinch herself to make sure it wasn't a dream.

She pulled out her phone, wanting to share the good news with Joel, but she stopped cold in her tracks. What would she tell him? That Nathan was miraculously better? Joel would want to know all the details, details she couldn't give him.

She regretfully put her phone away.

"You going to be all right there, Lanie?" Nathan bumped her on the chin, raising her gaze to his. "You just got all sad for a second there."

"I'm fine," she lied. "Just … tired." It was the best excuse she could come up with. And it was partially true. She was tired—tired of running from Alexander, tired of worrying about Nathan and her family, tired from a training assignment she hadn't even had to do yet.

She sighed.

At least Nathan was one less thing to worry about. Now she only needed to focus on getting through the weekend.

Chapter 19

"What do you mean you have plans?" Joel's voice asked through the line.

Saturday had arrived and Joel wanted to take her out on a date. A proper date. He wanted to treat her to dinner where she would have to wear something other than yoga pants and a sports bra. Then he wanted to take her out afterward—he hadn't said where, only that it wasn't for a training session.

It sounded wonderful and amazing and ten other adjectives that were used in place of great—and Melanie had to decline.

Her heart hurt and she felt like the biggest bitch in the world for turning him down. And on top of having to tell him no, she lied right to his face.

"I'm helping my brother," she told him. The lie squeezed her lungs, making it hard to breathe.

"How's he doing? Did he start using a notebook? Has it helped?"

His concern for her brother twisted the metaphoric knife in her gut even more. "It has. He's doing much better."

"Awesome! Maybe I can meet him one day."

She mumbled something that could have been a "maybe" then quickly ended the call.

Melanie shut her eyes and lifted her face to the warm sun as she stood outside her house. This had to be the worst thing on the planet she could do to someone, and still she was forced to do it.

Only a little longer. Once Juliet was paid in full, Melanie would come clean with everything.

She tucked her phone away and scanned the streets for her reason for turning Joel down.

Right on time a sleek black BMW pulled up to the curb.

The back window rolled down and Juliet poked her head out. "Ready?" she called cheerily.

Melanie felt as if she were marching down death row. But she doubted Juliet wanted to hear that from her newest soldier, so she remained quiet.

Remember what Nathan said. Stay positive.

She tried to focus on all the good things Nathan had to say about Juliet and her organization. How they'd brought in a woman who did what Melanie had done, only they explained his powers were gone now, permanently. He'd never be bombarded with visions again. He'd been so ecstatic.

Melanie tried to channel some of that excitement into herself, but it wasn't working. This situation was different than her brother's. In this case, she was the one taking the power. She didn't know how she felt about that.

But definitely not ecstatic.

You're going to help so many people, Lanie. I know you wished you didn't have your power at all but just think, your curse is going to change so many lives for the better. You're going to do so much good with it.

At the time Nathan's words calmed her, but now it was go time and butterflies were flooding her stomach.

She got in the car and instantly assessed Juliet's outfit. Melanie hadn't known what to wear, so she had opted for comfortable yoga pants, a simple tee, and a light jacket. Juliet was dressed in comfy slacks and sneakers. She had on a plain top that made it hard for Melanie to decide if the outfit was dressy casual or just casual.

"You're fine," Juliet said as if hearing her unasked question. "This assignment doesn't require much physical effort. There's no dress code required."

"Where are we going?" Melanie stared out the window as they drove down Pacific Coast Highway, her heart beating a mile a minute. Gray clouds hung low out over the ocean, making the water look ominous, while only a few miles in the sun shone brightly. It reflected Melanie's mood perfectly: a sunny exterior, but just out of reach waited an emotional storm.

She'd trained quite a bit over the past few days with Joel. She'd even say she felt mildly comfortable with her powers, but that was with Joel. This was completely different, and Melanie felt as if she were starting from ground zero all over again. She was frightened and she didn't even know why. Juliet wasn't projecting any outward hostility. She sat relaxed as could be in the leather seat. "You'll see," was all Juliet said. "We're almost there."

Melanie continued her assessment of the situation. In a strange way, it seemed to calm her, or at least offer a distraction.

The doors weren't locked. She took that as a good sign. They didn't intend to keep her here against her will.

Or it meant they weren't concerned with Melanie throwing herself out of a moving vehicle.

She frowned at the stray thought.

She hardly noticed when the car came to a stop. They had pulled into a residential area filled with houses and apartment complexes.

"What are we doing here?"

"Answering a house call," Juliet said before getting out.

The driver stayed where he was, not moving an inch. Melanie couldn't tell if he was even breathing, and then, as if he sensed her gaze, his head turned the slightest little bit so that those dark sunglasses stared right at her through the rearview mirror. Melanie hastily made her exit. Perhaps the man was some kind of cyborg. At this point she wouldn't put anything off as too far out there.

Juliet watched her with an amused smirk in place.

Melanie cleared her throat and pretended to dust herself off. The last thing she needed was Juliet to know how easily she was unnerved by her goons. "So what kind of house call are we making?" She tried to sound interested and not apprehensive.

"The helpful kind," Juliet replied, still giving Melanie nothing.

Melanie growled low in her throat but dutifully followed after the brunette when she started down the paved path into the apartments. They passed the laundry room, the pool, and ascended a set of stairs before reaching their destination.

Juliet knocked on the door to apartment 701A.

Melanie waited for a dog bark or the murmur of people on the other side, but there was nothing. Not a sound. It was eerie, and eerier still when the door cracked open soundlessly and half of a face peeked out.

"Yes?" It was a female voice.

One brown eye watched them warily, easily visible by the way her brown hair was pulled back from her face. It was hard to tell her age. Melanie guessed somewhere between twenty-five and forty.

"Charlotte Reese?" Juliet asked.

The gap narrowed, only an eye visible now. "Who wants to know?"

Clearly this woman did not want to be found. Melanie glanced around, half expecting someone to be watching, to report them to the police for disturbing this poor woman. But there wasn't a soul in sight.

"Ms. Reese, I'm Juliet Arden. We spoke on the phone."

The crack in the door opened wider until a full face appeared, followed by a body. Charlotte looked down at Juliet, clearly not having pictured the woman she'd talked to as being so short. "Ms. Arden, I expected you to be … " she paused briefly, "older."

Melanie hid her smile, as she could all but see the steam coming off Juliet's head. It must've been hard for Juliet to be such a high-ranking whatever she was and look like she was a middle schooler.

Melanie placed Ms. Reese somewhere in her mid-thirties. Now that Melanie got a better look at her, she could see the faint wrinkles around her eyes and mouth. Her clothes were casual but conservative and she wore no makeup.

"Please, come in."

Melanie followed Juliet's lead and stepped into the apartment of a neat freak. The place was spotless. No clothes lying around, no trash to be seen. Even the blanket on the couch was folded into a perfect rectangle, draped exactly halfway over the front and back of the sofa. There was an even number of pillows on both the couch and the large recliner chair, all arranged perfectly.

If ever there was a place that was the complete opposite of her own house, this was it.

When Charlotte motioned for them to take a seat, Melanie sat on the first couple inches of the cushions, too afraid of disturbing the pillows. Juliet had no such qualms and sat back completely on the couch next to her.

Charlotte lowered herself into the recliner, but she was seated on the edge as well, as if too anxious to relax.

"I didn't expect you so soon," Ms. Reese told Juliet. "Thank you so much for coming. Is she the one you were waiting for?" She pointed to Melanie.

Melanie sat up a little straighter, her attention riveted to Juliet. Finally, some answers.

Juliet didn't even glance her way. She nodded at Charlotte. "This is the woman I was waiting for. Ms. Reese, I'd like to introduce you to Ms. Vyntra. She'll be relieving you of your powers today."

Melanie's stomach dropped out of her body. She'd been expecting that, but when she'd been told she was going on a training assignment, she hoped against hope it wouldn't include this. She wanted to jump to her feet, put distance between them—maybe a whole block's worth of houses would be a good start—but her legs felt like rubber.

Juliet regarded her calmly. "This is your first training assignment. Ms. Reese, like your brother, lives her life in fear and pain. Only you can help her."

Melanie stared at Charlotte. She looked nothing like Nathan had. She wasn't strung out on drugs to escape horror-filled visions. The woman looked like a shining example of health. It appeared as if Charlotte had her whole life in order. Melanie got a better look at some of the books that were neatly stacked away. They were medical books. Clearly the woman was in the medical profession and wasn't hurting for anything. What could possibly be so horrible in this perfect little world?

"She doesn't need help." Melanie gestured to Charlotte and the living area around them. "There's nothing out of place, her eyes are clear, sane—where's the problem?"

Juliet shared a look with Charlotte. "Perhaps you should show her what you told me over the phone."

Charlotte got to her feet without a word. Melanie sat rooted to her seat. She hadn't liked the sound of that.

"Are you coming?" Charlotte asked her.

Melanie glanced at Juliet. "Aren't *you* coming?" she asked her boss.

"This is something you need to see all on your own. I can't always be there with you."

Melanie was stunned for a few seconds. Talk about feeding her to the wolves.

"Don't worry," Juliet reassured her. "I'll be right here."

Like that was any sort of comfort.

Melanie carefully got to her feet and followed Charlotte past the kitchen to the back of the apartment. The hallway was short, with a bathroom on one side and a closed door on the other. Of course Charlotte stopped at the closed door. "In here," she said.

Melanie braced herself. Couldn't give her warning for what was to come, right? That'd ruin the whole surprise.

She gave herself enough swinging room so that if anything jumped out at her from behind that door, she could get in a good punch.

The door swung in soundlessly, revealing a disaster. If they had tornados in California, Melanie might have thought one had hit Charlotte's place, but that wasn't the case. Which meant that all the broken furniture and torn clothes and damaged property was Charlotte's doing.

Melanie put a few feet between the two of them just in case the woman had some kind of anger management problem.

"What happened here?"

Charlotte went over to the pile of broken furniture. A wooden table was cracked clean down the middle, and a small box was resting on the edge, something silver sparkling in the low lighting. Charlotte picked up the box and brought it over to Melanie.

Again Melanie stepped back, keeping her distance. "What happened in here?" she repeated.

"I did." Charlotte's eyes were downcast, her shoulders slumped. She held out the box in her hands.

Surgical tools. Mangled surgical tools.

Chapter 20

"Uhh … " Melanie didn't know whether to run or feign interest. Luckily, she didn't have to do either.

"These were my tools," said Charlotte. "I'm a surgical oncologist, but ever since my powers manifested, I've had to take a leave of absence from what I love." She picked up a scalpel and turned it over in her hand. The handle was crushed, as if someone had smashed it in their fist. "I can't control the strength and I can't control when it happens. I've hurt so many people when I'm supposed to be helping them. Do you know how terrifying it is to be operating on someone, applying just the right amount of pressure to the scalpel and suddenly it cuts clear through bone?"

Melanie's stomach churned.

Charlotte continued, "I had to claim it was a cramp that caused my arm to spasm. My insurance has gone through the roof. I've nearly lost my job. I can't seem to stop it. My boyfriend left me because we had an argument and I was so mad, I slammed my fist on the table. It practically shattered under my hand." That explained the broken table at least. "Josh freaked out and never looked back, said I was crazy, on drugs, and needed to get help. But that's the thing, I'm not on drugs. I don't take steroids. I just have this unbelievable power sometimes that," her voice caught, "that destroys everything it touches. Literally."

Melanie felt her heart crack open a bit. She could sympathize with Charlotte, more than she probably knew.

"When Ms. Arden got in contact with me, telling me she could help my problem, I thought it was too good to be true. No one does something for nothing."

So Juliet wasn't charging Charlotte anything? Melanie stored that little bit of information away for later.

"But she told me about her organization and how they help people like me, how I could have my life back. I could finally return to my job, to what I love." Those doe-brown eyes rose to Melanie's. "She said it all depended on you, their new recruit. I had to wait for you, but I didn't mind. I understand a waiting list."

There was so much hope in her eyes that for a moment Melanie couldn't speak past the lump of emotion in her throat. She wanted to tell Charlotte that she wasn't alone. Charlotte was one of them, and Melanie finally understood what Joel had said that first time she'd spoken with him, how she was a part of their world now too.

People like me.

"Will you help me?"

Nathan had been so happy afterward. Juliet helped Nathan. Now Melanie had the opportunity to give this woman her life back.

"I can try," she said. She didn't want to give the surgeon false hope.

Charlotte's face brightened. "Thank you." She grasped Melanie's hands in hers and squeezed in thanks.

Melanie tried to smile, but it turned into a wince of pain as Charlotte's fingers continued to tighten.

Melanie tore her hands away.

Charlotte's eyes were wide with shock and she dropped her gaze, her hands going around her back. "I'm so sorry."

Melanie massaged her hands. "It's okay. No harm done." Though she'd probably have a few bruises tomorrow.

"Where do you need me?"

Melanie eyed the disaster zone. "Let's go back out into the living room."

Charlotte nodded and closed the door behind her, leaving that part of her life locked away where no one could find it.

Melanie felt a wave of sympathy for her. How many superpowered individuals were there in the world? How many didn't have anyone to talk to, no one to help them?

Joel would have jumped at the opportunity to meet Charlotte and teach her as much as he could about their kind. The thought of him flitting around the room in an excited frenzy made her smile. She rubbed her chest.

When they entered the living room, Juliet got to her feet. "How'd it go?" Her blue eyes scanned Melanie as if for any injury before settling on her face where they remained, studious.

Charlotte was the one to answer. "She agreed to help me," she boasted, positively glowing with joy.

Juliet smiled, but her eyes remained glued on Melanie. "I'm very glad to hear that, Ms. Reese."

Melanie swallowed nervously. She'd gotten this far, now what?

Juliet seemed to take pity on her and led Charlotte onto the sofa then tugged Melanie to her side. She placed Melanie's hands on Charlotte's arm and gave a meaningful squeeze. "You hang on to her, okay? No matter what, don't break contact until I tell you to. Got it?"

Melanie nodded numbly.

Her heart was pounding furiously and she wanted to apologize to Charlotte for her sweaty palms.

She wished Joel were here.

But he wasn't, and Juliet would have to do as a substitute.

"I want you to close your eyes now, Melanie," Juliet instructed. "You, too, Charlotte."

Melanie did as she was told and assumed Charlotte did as well because Juliet didn't say anything more on the matter. "Now, Charlotte, I need you to stay calm and relaxed. Melanie"—she tensed—"I need you to concentrate and reach for your powers."

Melanie tried to do just that, but like at the beginning, she couldn't activate them. She swallowed thickly. She couldn't get performance anxiety now.

A few more tense seconds passed before Juliet silently spoke up. "Melanie?"

"Give me a minute," she whispered back. She thought of all the times she'd been with Joel, and how easy it had been to call forth her powers then. There was that time she'd accidently helped Nathan … well, she wanted to do that now. Why wasn't it working?

Okay, she needed to focus. With Nathan her powers had activated because she was afraid for him. She tried to conjure those feelings again, how terrified she'd been, the feeling of helplessness, her throat closing off and an invisible weight pushing down on her lungs …

Her neck didn't tingle.

She axed that idea.

"Melanie?" Juliet's voice was a tad impatient.

She wanted to growl, but kept it to herself. "Working on it," she hissed and blocked out the waves of irritation she felt coming from Juliet's direction.

Clearly, trying to recreate the feelings of fear didn't work. Melanie needed something else. She went back to her lessons with Joel, picturing his house, the kitchen, the table, the nerdy movie posters, everything. She instantly felt more at ease. Taking it as a good sign, she continued, imagining herself seated at his kitchen table directly across from Joel, his midnight- blue eyes sparkling, a bright white smile just for her.

Her stomach fluttered and the back of her neck tingled.

Melanie grasped onto her powers with both hands, metaphorically speaking.

"Got it," she told Juliet.

"Good." Juliet's tone was clipped. "Now pull Charlotte's power into yourself, feel it flow into you."

Melanie did as Juliet said, but she took her time. She put into effect everything she'd practiced with Joel. She drew from

Charlotte's arm at first, then moved her way up into her chest, taking the brunt of Charlotte's power, easing it away from her so that she'd never hurt another patient accidently during surgery.

Melanie's hands started to burn. "I think I should let go now—"

"No!" Juliet shouted. "Do not release her."

Melanie frowned, her hands hurting from the heat that was coming off them or perhaps from what was coming into them.

Her heart rate picked up. "I don't like this, Juliet—"

"Just a little longer, Melanie, you're almost there. Keep pulling."

"I really don't want to do this anymore." She started to release her hands, but Juliet's own wrapped around them.

"Think of all the people you're going to help, think of Charlotte. Just hang on a little longer."

"It doesn't feel right." The burning pain was nearly unbearable now and she clenched her jaw, her eyes popping open.

Juliet knelt in front of her, her hands on top of theirs, keeping the contact. Charlotte was still lying on the couch but—"Oh my God, Juliet, look at her face. She's in pain!"

Melanie tried to stop the flow, but she was panicking. Her heart was beating out of control and she couldn't rein in her powers even if she wanted to.

"Let go of me." Melanie tried to throw Juliet off. "I could be killing her. What are you waiting for?"

Charlotte's body arched off the couch, her mouth open in a silent scream.

"That." Juliet released Melanie's hands and jumped away.

She didn't see anything more. A bright light, like someone taking a surprise photo with the flash on full blast, momentarily stunned her. She might've blacked out because next thing she knew, she was on her back, staring up at the popcorn ceiling.

Juliet hung over her, concerned. "How're you feeling?"

Melanie narrowed her eyes, wanting to strangle the curvy brunette. "How am I feeling?" she mocked. "What the hell is wrong with you?"

She shot up to a sitting position and the world took a spin. She flung her arm out blindly in an attempt to grab anything to center herself. She hit something that grunted, probably Juliet. *Good.*

Something slick and cool pressed into her hand. "Drink this," Juliet commanded.

Melanie felt like telling her to shove her orders up her ass, but the world was still spinning so she did as she was told.

It took a few minutes of sitting on the floor and sipping water before she could see straight again. When the world was still once more, she blinked a few times and shook her head just to make sure. When all was well, she pinned Juliet with a glare.

"What was that all about? I've never hung on that long before or taken that much. You have no idea what the ramifications are."

Melanie's anger spiked when Juliet smiled at her words.

"What's so damn funny? You could have hurt Charlotte."

Speaking of Charlotte, she turned to check on the woman and found her on the sofa, eyes closed.

Her stomach clenched. "She's not dead, is she?" Oh god, she couldn't deal with that.

Juliet's smile deepened. "No, she's not dead. She's just unconscious and she'll be fine once she wakes up. She'll be a little disoriented like your brother was, but she'll be right as rain in a few hours, after a day at most. And I was smiling, Melanie, because I do know the ramifications. This is not my first rodeo, as some people would say. This has been my eleventh mission when it comes to … relieving another of their powers. I know what to do, what to expect, what signs to look for, and you did everything perfectly. Nothing was amiss. I know it'll take some getting used to, but you did wonderfully."

Melanie shakily got to her feet. "Wonderfully? Are you kidding me? Did you see what happened to Charlotte? She looked like she was in pain. She passed out, for cripes' sake!"

Juliet calmly got to her feet as well. "That's how it happens. When she came off the couch, that's the sign you wait for. It's the visual signal that the last of her power has left her body."

Juliet's words sank in slowly, taking a minute to get past the anger. "So I just did what you did to Nathan? That woman's powers are gone now?"

"Gone from her but not from you. You see, you have them now. Permanently."

The blood drained from Melanie's face and her knees gave out.

Juliet caught her, but Melanie still had a couple inches on her and they both toppled into the recliner chair, Melanie half sitting on Juliet.

Melanie hardly noticed. "You mean—? I have—" She couldn't finish her sentences.

"The powers have gone into you," Juliet told her, surprisingly gentle. "You now have Charlotte's super strength ability."

Melanie wanted to laugh. A mad, hysterical laugh at the comic book her life seemed to have become.

"So, I'm like Wonder Woman or something? Am I going to be able to fly soon too? Do I get a whip or lasso or whatever it is she carries around?"

Juliet awkwardly patted her arm, as Melanie was still seated atop her. "Take it easy. I know it's a lot to process right now, but you're going to be fine. This new power is like having your first one. It'll only come to you when you activate it. This is also where my knowledge gets a little fuzzy, but I think it's a bit more difficult to summon this new power than your original. We have another like you who can help you with any questions you might have."

Melanie stared down at her hands. They looked the same, only now she could harness unthinkable strength. Would she suffer the same fate as Charlotte? Accidently hurt someone in a moment of gentleness?

Her mind instantly went to Joel—hurting him during a tender moment together.

She felt sick.

She hadn't asked for this. She didn't know she'd gain the ability permanently.

She could barely stand the idea of her own power. Now she was going to have to deal with multiple abilities?

Only minutes ago there had been such hope in Charlotte's eyes, joy at knowing she was going to be fine.

Who was going to save Melanie?

Tears burned her eyes, from anger or sadness she couldn't tell, but she refused to let them fall.

"Take me home," she ordered Juliet.

For once Juliet didn't argue. Maybe she realized how unstable Melanie was. Maybe she feared for her life because she was in the presence of a woman with uncontrollable strength.

Melanie laughed humorlessly to herself as she let Juliet up. She was the Hulk. Would she turn green now when she got mad? Would she lose all sense of reason and attack those she loved?

When Juliet dropped her off at home, Melanie went straight to her room. She shut the door and called Joel. She didn't care anymore. She needed someone to talk to.

Voicemail.

Frustrated all over again, she threw her phone into her pillow, the tears she held back earlier falling freely.

The door to her room opened slowly and Nathan appeared, holding a plate with a sandwich. "Lanie?"

She sniffed pathetically and that was all it took.

Sandwich forgotten, Nathan enveloped her in his arms and held on, not saying a word as the tears swamped her soul.

Chapter 21

Melanie's number popped up on his phone.

"No calls, Kegler," Cali hissed at his side. Her dark hair was pulled back into a ponytail, her eye makeup accentuating her dark eyes. Those eyes looked at him nervously, and he knew she only snapped at him because she was worried for Felix.

Earlier that day Niella had gotten a Dream about where one of their suited friends was located. The guild hadn't hesitated—they moved out, not wanting to miss their opportunity.

But that wasn't the only thing contributing to Cali's nervousness. Jente was missing. Whether it was his own choice to go to ground or someone had taken him was anyone's guess. Cali had tried to get ahold of him again and again, but to no avail.

It didn't bode well and had the entire guild on edge.

Now the two of them stood outside the building Niella had sent them to. They'd found it relatively easily, and Felix and Merrick had gone inside. Joel was still feeling sore about being left behind with Cali, but they had all ganged up on him, saying he wasn't fit enough after his accident earlier in the week. Sure, his muscles were still stiff from the wreck, but he didn't think it was that bad. He could have helped out more instead of being sidelined.

He tried to find his silver lining. At least he wasn't stuck at the clinic like Sydney, Luke, and Niella.

"I don't like this," Cali said after a few moments. "What if they were attacked?"

He shook his head. "We would have heard something if there was a struggle. I think they encountered a computer they could hack and they don't know what to do with it."

Cali shot him an arch look. "Get over it, Joel—you weren't going in there. You can hardly turn your head."

"I can too," he protested and started to do just that. He winced before he even got his chin to shoulder.

Cali snorted. "Uh huh. Now cut it out before you hurt yourself."

They waited for ten more tense minutes before Joel started to get anxious. Cali bounced next to him, unable to control her nerves.

Their eyes locked. "We should go in there," he said.

"Agreed."

They started out hunched over, hugging the edge of the building until Joel realized they'd attract more attention that way. It was broad daylight; one didn't sneak the way they would at night.

"Stop, stop." He grabbed Cali. "We need to act like we own this place. If anyone drives by, they won't notice a thing."

She eyed him suspiciously. "And when did you become a special ops expert?"

"It's not that hard, Cali." He proceeded around the building, standing tall, scanning for any cameras. "You just have to pay attention when you watch all those movies Felix and I like to marathon."

She scoffed behind him. "I can't believe you have a girlfriend."

He thought about that for a moment. He didn't know if Melanie was his girlfriend. He knew without a doubt that she was his Mirror Mate, but like Melanie said, they didn't have control over that. Would she want to be referred to as his girlfriend? That would be something she *did* have control over.

He'd ask her next time he saw her.

His phone burned in his pocket and it ate at him that he'd had to ignore her call. What if it was something important? What if she was in danger?

He shook his head. It was Saturday afternoon. She was safe.

"Earth to Kegler," Cali whispered. "What the hell, man? You can't go off daydreaming in the middle of a mission. What kind of operative are you?"

"Sorry." Joel rubbed his arm where she'd pinched him mercilessly. "And ow."

"Serves you right. Do you see anyone by that back door?"

They'd made it around the building to the back door propped open with a small stick—either Felix's or Merrick's handiwork.

A car engine sounded around front.

Cali cursed. "I think they're back."

"What the hell are you guys doing here? You're supposed to be our lookouts." Merrick's ice-blue eyes flared as he stared down at them. He held the back door open as Felix emerged a few seconds later, printed documents under one arm.

Felix stopped dead when he saw them. "Cali? Joel? Why are you guys—?"

The glass door shattered, a rippling wave seeming to shake the very foundation. They all recoiled as the shards rained down around them.

"Shit." Joel felt the glass cut against his skin. "What was that?" He looked around for a bullet, a rock, something that could have destroyed the door so effectively.

"Sonic boom," Cali shouted, her hands covering her ears. She was the only one.

Joel, Merrick, and Felix all exchanged glances. They hadn't heard anything, only felt the force, which meant there was another Silencer like Cali around.

Felix, Merrick, and Joel popped up as one to take a good look at what they were up against.

Joel recognized their suited friend, but the Asian woman next to him was new. She also wasn't dressed in formalwear. Her hand was pulled back, ready to throw another sonic blast at them.

Merrick's hands came down on Joel's shoulders. "We're leaving, now!"

Felix was already ahead of them, ushering Cali away as quickly as possible.

The woman didn't run after them. Her face was pinched in concentration and she brought her arm up in a quick move.

Something shimmered at the corner of Joel's vision and a few seconds later Merrick cursed as he ran face first into some kind of invisible barrier.

Joel stared. "No fucking way." There was no way that woman had shot a sonic boom at them and then erected some invisible wall.

Adrenaline pumped through his veins. Joel grabbed Merrick, blood gushing from his nose, and steered him away from the wall.

He continued to glance over his shoulder and watched as the woman tried again and again to summon the barriers but to no avail. Frustration marred her face.

Curious.

She threw sonic blasts out like they were no big deal, yet she wasn't comfortable with these powers? If Joel didn't know any better, he'd think she was just starting to use them.

"Hurry up!"

Felix's voice broke Joel's thoughts, and he and Merrick rushed to the Hummer.

"What happened to him?" Felix jerked his chin in Merrick's direction as he slammed his foot on the gas. "You take a sucker punch at him or what?"

He glared at the back of Felix's head. The jab would've been more accurate a few months ago when Joel had still felt torn up about Sydney leaving him for Merrick, but he didn't feel that way anymore and he wanted the guild to know that too.

Merrick beat him to the punch. "Joel and I are good. He didn't hit me, he saved me. That woman had some other power I've never encountered before. She summoned this invisible wall. I ran right into it."

"Illusionist?" Felix asked.

Joel and Merrick shrugged.

An Illusionist was someone with the ability to create anything with a wave of a hand. The catch with Illusionists was that their creations weren't corporeal unless the Illusionist was full-forced. There was no way that woman could be a full-forced Illusionist and a Silencer.

Cali echoed Joel's sentiments.

"How is that even possible?" She spoke up from the passenger seat. "She threw that sonic attack at us, so how can she turn around the next minute and summon some magic wall?"

Felix frowned and Joel waited as his friend tried to piece together the same puzzle he was trying to wrap his mind around.

"I don't know," Felix said after a few seconds.

"Hopefully, we'll find some answers in the documents we confiscated," Merrick said.

"Hopefully," Joel echoed, a sinking feeling in his gut.

Chapter 22

Melanie found Joel sitting alone on one of the benches near the basketball courts at the community center. He got to his feet as soon as he saw her.

"I'm so sorry I missed your call yesterday. Is everything okay?"

He'd called her late Saturday night, apologizing for his moment of silence, mentioning a bunch of paperwork he needed to go over with his guild that night, and as an alternative to their date he'd suggested a basketball game today with two of his guild members.

"Everything's fine. I was a little stressed yesterday and needed someone to vent to." It wasn't a lie. After crying her eyes out to Nathan, she'd told him everything and he'd helped her work through it. He'd pointed out the importance of her work again, how she was curing so many people and giving them the best gift of all: their lives back. He'd pointed out that she was learning to control her main powers and that it should transfer over to all the other powers she might collect on the way. It made her feel a tiny bit better. She'd had all morning at work to come to terms with it. In hindsight it was probably a blessing that Joel had missed her call. She would have told him everything, and that would have been disastrous.

Her eyes caught on his forearms. New cuts littered his skin, some covered with bandages.

"What happened to your arms?" She rushed to him and gently ran her fingers along his skin. As always, her gut clenched at the contact and her body ached for him.

His eyes flashed with desire. "It's nothing," he said hastily. "A cat got loose at Sydney's clinic and we all had to help catch it."

The scrapes didn't look like claw marks—some of them were too fine—but Melanie left it.

"Speaking of your guild, how did the paperwork go?" she asked him.

His expression darkened. "Disconcerting."

He didn't elaborate.

So, she wasn't the only one keeping secrets.

Before she could ask any more, two new people came onto the basketball court. Joel smiled and waved. These must've been part of his guild. Wow, they were gorgeous.

Was there some kind of pretty rule to get into their guild?

"Melanie, I'd like you to meet Felix Del Valle and his fiancé, Cali Crazar."

"You know," Cali said, "when we get married, I'm going to make it a rule that I come first in the introductions and you can follow as my husband."

Felix grinned. "Joel just likes me better so he says my name first."

They were both tall, which meant this was going to be a one-sided basketball game. They also shared dark hair. Cali wore her hair back in a ponytail, her side bangs pinned out of her onyx eyes, which were made more pronounced due to the smoky makeup she wore around them. Her build was somewhere between a model and an athlete. Cali didn't suffer from large breasts either. Melanie felt a twinge of jealousy.

Felix had a short haircut and five o'clock shadow. His skin was bronzed and his eyes were the brightest blue-green she'd ever seen. He was built like a football player, broad shouldered and nothing but hard muscle. Melanie narrowed her eyes at him—was he was one of the guys in high school who used to pick on Joel?

"Nice to meet you, Melanie." Felix stuck out his hand, instantly destroying her ill-mannered jock theory, and she noticed a faint coating of something white around his fingertips.

He caught her staring and brought up his hand to examine it himself. "Damn, thought I got all the flour out."

"Flour?" she asked.

Cali patted her fiancé on the chest. "He's got the manliest job around. He's a baker."

"Thanks, future wife," Felix drawled.

Cali winked up at him. "You can butter my biscuit any day."

Joel made a disgusted noise. "Save it for the honeymoon, would you?"

Melanie found herself smiling along.

The basketball game started out innocently enough. It was the perfect day, bright sun, few clouds, and a wonderful cooling breeze from the ocean. One second Melanie was passing the ball to Joel, the next it disappeared then reappeared in Felix's hands.

"Hey!" Joel shouted. "No powers, cheater."

Felix gave him a cheeky grin. "It's not cheating. It's called using my advantage." He threw the ball to Cali, who scored.

A glint came into Joel's eye, and he took the ball and passed to Melanie. She was still trying to wrap her mind around what Felix had done with nothing but a swipe of his hand. Sure, she remembered the brief description Joel had given her of all the guild's powers, but it was entirely different to see them in action.

Joel raced up court and she passed to him. In a burst of speed, Felix came up the middle and stole the ball. Quick as lightning, Joel switched direction and grabbed Felix's arm, only for a second. Felix continued toward his own basket.

Melanie laughed. "Traveling!" she shouted at him.

Felix stopped dead and stared at his hand where Joel had Locked the ball to it. "Hey now, that's playing dirty."

"You started it," Joel said arrogantly.

Melanie felt the testosterone go up in the air.

"Fine." Felix held out his hand for Joel to Unlock the ball. "New rules."

"This should be interesting," Cali, standing next to Melanie, said under her breath.

Joel grasped Felix's hand. "New rules," he agreed as the ball fell free from Felix's grasp.

Melanie didn't know what to make of any of this. Joel held the ball and came over to her. Cali moved to Felix.

Joel blocked them with his body. "Take some of my powers. We need to even the playing field," Joel whispered to her.

"What?" Trepidation ran down her spine.

"It'll be a good exercise session for your powers too," he said. "Take a little bit and when someone tries to take the ball from you, Lock it to your hand so they can't snatch it." A competitive glint came to his eye. "Then maybe try and Lock their limbs so they can't use an arm or something."

"Now *that* is playing dirty," she whispered to him.

He shrugged. "This is war. Felix is giving similar instructions to Cali."

Melanie leaned to her right to glance around Joel. Sure enough, Felix stood hunched before Cali, his hands moving animatedly.

"What can Cali do again?" Melanie asked.

"She's a Silencer, so she can manipulate and control sound. I'm not sure how she's going to use that to her advantage, but we need to be cautious."

Melanie refrained from rolling her eyes. Joel was treating this as if it were an actual battle. *Boys.*

She had to admit though, their energy was contagious. When Joel held his hand out to her, she hesitated only for a second before reaching out to take a bit of his powers.

"Ready?" Joel asked when she'd released him.

His blue eyes sparkled.

She stood taller and gave him a quick salute. "Ready, sir."

Pride shown on his face and he quickly gave her a kiss on the cheek. "That's my girl."

His words warmed her, but the time for pleasantries was over.

It was game time.

It didn't take long to figure out how Cali was using her powers to their advantage. Melanie saw her lips moving but no sound was coming out, then Felix's mouth would move and still she couldn't hear. Somehow they were communicating without her or Joel being able to hear it.

They shared a worried glance. This wasn't good.

Team Tall, Dark, and Gorgeous, as Melanie was mentally referring to them, scored five points in a row on them. Her own competitive nature started to spark as she took the ball down court to Joel. She saw Cali come up on her left, she faked to the right, and quickly threw to Joel.

Cali's lips moved and she shot out her arm.

As if hit by some invisible wind, the ball sailed past Joel, right to Felix. Felix took off and scored a three-pointer.

The spark of competition inside Melanie grew to a flame.

She walked over to Cali and touched her on the arm. "How'd you do that? It was amazing," she gushed.

Cali preened under the attention. "Thanks. Just another skill that comes with the territory."

"Ready, Melanie?" Joel called from down court. He gave her a knowing wink and she smiled to herself as she jogged down for a pass.

Cali kept pace with her, but when she went to block the ball, her arm didn't budge.

Her lips moved and Melanie didn't need sound to read them. "What the hell?"

"Problem?" Melanie asked sweetly.

Cali's dark eyes narrowed, and before Cali could say more Melanie passed to Joel, who was already up court to narrow the gap between their scores.

Joel laughed as Cali ran, her upper arm frozen to her side, to where Felix stood with the ball. Her expression was murderous.

Felix tried and failed to hide his smile, which earned him a smack on the shoulder with Cali's good arm.

"Nicely done," Joel said. "She didn't even realize what you were doing till it was too late. That's what I call finesse."

"I feel a little bad. How long will it stay like that?"

Joel shrugged. "Until you Unlock it. If you're feeling really torn up about it, you can let her go when we take the lead."

"You're horrible," she said, but the smile on her face belittled her words. "Are you going to get Felix?"

Joel threw his head back and laughed. "Now who's the bloodthirsty one?"

The game took on a mind of its own after that.

Felix started using his powers more to make up for Cali's one-arm disadvantage. Cali weaved around the court in an attempt to keep Melanie at bay. Melanie got only close enough to Lock Cali to the concrete once, but her concentration was spotty at best and the hold lasted just a second.

Cali jumped away from her. "We're switching, Felix, You're taking Melanie now. This girl is ruthless. I think she's better than Joel."

"I heard that," Joel called.

"That's 'cause I wanted you to." Cali stuck her tongue out at him.

They switched partners. Melanie was winded within seconds trying to keep up with Felix's long legs. Cali had been closer in height so the difference wasn't as obvious, but with Felix she was screwed. It didn't help matters either when he gave her winks or smiles as he scored on her. Her competitive side was starting to get annoyed.

"Need a break there, Melanie?" Felix asked playfully.

Her chest heaving, she glared at him. "I can go all day," she told him boldly.

His brows rose. "Is that so? Here." He threw her the ball for a check despite the fact they were playing full court. He moved up the sideline, and Melanie felt a small tingle at the back of her neck as she tossed the ball back to him. It shot out of her hand like a cannon and she realized her mistake as it happened. Felix caught the ball with an "umph" and fell into one of the benches that lined the court.

Cali and Joel turned at the sound.

Melanie stood frozen to the ground. She hadn't meant to use Charlotte's powers. She wanted to ask Felix if he was hurt, but she didn't want to risk exposing herself.

I kinda already did.

She swallowed thickly as Cali and Joel jogged over.

"What the hell are you doing?" Cali asked, hands on hips.

"You tired, Felix? We can end the game right here if you like," Joel said with a smile and waggle of his brow.

Felix got up and rubbed his back and butt. "I'm fine." His gaze touched on Melanie for a second before moving onto his friends. "I just lost my footing."

The rest of the game went by in a blur. Melanie kept her focus solely on making sure she didn't accidentally shove a basketball through someone's chest.

By the end they were all sweaty and exhausted. They lounged on the benches, talking and drinking.

Melanie Unlocked Cali's arm from her side.

"So what's your power again?" Cali asked. "Are you a Locksmith like Joel?"

Melanie fiddled with the leather bracelet on her wrist. "No. I can temporarily borrow someone's powers."

She waited for fear or disgust, but Cali simply nodded. "That's cool." She stuck her hand out. "Take mine."

Melanie recoiled. "It's okay, I'm a little tired."

"Oh, come on." Cali wiggled her fingers. "Just a little bit. I want to know what it feels like, and I'm sure you want to practice using someone else's powers other than lame-ass Joel's."

Joel arched a brow. "Lame-ass? Really, Cali? Your material is going down the drain." He tsked and took a long swig of his Gatorade.

Cali glared at him. "You were more fun before she gave you confidence." She jerked her head in Melanie's direction.

Joel saluted her with his Gatorade bottle. "Your days of getting a rise out of me are over, evil tyrant."

Melanie took a tentative sip of water, thinking she'd dodged Cali's bullet.

She thought wrong.

As soon as Cali finished smart-mouthing Joel, those dark eyes were back on Melanie, her hand stretched out before her.

Melanie stared at it. She could probably fight all day long and Cali still wouldn't give up.

"Might as well," Joel said to her. "It'll give you more practice."

She mustered a smile. Little did he know that they were giving her exactly what Juliet would want.

No. She wasn't going to go that far with it. She'd take a little bit of Cali's powers, enough to satisfy both their curiosities, and then she'd be done.

Cali's nails were done a dark purple and her fingers were slender. Artist hands.

Melanie closed her eyes, and with Joel so close, his heat warming the right side of her body, she conjured her powers easily. She imagined a stream, trickling into the ocean, and took the tiniest bit from Cali.

"That's so strange," she heard Cali say. "It feels like I'm touching a live wire or something."

Melanie released her instantly.

Disappointment crossed Cali's face but interest replaced it within seconds. "Can you use them now?"

Melanie focused. How was she supposed to shift through the different powers and know when she had the right one?

Her neck was buzzing from her active powers.

"I don't know," she said at last, unsure how she was supposed to use a Silencer's abilities.

Cali and Felix had knowing smiles on their faces.

"What?" she turned to Joel.

His lips moved but no sound came out.

"What?" she said again and worked her jaw to try and pop her ears.

His grin deepened. This time he moved his lips slowly. "You're using Cali's powers."

Being in her own little sound bubble was a little disconcerting. There was no noise whatsoever, no wind, no cars, no sound from the people around the corner on another court.

It felt lonely.

"Is it gone?" she asked after a moment.

"I think so," Joel said. "I can hear you again."

She relaxed. "Good. That's a strange power," she mused to herself.

Cali shrugged. "It was really helpful when I needed peace and quiet to work on some of my paintings."

Felix leaned around her, hand outstretched. "Me next," he said like a little kid.

Melanie couldn't help it. She laughed. "Fine." She pretended to be put out and grasped his much larger hand. It was warm and soft but missing all the scars she loved to trace with her eyes.

She reached for her powers, but Cali quickly disentangled their hands. "Wait a minute," she said. "Is it really a good idea to have her take your powers, Felix?"

His blue-green eyes widened. He quickly took his hand back, his gaze dropping with embarrassment. "Sorry, I should have realized."

"Realized what? What's going on?" Their faces betrayed nothing. "I don't understand."

Joel's hand came to rest on her thigh. A spark of awareness shot through her and she saw the answering call in Joel's eyes, but like her, he pushed it down. "Felix's powers are … different. If you don't know how to control them … "

"People could get hurt," Felix finished for him, looking both ashamed and angry.

"What do you mean? I saw him on the basketball court earlier. He made the ball vanish and reappear. What's the big deal?"

"The big deal is that I'm an Eraser and got my name because I used to cause things to vanish, for good. I only got my ability to bring things back when I became full-forced. If I transferred my powers to you, who knows if you'd have the ability to make things reappear. If you accidently Erased one of us and couldn't bring us back … Well, let's just say we never want to find out."

Melanie stared at Felix as she let his words sink in. "That must've been frightening," she said.

They all gave collective nods, Felix mostly. "It was, still is."

"Have you ever tried to Erase someone and bring them back?" she asked carefully.

His head snapped up so quickly she winced.

"Never."

She jumped at the vehemence in his voice.

She held her hands up, palms out. "Okay."

Joel squeezed her thigh sympathetically. "It's not a matter of fearing that he wouldn't be able to bring them back. It's a matter of where they go."

Unease crept down her spine. "Where do they go?"

They all exchanged worried glances. "We're not sure," Cali answered her.

"Then how do you know it's somewhere bad?"

Cali wordlessly handed Felix the basketball resting beneath their bench. Felix took the ball and glanced around to make sure no one was watching.

Melanie couldn't help it; she scanned the area too.

When it was deemed clear, Felix inhaled deeply and waved his hand. The ball vanished, but unlike on the basketball court he didn't bring it back right away. He seemed to be waiting for something.

A minute or so later he waved his hand again. The basketball reappeared at his feet.

Melanie drew back from the sight, Joel's hand steady on her leg. "It's okay," he murmured.

When she overcame her shock, she leaned forward. "What the hell happened to it?"

The ball was covered with a faint pink mucus. It looked to be steaming, and the hiss of deflating air met her ears. There was a long gash in the side of the ball that looked suspiciously like claw marks.

Her eyes met Felix's. They were steady, but deep within she could make out the hint of fear. She'd seen that look in the mirror enough times these past few weeks.

Her heart went out to him and in the far recesses of her mind, she wondered if Felix wanted to be free of his powers.

Chapter 23

That night Melanie fretted over what she was going to wear. Joel had dropped her off after basketball and invited her out for dinner. Just the two of them. Their first real date.

And she had nothing to wear.

"Damn," she said under her breath and threw the shirt she was holding against her chest over her head where it landed with all the other rejected tops.

"Hot date?" Nathan had snuck into their room.

"The door was closed for a reason." She glared at him.

He leaned back against the wall, a smile teasing his lips. "You totally have a date. Need helping picking out an outfit?"

"Ha. Like you would be any help."

He shrugged. "Fine, but I think you'd look best in that loose floral skirt you put in Mom's closet for safekeeping."

She paused mid reach into her closet. She'd forgotten all about that skirt. It had been one of her favorites, which was why she kept it from her room. She hadn't trusted Nathan with all of her possessions.

"See," he said. "I can be helpful." He turned and left.

She hastily followed after him. He was already in the hallway closet, sifting through the mass of clothes stored within. He pulled out the skirt in question and held it up for Melanie.

It was perfect.

Knee length and decorated with pale pink and blue flowers, it had captured her attention instantly when she'd seen it at the store. She'd splurged and bought it at full price, not wanting to risk losing it.

"How did you know this was here?" she asked. She distinctly remembered that he'd been zoned out of his mind when she'd got home the night she bought the skirt.

He looked uncomfortable. "I saw this."

Her fingers tightened around the skirt. "Saw this, as in you stumbled through the closet and saw it?" But she could already tell by his expression that wasn't the case.

She lowered her voice. "You *Dreamed* of me in this outfit?"

He avoided her gaze and rubbed the back of his neck. "Yeah."

Melanie didn't know how she felt about that. "What else did you see?"

He shrugged. "Not sure. Over the last couple days it's like my mind finally has time to catch up to everything it saw over the past few years. I remember things that I know I didn't see with my own two eyes. I just saw you in this." He gave another shrug. He couldn't quite look her in the eye, and he disappeared to the kitchen before she could say more.

She shook off her unease. So Nathan saw her in this outfit, no big deal. She might have worn it to something else when he had the vision. She made her own destiny. With her spirits lifted, she marched back into her room.

She had the perfect blue top to go with her skirt. She debated whether or not to wear cowboy boots but ultimately decided to wear heels instead.

She borrowed some of Aunt Bertie's makeup and threw on a hint of lip gloss and a layer of mascara. It made her eyelashes feel heavy, but it was worth it. There wasn't much she could do with her hair; the bob went to her jaw and was too short to curl. She settled on running the hairdryer through it a few times and teasing the hair to give it volume.

There. Done.

She stepped back from the mirror and admired herself.

She hoped it was enough. The doorbell rang and her heart leapt into her throat. She snatched her purse from her room and ran for the door so no one else would answer it.

Unfortunately, the entire family was home on a Sunday evening, and as she rounded the corner of the hallway she saw her father open the door.

She came to a screeching halt as the two men at the door eyed each other.

Joel looked amazing. He wore black dress slacks and a navy-blue, long-sleeved button up that had thin, pale blue strips running vertically through it. The sleeves were rolled up to his elbow, exposing the scars both old and new on his arms. He was freshly showered and shaved, his damp hair looking as if it was combed back but starting to develop a mind of its own as it dried.

His black eye was nothing but a yellow-green mass on his face, and she could see her father zeroing in on it as well as the fresh cuts on his arms.

She hurried to the entrance, passing the kitchen where her mother, aunt, Paul, and Nathan stared openly. She grimaced and rushed to her father's side before he could say anything.

"Hey," she said to Joel and smiled. He wore cologne, a faint woodsy smell that made her take in another lungful. "You clean up nicely."

Joel blinked and gave himself a small shake. "So do you. Wow."

Melanie's cheeks heated with pleasure.

"It's Sunday night." Her father's voice broke the moment. "We're having a family dinner."

Melanie whirled on him. "I'm going out to dinner. You can split my portion between the five of you."

She brushed past her father, but he caught her wrist. "Melanie, you should not be hanging around this man. Look at him." Her father gestured to Joel, who had stiffened but refused to drop his chin. "He's dangerous. I won't have my daughter going out and getting herself into another car accident, some knife fight, or worse."

Joel's eyes darted down to his arms and he cringed.

Melanie tore her hand from her father's grasp. "Joel would never hurt me. And I'm past the age when you can tell me who I can and cannot see."

She stormed past Joel as he gave a quick nod to her father before following. He lunged before her to open the car door and she smiled at him. "Thank you."

"My pleasure."

He hustled around to the driver's side and started the car. Melanie watched her father's silhouette as they drove off, getting smaller and smaller until it disappeared completely.

She deflated into her seat. "I'm so sorry about that. My father can be … "

"Protective? Intimidating as all hell?"

She laughed. "Yeah, something like that. Please don't listen to him. You look amazing tonight." She rested her hand on his forearm, feeling the scars beneath her palm. She traced one with her thumb absently, not realizing what she was doing until they came to a red light and Joel pierced her with a heated look.

His eyes flashed in the streetlight, a deep blue as to be almost black. The air in the car crackled and the hair on her arms rose. Her pulse jumped. She should pull her hand away but she couldn't. She wanted to feel his heated skin against her. She loved the feel of his muscles bunching beneath her fingers as he gripped and released the wheel.

The light turned green. The spell broke. But that didn't stop the fact that the car suddenly felt two sizes too small.

As soon as they parked Melanie jumped out into the night air. If she spent any longer inside that car they'd never make it into the restaurant. She was achy and needy and out of control. She inhaled the fresh scent of the ocean water so close by and let it calm her. The cool breeze ruffled her hair and she welcomed it.

The restaurant was small and quaint, with dim lights and deep red walls, the back wall filled with wine bottles.

"Wow," she muttered as they were led to their table. Joel's hand rested on her lower back and the heat radiating from it seeped into every pore.

Melanie never had to ask for her water to be refilled, her steak was cooked to perfection, and the plates came and went off the table in a blink of an eye.

"That was amazing." She leaned back in her chair, pushing the last of the mud pie toward Joel. "Please finish that."

"You sure?"

"Yes, I'm stuffed. I'm going to have to up my yoga to five times a week next week."

He shoveled the pie into his mouth. "I think this is the first time I've ever seen you not in yoga pants."

She grinned. "And this is the first time I've never seen you in a graphic tee shirt."

He pulled nervously at the collar. "I miss my graphic tees. These are a little constricting, and promise not to tell anyone, but I had to have Cali help me pick it out. As an artist she has a good eye for colors. Said this would," he batted his eyelashes, "bring out my eyes."

"Well, she was right. How're they doing by the way? Is Felix all right?"

Joel tilted his head fractionally. "Why wouldn't he be?"

She glanced around the restaurant, but every other couple was deep in their own little world. She dropped her voice anyway. "Because of what happened earlier, with the basketball?"

Joel waved it off. "That wasn't the worst incident, trust me. One time he Erased Syd's car—she was none too happy about that—then brought it back. We all kind of freaked out at the sight of it. It was covered with a pink mucus and dust, with dents all over and scratch marks that didn't look of this world. We learned that he also brought back an actual animal inside, if that's what you want to call it. We referred to it as the demon cat."

Her expression must've betrayed her because Joel reached for her, concern on his face. "Are you okay? Don't worry, it's nothing to be afraid of. Felix put it back wherever it came from. He gains more control every time he uses his powers. We all trust him."

"But does he trust himself?"

Joel sat back. "What does that mean?"

"He must be terrified all the time, wielding that kind of unpredictable power."

"It's not unpredictable. He's got control over it."

She stared at him. "And what happens if he brings back another monstrosity when he uses his powers? If he keeps using them all over the place, it's only a matter of time."

Anger sparked in his eyes. "Hey now, Felix doesn't use his powers *all over the place*." He gestured with his hands. "He's very conscientious of when he uses them and who he's around."

"He used them during a basketball game," she pointed out. "That kind of carelessness is dangerous."

He gaped at her. "Carelessness? He brought the ball back instantly. That's not carelessness, that's being mindful of what he's doing and understanding his ability's limitations. You saw him demonstrate the knowledge of his own power. He kept the ball longer and it came back in ruins, which was why he didn't keep it there longer than necessary during our game."

"And did you see the look in his eye when that basketball returned destroyed? He's afraid of his own power. What kind of a life is that? What if he could get help?"

"Felix has had a long time to deal with his powers. He doesn't need help. They aren't a curse, Melanie. You can't keep focusing on the bad."

It was a direct hit. Her mouth snapped shut.

Was he right? Was she nothing but a biased party who would never see her abilities as anything more than a negative?

That afternoon on the basketball court had been the first time she'd felt accepted, like she could belong. Was she holding herself back from happiness by refusing to accept her abilities as part of who she was?

"Shit, I'm sorry," said Joel after a few silent seconds.

"No, I—"

"Son of a bitch," Joel cut her off.

"Excuse me?" Melanie's gaze shot up, but Joel wasn't looking at her.

She jerked her attention to where Joel was staring out the window.

Alexander.

He stood on the curb, probably waiting for a bus or taxi. He smiled when their eyes met. Melanie felt her temper rise.

"Give me your hand." She laid her arm across the table, palm up for Joel without even looking his way. She didn't want Alexander to get away. Not this time.

She'd tried everything—avoidance, contacting the police—and she was sick of it. If she ever wanted her life back, she needed to stand up for what she wanted. And she didn't want Alexander.

She turned to Joel.

Her neck prickled with her powers.

"What are you planning on doing?"

"I'm taking hold of my supernatural ability. I'm going to do what you suggested and scare him." She wanted to use her powers. She wanted to give them the chance that Joel kept inspiring within her. She couldn't have someone fight her battles for her. If Joel faced Alexander, her ex would just misinterpret it as Joel was keeping Melanie from him. She knew she wasn't supposed to confront Alexander—that it could only encourage him—but she had to try something.

Joel studied her for a moment before giving her his hand. "Remember," he said calmly, "control. A little bit goes a long way. I'll take care of our check, then I'll be right behind you."

She nodded and wrapped her hand around his. She did as he asked and controlled the pull of his power into her. The heady sensation flooded her body. She amped up the trickle of power into her until it was a steady flow, and when that wasn't enough, she—

Joel yanked his hand away. "That's enough." He shook his arm and cradled it to his chest, eyes guarded.

Melanie didn't have time to question what she saw in his face. She left the restaurant, hunting for Alexander. He wasn't by the curb any longer. She jogged down the sidewalk as best she could in her heels and stopped when she saw something out of the corner of her eye.

It was him.

He slipped into a parking lot.

Melanie followed, her neck practically throbbing. She needed to come up with a plan. She'd never willingly walk into Alexander's arms and he knew it too. If she tried to instigate any kind of contact, he'd know something was up.

But what did it matter?

A quick touch was all she needed.

She could jump him.

She shook the thought away. If she missed, her opportunity was lost. She couldn't risk it.

She had to act like normal but with a hint of vulnerability to draw him out.

"Alexander?" she called hopefully into the evening light. The sun was setting, casting long shadows and brilliant yellow and orange colors. The wind had picked up and her skirt fluttered around her legs, as restless as she was.

He didn't respond.

Had he kept going?

"Alexander, please, I need to talk to you." She swallowed her pride and continued. "This can't be a coincidence. I keep running into you. Something wants me to see you. To speak with you."

He stepped out from behind an Escalade, a smirk firmly in place, arms crossed. He didn't come any closer. He was too far for Melanie to touch, so she kept her pursuit slow, taking baby steps toward him.

"Why are you here?" she asked.

"Like you said, we keep running into each other. It's uncanny, isn't it?"

Uncanny, my ass. He was a stalker, plain and simple, which meant he knew where she was and who she was with.

The familiar lick of fear that accompanied that realization went through her, igniting her anger. She was done fearing him. Done looking over her shoulder and worrying.

She got a few feet closer. "Yes, very uncanny," she drawled. "I've tried to move on. I pushed you away as best I could, but you keep coming back."

This time he came toward her, narrowing the gap between them. "I'll always come back for you. You're mine." He grasped her upper arms. "My soul mate."

She clenched her jaw. It was Alexander's fault those words were tainted. She briefly wondered how she would have reacted to meeting Joel and learning everything she had in the past couple of weeks if she'd never encountered Alexander. Would she have accepted the idea of Mirror Mates? Embraced it?

She'd never know, and it was all this man's fault. She wanted to jump from his touch as his fingers dug into her skin.

"You really will never leave me alone, will you?" She took his hands in hers and lowered his arms to his sides. "You just don't get it, do you? When a woman says no, all you hear is yes. You crave the power you get when you see the fear in our eyes. Well, I'm here to tell you that I'm done being afraid of you." She reached for Joel's powers and visualized shooting them straight through Alexander's entire body.

His eyes widened, his body instantly stiffening. "Wh—what have you done?" His eyes darted around wildly, though his head never moved.

She stepped back, admiring the way he looked like a kid ready to do a pencil dive into a pool.

"What I've done," she said, "is show you that if you come near me ever again, you'll feel more of my anger than what I've demonstrated today."

Alexander's breaths started coming quicker. "I-I can't—I can't—"

"Move?" she interrupted with a sickly sweet smile. "No, you can't, because I won't let you, just like you never let me have a life when I tried to get away from you. You trapped me into this cage of fear." She stepped into his face, rage burning through her as she saw everything she ever hated about her life in him. "Now I'm returning the favor. And if I ever see you again, I'm going to do more than trap you. I'll imprison you permanently!"

"Melanie!"

Strong hands tore her away from Alexander. His eyes were bloodshot, his face purple, a strange wheezing sound coming from him.

"Jesus, what the fuck are you doing?" Joel stared at Alexander in horror.

"Can't," Alexander's voice was ragged, " ... breathe."

His eyes rolled into his head and he dropped like a board.

Melanie screamed at the sickening thud.

"Call 9-1-1," Joel shouted at her as he rushed to Alexander's side. He hovered over him, hands on his body. "What did you do to him, Melanie?"

"Nothing." Tears tracked down her face. "I just Locked him like you said."

"I didn't tell you to do this!" Joel shot back. "Shit! His chest isn't moving. You Locked his lungs, that's why he can't breathe—his rib cage and lungs can't expand."

Joel shut his eyes and kept his hands firmly on top of Alexander's chest. A few moments later his chest lifted, expanding completely to suck in as much oxygen as possible.

She waited for Alexander's eyes to snap open, for him to jack-knife into a sitting position and accuse her of nearly killing him.

He didn't move.

A small pool of blood started to spread on the cement behind his head.

Joel noticed it moments after Melanie. "Shit." He glanced her way. "Did you call the ambulance yet?"

She jolted into action. Her hands shook so much she nearly fumbled her phone twice. She told the dispatcher only the bare minimum.

"Are they on their way?" Joel asked as he stayed crouched next to Alexander. His hands kept clenching and unclenching, as if he was fighting the urge to pick him up and assess his head injury.

"Don't move him," Melanie told him.

Joel's jaw twitched. "I know, but what if it's serious? We can't just stand here—we should try and stop the bleeding."

"The ambulance is on its way." Already in the distance she could hear the wail of the sirens.

"Shit." Joel shot to his feet and rubbed his face. He turned on her. "What the fuck happened?" He paced back and forth. "And don't leave anything out, because we need to get our story straight for the hospital." He paused and swore again. "And the police."

Chapter 24

Joel found himself in the ER.

Again.

And he still wasn't quite sure how it had happened.

He stared down at his hands. A smudge of blood ran along the outside of his thumb. The paramedics had given him wipes for his hands after helping cart Alexander into the ambulance. He'd missed a spot.

He stared at the dark red splotch as it dried.

Alexander was in the ER. Because of him.

No.

Because of the silver blonde next to him.

Melanie sat hunched over in her chair, arms around herself, rocking. Joel had tried to console her, but she shrugged off each and every one of his attempts.

His phone vibrated in his pocket, and with one last look at Melanie, he left the no cell phone area.

"You answered," Felix's voice came over the line. "You weren't supposed to answer. You're supposed to be getting lucky. How was the date?"

"Fan-fucking-tastic. I'm back in the ER."

"What?"

Joel held the phone away from his head. "Quiet," he hissed when Felix's outburst was over. "I'm back in the ER. I'm okay. It's Melanie, she had an … episode."

Felix was silent on the other end. "What kind of episode?" he asked at last.

The kind where she nearly killed her stalker ex-boyfriend.

"Doesn't matter," Felix cut in before Joel could open his mouth. "We'll be there soon."

"What?" Joel checked his voice as a few nurses sent him dirty looks behind the reception desk. "No, there's no need. Really."

"Joel," Felix said patiently. "We weren't there for you the last time. This time we will be. So sit tight, you can explain it all when we get there." A smile came into his voice. "That way I don't have to relay the whole thing to the guild."

He hung up before Joel could sputter another word. The whole guild? Shit. He rubbed his jaw. He shouldn't have answered his damn phone.

Melanie looked up as he returned to his seat next to her. "Who was on the phone?" The tip of her nose was pink. Her crystal blue eyes were puffy and red from crying. But behind the worry and remorse he saw a flicker of revulsion. Not at him, but at herself.

He felt helpless. This wasn't a physical battle he could win for her. He was stuck on the sidelines as she battled whatever inner demons were haunting her. It tore him up and emotion clogged his throat.

He cupped her face and was relieved when she allowed him to. He rubbed his thumb across her cheek. Already he felt so much for her.

Logic told him to be cautious. He'd admitted she was his Mirror Mate, but he still refused to jump without looking, to risk his heart without testing the waters. He'd been bitten in the ass too many times when he rushed headfirst into things. This time he was going to do it right.

"How are you holding up?" he asked gently.

Her face crumpled, and she shook her head as if too afraid to speak. He pulled her to him and reveled in the feel of her in his arms. "I will always be here for you," he told her fiercely. "Also," he said after a few minutes, "you should know that the guild is coming soon."

She leaned back, her jaw slack. "The guild? As in … the entire guild?"

He nodded.

"Why? What did you tell them?" Her face went pale. "They're going to think the very worst of me."

"Hey." He grasped her shoulders and waited until her eyes reached his. "They will understand you better than anyone. They're concerned, that's all." He paused. "Well, they're also nosy, and overwhelming, and can be a complete pain in the ass sometimes, but they know what you're going through. I'm sure with so many heads together we'll be able to think of something to keep this from happening again."

She glanced away, something flickering in her eyes too quickly for him to make out. "You're right," she said quietly. "This will never happen again."

Something in her tone didn't sit well with him. "Melanie?"

She tilted her head and looked at him, her eyes no longer clouded. Instead they blazed with conviction. "You were wrong earlier when you said powers weren't a curse. They are. I tried to use them for good, I really did, Joel, but you saw what happened." She moved her arm to indicate their current location. "Look at where we ended up when we used them. We think we're using them for good, but all we really do is hurt one another. We use them to instill fear in others, or win a game, or to come out ahead in life. We never really use them selflessly. Money, power, those are the real reasons. What kind of good can we actually do with them?"

He shook his head. "You don't believe that."

"But I do."

"No. You don't. You're scared right now. But in our group, the Guild of Truth, we use our abilities to fight the evil that would use theirs against others."

Now it was her turn to shake her head. "And who are you to say that the others are wrong and you're right? This isn't black and white, Joel. This isn't a comic book where you're the hero and everyone else is the villain. I'm sure other people have their own reasons, their own *good* reasons, for doing what they're doing. You can't condemn them because they're different. No one deserves this kind of power."

Joel frowned. "What are you talking about? I haven't condemned anyone. Who—?"

He was cut off as the ER doors opened and six familiar faces came in.

Their timing couldn't have been worse. As usual.

Joel sighed and got up to greet them.

Felix was first to him. He grasped his hand and brought him in for a hug. "How're you holding up?"

Joel gave a half-hearted shrug. "I've been better."

Felix studied him for a moment, his eyes going to Melanie and then back again. He dropped his voice. "Can I talk to you in private later?"

The rest of the guild buzzed around them. Cali went to Melanie, effectively bringing all the other females along, including a grumpy-looking Niella.

Joel continued to stare at Felix, unease working its way into his system. "Sure," he said at last.

Felix gave a stiff nod and headed toward Melanie, his seriousness replaced with an easy smile and a sympathetic touch.

Joel shook himself.

"Hey." Merrick clapped him on the shoulder. "We came as soon as we heard. Everything okay?"

"For now," was all Joel could think to say. He didn't know where they could all go that would offer them a safe place to talk.

He turned to see how Melanie was taking the sudden onslaught. Her smile was stiff, not quite reaching her eyes, but she kept it firmly in place as she shook Sydney's hand. When Syd stepped away to give Niella room, Melanie's face paled as if she'd seen a ghost.

She wobbled on her feet.

Joel rushed to her side, tucking his hand beneath her elbow to keep her steady. "You okay?" he whispered into her ear.

"Huh?" She stared at him as if she didn't know how he'd gotten there.

Melanie's attention went back to Niella, who was watching her carefully behind her red glasses. "Have we met before?" Niella asked. "You appear as if you know me."

That couldn't be right; Joel was certain they'd never met. *I've only known Melanie a couple of weeks though.*

True, but if it was as simple as running into Niella at the supermarket, why did Melanie look so horrified?

Unbidden, Joel's eyes met Felix's. His friend's mouth was set in a grim line, eyes hard.

Sydney took control of the situation. "Maybe we should give Melanie some space."

Joel shot her a grateful look. She smiled in return and ushered everyone over to a row of unoccupied chairs.

Joel turned Melanie around to face him. "What was that? Have you met Niella before?"

She shook her head. "No."

Joel released her. She was lying to him. He could see it in her eyes. But why would she lie about meeting Niella? Sure, Niella could be a little … prickly, but if she'd treated Melanie badly, he wasn't going to get mad at Niella or cause a scene at the ER or anything.

"Miss Vyntra?" A nurse came out to the waiting room.

Melanie hopped on the distraction. "Yes," she practically yelled, then lowered her voice. "Yes, I'm here."

The nurse gave her a strange look and flipped through her clipboard. "If you would come with me, we have a few more questions."

Melanie followed without a backward glance.

Joel watched her disappear behind the emergency doors, feeling as if he'd swallowed a brick.

He felt more than saw Felix come up beside him.

"I don't know if I'm in the mood to talk, man," Joel said.

"I understand that, but what just happened only adds to my suspicions."

At that Joel whirled on him. "Suspicions?"

Felix steered him away from the others and out of earshot of any other ER patrons.

"Yes, suspicions," he said once they were tucked away in a corner. "Do you remember that woman we encountered on Saturday who seemed to have numerous powers?"

"Yeeesss."

"I've been wondering how someone could wield multiple powers at once. And then I met Melanie."

Joel didn't like where this was going. "What is that supposed to mean?"

"Remember those documents we stole? The names with different powers associated next to them and some of the people crossed off, like they were taken out? Don't you find it suspicious that the company we stumbled upon happened to have someone like Melanie? A ... " he thought for a moment, "a Siphoner, and that you saw the same men of that company hanging around Melanie? You thought they were after you, but what if they weren't?"

Joel's hands balled into fists. "Are you implying that Melanie is a part of that organization?"

Felix held up his hands, palms out. "I'm only relaying to you my suspicions. You read the documents we took from the mystery group. They were detailed records about supernaturals, more detailed than the records we found in Vander's possession. Whoever this organization is, they researched their targets' backstories, their powers, their weaknesses. What that woman demonstrated fits with the list of powers that were crossed off."

Joel gritted his teeth. "I fail to see how this involves Melanie."

Felix straightened his shoulders and took a deep breath. "Melanie has displayed more powers than just her own."

Joel frowned. "What are you talking about? Of course she did, she took mine and Cali's."

Felix shook his head, eyes sad. "I'm not talking about those. I'm talking about today on the basketball court. When you and Cali found me on that bench, it wasn't because I lost my footing. When Melanie threw the ball at me, it hit me like a ton of bricks, as if she possessed some insurmountable strength."

"That's not reasonable proof," Joel responded instantly. "She could have thrown it with a decent amount of strength and you simply caught it funny, making it seem like she threw it harder than possible."

Felix opened his mouth as if to argue but gave a small shake of his head. "Fine. What about her reaction to Niella?"

Joel didn't have an answer for that one.

Felix pressed on. "Did you recognize anything funny about her reaction? Like that was how Niella used to respond to people she'd Dreamed about?"

"You think Melanie Dreamed about Niella? That's impossible. She doesn't have access ... " He drifted off because Melanie did have access to a Dreamer. Her brother.

No.

He shook his head.

He would not believe that Melanie would seek out her brother's powers. She barely accepted taking Joel's powers when he offered.

But the doubt was set. Felix's words wormed their way into his thoughts and he couldn't cast them out no matter how much he tried to shake them.

What if she was getting power hungry? What if she was going from one extreme to the other?

He recalled the way she'd hung on to him at the restaurant, how he'd had to break the connection because she was taking so much from him.

"You know I'm right, don't you?" Felix said quietly.

Joel jerked his gaze up to him. "No," he spat. "You're wrong. She would never do that." *She'd never do that to me. She'd never betray me like that.*

Felix watched him with sad eyes. "I'm sorry, Joel."

Joel stepped back from him. "Stop it. You're wrong. Stop spreading lies about my Mirror Mate."

Felix's body stiffened. "I'm not spreading lies. I'm trying to help you, for fuck's sake."

"Well, you're not."

Felix jerked as if Joel had physically punched him. "Joel, I know you care for her, but you can't ignore signs—"

"I think you should leave." Joel cut him off.

Felix blinked. His mouth opened. Closed.

"Fine." Felix's jaw clenched and he brushed past, sending Joel stumbling as his shoulder knocked into his.

Cali was already on her feet before he reached her.

Had she been listening?

Joel ground his teeth.

What did he care anyway? If she believed as Felix did, he didn't want her here either.

He hung back from the rest and watched as Felix gave a quick goodbye. Niella and Luke ended up leaving with him and Cali. Joel tried not to let their leaving feel like a personal attack. Niella and Luke didn't know what was going on—at least Luke didn't. With Niella, it was anyone's guess.

As one, Sydney and Merrick turned from Felix's exit to stare at Joel.

Great, he was left with the last two people on earth he'd ever want to discuss matters such as this with. Instead he sat and stewed in his own thoughts, trying to console himself. He'd done everything right—no rushing in without looking. He would have seen the signs himself, right? He couldn't be blindsided by a woman again, could he?

He just didn't know anymore.

Chapter 25

Melanie came out of the ER to find the waiting room empty.

Where had the rest of the guild gone?

That woman with short hair and glasses was for certain the same person she'd seen in her vision that night she'd accidentally taken Nathan's powers. Anxiety made her stomach queasy. She didn't want to see her, to be honest. She didn't want to see that look in her eyes that said she knew Melanie was lying about not knowing her.

Of course she'd know you were lying. She's a Dreamer.

Did that mean she knew her time was nearly up?

Melanie doubted it. No one could remain that cool and detached when they knew their death was on the horizon.

If Melanie knew the end was near, she'd be off exploring the world, spending as much money as her credit card would allow.

Niella had no idea what was coming and Melanie was torn with what to do. She couldn't tell her. The last thing she wanted to do was freak her out or scare her off. Melanie didn't think she'd want to know if she only had a few days to live, but at the same time, how could she save Niella if she didn't talk about it?

Make sure she's not home the night of the accident.

And how was she going to do that? Aside from kidnapping, she didn't think Niella would want to go anywhere with her. Especially after Melanie's reaction to her today.

Then get close to her.

She was beginning to sound like Juliet.

Hmmm, would Niella want to be cured of her powers?

I could cure her of her powers.

True, but that was one power she didn't want. Perhaps Melanie could ease the burden for a bit like she had with Nathan that one night. Maybe she could help Niella without taking her powers, and if Niella expressed interest, she could involve Juliet.

It wasn't a perfect plan, but it was better than nothing.

Now she only needed to find her target.

Where had everyone gone?

Did the police come and take Joel away? It would explain why the whole guild seemed to have disappeared.

Melanie was getting ready to call a cab when Joel stomped through the front entrance. His movements were jerky; he was clearly too tense to function properly. He caught sight of Melanie and his fierce expression softened.

"Hey." He reached out when he was within arm's reach to tuck her hair behind her ear.

Her heart skipped a beat. "Hey. Where'd everyone go?"

His face darkened for a moment. "They left."

"Just like that?" That didn't sound like the guild Joel had described. And the little bit she'd got to know of Sydney and Niella didn't warrant that kind of behavior either. Sydney had been so genuine with her concern, sounding as if she'd wait as long as it took until they were cleared to leave. "Did something happen?"

What if Joel had told them the whole story of how they'd come to be in the ER? The guild probably thought she was a monster.

Her worry must've shown because Joel shook his head and rubbed her arms, effectively causing goose bumps. "Nothing happened. I knew it wasn't the best time for you to meet them so I asked them to leave."

Her shoulders sagged in relief.

"What did the nurse want to talk to you about? Are we free to leave?"

"Yeah, she wanted a little more information about Alexander. I told her as much as I could; I don't know him well enough to provide allergies to medicines or anything like that. They're notifying his family. He's stable and will be fine in a couple days.

I'd like to be gone before his family shows up though. Plus, there is a restraining order against Alexander and I'm pretty sure I violated it enough tonight."

Joel's lips twitched. "We should probably get out of here then."

To her relief, he took them back to his place. She didn't feel like being questioned by her parents, or in her case, lectured by her father on choices for male companions.

"I'm going to grab a quick shower. Do you mind waiting?" Joel stared down at his hands where there was a faint smudge of blood on them.

Melanie's stomach lurched at the sight. "Go ahead. I'll be here." She sat down on his couch. A few minutes later, the soothing sound of running water met her ears and she allowed herself to relax, grateful for the respite away from everyone. Her head fell back on the sofa.

She wanted a shower herself, to scrub away the memories of Alexander's face, the sound of his body hitting the pavement, the scent of blood as they'd loaded him into the ambulance.

"Stop it," she ordered herself.

But her brain wasn't listening. Like a broken record, the memory continued to play in her mind.

What had she been thinking?

She hadn't. That was the problem. She'd been upset at Joel constantly telling her that powers were a gift, something to be treasured. Then she'd seen Alexander and decided to put Joel's words to the test.

She should have known better.

Juliet and her group were right. Powers did nothing but hurt others. She was no better than any of the people Juliet had shown her. The only problem was that they needed Melanie to stop the others. She was stuck, forced to keep her own powers to better the world.

She sighed and thumped her head repeatedly against the sofa.

"You feeling okay?"

Joel's voice scared the hell out of her. She whirled to find him at the base of his stairs, damp hair, low-riding sweat pants, and no shirt.

Her mind went blank.

She could do nothing but stare. It felt like forever since she'd seen him like this, nothing but skin and sinew and sex. Because that was exactly what she was feeling, what she was pretty sure he was telegraphing to her. And she was more than ready to jump on the bandwagon.

A small smile beckoned her to him. Like a moth to a flame, she got up from her seat and went to him.

His arms slid around her waist. This close, she could smell his shampoo. It smelled of the ocean, sea salt, and something else she couldn't put her finger on. The heat of his body warmed her, and she leaned into him, eager for more contact between them.

His lips descended on hers, hot and hard, desperate for something. She could do nothing but hang on as his mouth plundered hers. When he pulled away she blinked, dizzy.

His dark blue eyes stared down into hers, searching.

"What is it?"

He shook his head. "Nothing, just … do you keep secrets from me?"

Her heart skipped a beat, but she owed it to him to be honest. "Yes, but one day I'd like to not have to. I'd like to tell you everything, if you let me." Because what they had together could be something worthwhile—could be more than what she first thought was only a strong attraction. But she had to finish with Juliet first. She needed to clean her slate so she could start fresh with Joel.

She cupped his face and brought his lips down to hers.

When her lungs started to burn she pulled away.

Joel had a lopsided grin on his face. "I'll let you do more to me than just tell me secrets. But while we're on the topic, do these secrets you're going to tell me happen to be about your wildest fantasies?"

She gave him a sly look and took his hand in hers to lead him up the stairs to his bedroom.

She gently closed the door with a soft *click*. She leaned back against the wood and took her fill of Joel's body.

"How do you stay so fit if you sit in front of a computer all day?" she asked, genuinely perplexed. If that were her job, she'd be as big as a house.

She pushed off from the door and circled him, wanting to take in all angles of his body.

Joel didn't move, simply tracked her with his eyes. "Yoga," he answered with a cheeky grin.

Melanie found herself smiling back at him.

She continued to circle him, letting one hand reach out and trace along his skin. His muscles flexed beneath her finger and she watched with rapt attention as his abs contracted, his back, his biceps. On her second go around, she dropped her hand to the waistband of his sweats, proudly displaying that V shape. She gave a few experimental tugs, but she'd have to stop completely if she wanted to undress him properly. She wasn't ready to give up the hunt, circling her prey. It stoked the flame within her hotter, and she could see a similar effect on Joel. His eyes watched her every move. Her caresses made his eyes dilate. He licked his lips as if preparing for a meal and Melanie's sex throbbed at the action.

"Need some help?" His voice came out husky. He gestured to his sweats.

"Yes." Her voice was just as throaty, and when he went to shove them down in one swoop she placed her hand on his forearm. "Slowly," she told him and watched as the fire in his eyes danced.

Her breasts ached, her whole body hyperaware of him. She wanted to jump him right then.

Not yet.

Joel did as he was asked, making a show of losing his sweats and loving every minute of it. So was she.

When he stood naked before her, she granted herself one taste. Their lips crashed together, sparks flying.

Melanie had a faint recollection of moving. Her back hit a wall, her rump dropped on the edge of a desk or dresser of some sort. A crash. Her skirt lifted. A tear of fabric. Joel's hot body between her legs.

Her mind reeled. She arched toward him, her body aching. When he slid inside they both groaned. Her legs tightened around his waist, her arms clamped around his neck.

"Don't ever leave me," Joel breathed against her neck. His voice so low she wasn't even sure if she'd heard right.

She opened her mouth to ask when he began to move within her.

Pleasure streaked through her. Her head fell back against the wall. Joel lifted her off the desk/dresser.

"Not yet." Melanie shot her arm out to keep herself in place. Another crash as something fell to the floor.

Joel didn't seem to notice. Instead he pulled her to the very edge of the wood.

Her thoughts scattered to the wind as Joel thrust deep within her, over and over until she was poised right at the sexual edge. She dug her nails into him. His mouth fused to hers, tongues tangling.

Her world burst apart, her muscles contracting as she came.

She nearly bowed off the woodwork. Joel rode her through it, pumping into her again and again until he found his own release.

"I'm going to need to up my home insurance or something," he said after a few moments, surveying the damage littered on his floor.

When Melanie finally got control of her limbs, she leaned over to stare at the broken picture frame, books, figurines, and a plastic bowl that spilled all sorts of computer parts and tools everywhere. "I didn't realize I was such an expensive date."

Joel chuckled and buried his face into the crook of her neck. He inhaled deeply, his whole body relaxing as he exhaled.

Melanie ran her fingers through his hair. "Are you okay?" Now that she wasn't in a lust clouded frenzy, she could recall the almost desperate way Joel had made love, as if frightened to lose her.

"I am now," Joel mumbled against her skin. He pressed light kisses all along her neck and she moaned. She shifted against him only to notice that she still wore her clothing.

She stared down at them in bewilderment. "Why am I still dressed?"

Joel laughed. "I don't know. Let's remedy that, shall we?"

He picked her up and brought her to the bed, gently laying her down. He towered over her and gave her a devilish grin as he slowly pulled her skirt from her body. Melanie felt an odd flash of embarrassment as she lay there half-naked before Joel, which didn't make any sense considering he was naked as the day he was born. In an attempt to get rid of the awkward sensation, she threw her shirt off. It didn't help. She went to unlatch her bra only to have Joel stop her.

"What's the hurry?"

Her cheeks heated. He leaned over her and effectively turned her on with how slowly he removed her bra. First he fingered the straps, letting his fingertips trace along her skin before guiding the material up and over her shoulders. Once they couldn't go any further down her arms, he moved his hands back to her chest, tracing the edge of the lacy cups and following the fabric around to the back where he impressively opened the clasp in under five seconds. A record, she was sure.

He pulled the clothing from her body slowly, like someone unwrapping a gift and wanting to savor it. When she was completely bare to him, he threw her bra to the floor and took her in.

Melanie had always been self-conscious of her breasts. They'd developed way before high school, and all the other kids used to make fun of her ample chest. When she reached a grade where large boobs were coveted, she was the target of everyone's jealousy. She'd never liked them; they got in the way, and they drew too much attention. But right then, she didn't mind so much. She didn't mind at all.

Nor did she mind when he flopped down next to her on the bed and began tracing them with his fingers, lazily drawing circles and other miscellaneous shapes.

She turned on her side to face him, her fingers seeking the scars on his forearms. "Do you remember how you got each one?" she asked.

"To be honest, I got so many of them at the same time that I've forgotten what caused what."

She yawned as the events of the evening started to take their toll. "Tell me what you remember," she said, her eyelids starting to droop. She heard Joel's soft chuckle, felt the brush of his fingertips along her skin, and as she drifted to sleep, he told her about his time with his father, working on the car.

Chapter 26

Joel called into work the next day to tell his IT department he'd be working from home because he'd caught a bug and didn't want to spread it around. He probably could have thought up a better lie, said he was hurting from the car accident, but no one ever asked questions. They knew he'd get his work done whether at the office or home, and working from home gave him ample opportunity to make sure Melanie was taken care of.

He flipped another pancake and waited for the smell of fresh-cooked breakfast to work its magic and wake Melanie from upstairs. It was going on eight o'clock and he had no idea if she had work that morning or not. She didn't mention it during dinner last night before everything went to hell in a hand basket.

"That smells amazing."

He glanced up and found Melanie dressed in nothing but his t-shirt, standing at the edge of the table.

His tongue stuck to the roof of his mouth for a good minute. The hem of his shirt flirted with the middle of her thigh, bringing with it memories of last night and what he'd been doing between those thighs. His cock stiffened. He gave himself a small shake and regretfully pulled his eyes away. "I made plenty, eat up."

She took a seat at the table, and he tried not to think about how the hem of his shirt would be riding up those legs, barely covering her. If he leaned over slightly he could probably see—

"Joel?"

He jumped. "Hmm?"

"You're burning the breakfast."

"Shit." He hastily dumped the blackened pancake into the sink and turned on the microwave fan before the stench triggered the fire alarm.

Too late.

The blare of the alarm sounded and Melanie clapped her hands over her ears, a grin spread across her face.

Joel grumbled to himself as he snagged a chair. He hopped up and pulled the battery from the alarm. The beeping stopped immediately.

"Sorry," Melanie said. "I didn't mean to distract you. I can leave and come back in something more appropriate if you like."

"Don't you dare," he growled. He finished with breakfast and took the seat opposite her. "Look, I'm sorry if yesterday I came off a little ... needy." He hated saying the word, but after Felix planted the seed of doubt, he felt off kilter.

He'd been wrong about Sydney being the one for him, and after her deceit for three months he was a little sensitive. He could admit that, and now that he'd found Melanie ... well, he didn't want to be wrong about Melanie. And he didn't mean Mirror Mate wrong—he knew she was his Mirror Mate—but that didn't mean she was perfect for him in every way. He was afraid of being wrong about her personality, who she was.

One deceitful woman he could deal with because Sydney's circumstances were extenuating, but two women? He'd be dubbed the worst judge of character for all time. Not to mention it'd only solidify his streak for jumping into situations without looking first. Was he an idiot to offer so much to Melanie—his friends, his resources, his bed?—before really knowing her?

Melanie put her fork down and reached across the table for him. His heart quivered in his chest at the contact. "I understand that you were scared yesterday. I was, too, and it's only natural to assume I'd turn tail and run after that fiasco, but I'm not going anywhere." He relaxed. "In fact," she continued, "I am wondering if I could perhaps get closer to Niella."

He started. "Niella?"

"Yeah." Melanie shrugged. "She's like Nathan, so perhaps I could try helping her. You said she was getting worse, right?"

Joel didn't know why he suddenly felt the needed to keep his mouth shut about Niella.

This is all Felix's doing.

"She's … doing okay," he yielded.

"Well, Nathan is doing better, so maybe if she had someone to talk to, she'd feel more hopeful."

Joel couldn't fault her logic, but there was one problem. "Niella isn't exactly the talkative type."

"Neither was I if you recall. I know myself, which means I'll know how to approach her. It can't be that bad."

Oh, it was going to be bad all right.

• • •

"You want me to do what?" Niella asked, arms crossed, a very pissed expression on her face. Joel scanned the lobby of the clinic to make sure no one had come out of the patient rooms at Niella's outburst.

"Keep your voice down. It's not like I'm asking for a million dollars."

"You'd be better off asking for a million dollars."

Joel chose to ignore her. "Melanie wants to get to know you better. She wants to get involved with the guild."

"By talking to me?" Niella's gave him a flat stare. "She feels sorry for me and wants to act as a therapist. No thank you."

She rolled out from behind the reception desk, conversation closed.

"Wait, wait, wait." Joel grabbed both sides of her wheelchair to keep her from escaping and from running over his toes. She'd done that before. "I'm not being entirely truthful here. I want you to entertain Melanie because I want you to do some information gathering for me."

Niella arched one perfectly sculpted brow. "You want me to *spy* on her?"

Joel winced. "Not spy—" At her expression, he sighed. "Fine, I need you to spy. But it's not what you think," he added hastily.

Niella crossed her arms. "By all means, please tell me, what I am thinking? I didn't know you developed telepathy."

Joel ground his teeth. Why the hell did Niella have to make everything so damn difficult?

He reached for patience. "Okay, it's not that I don't trust her, it's just … "

Niella's face softened. She uncrossed her arms. "You can tell me."

Joel let go of her chair and paced a few feet before rubbing his hand along his jaw. "Felix put this idea in my head that maybe Melanie might not be so innocent when it comes to these new suit guys we've been seeing."

Her hazel eyes widened.

Joel pressed on. "I don't believe him," he said sternly. "Melanie would never do that to me, but I have been known to leap without looking, and the thoughts are there, and when she asked to hang out with you … I just thought this might be a good opportunity—"

"To prove Felix wrong?" she supplied gently.

Joel pushed both hands through his hair. "I'm being paranoid, aren't I?"

A dog and its owner came out of one of the patient rooms, and Joel hung back while Niella took care of payment and setting up a follow-up appointment. Once the door closed behind them, she wheeled herself out from behind the desk. "I don't think Felix would accuse Melanie of anything if he wasn't genuinely concerned." She held up her hand to halt his protests. "That doesn't mean I'm siding with him. I'll do what you ask, but I can't say how long I'm going to last. If she starts trying to psychoanalyze me," she snapped her fingers, "It's over."

"Deal. Thank you so much, Ell—"

"You owe me."

He nodded. "Of course, whatever you need."

"I'm not talking about fixing my computer. I'm serious." Her eyes bore into his and a strange sensation crept up his spine. "I'm going to ask you for something and I expect no hesitation, no questions asked. Got it? That's my request."

Joel swallowed thickly. "Deal."

"Good." She looked away, the serious glint in her eye gone. "So when do I have to endure this farce?"

He pulled out his phone. "She was really hoping for tomorrow night. She has to work a double today."

"Tomorrow?" she squawked. "I was going to watch the finale of *The Bachelor*."

Joel grinned. "You'll just have to record it. We'll meet you outside after closing."

Niella wheeled herself back behind the reception desk, grumbling all the way.

• • •

Melanie stared down at her cell phone screen.

We're golden. Niella's in, meet us at Sydney's animal clinic tomorrow after 6.

He'd pasted a Google map image with the address.
The following message was hours later.

How was the double shift? Don't run yourself too ragged. If you need a pick me up, just ask. ;)

Melanie's stomach cramped. She hated lying to Joel.

Only a little longer and you can come clean.

"I'd say no cell phones on the missions, but you did so well today that I think I'll make an exception." Juliet took a seat next to her out on the curb.

Night had fallen and the steady drone of cars passing on the street made for a good distraction. Melanie watched a few taillights go by before she turned to Juliet. "Please don't congratulate me on a job well done. I'm not a dog; positive reinforcement won't get you anywhere. I told you why I'm doing this. That will have to be enough."

Juliet rolled her blue eyes. She wore jeans. Jeans! In regular clothes she looked much younger than Melanie. "I know you're not a dog, Melanie. But you do deserve some praise. We stopped a con artist because of you."

Melanie stared down at her hands. She flexed them, expecting to feel the new power she possessed moving under her skin, but her hands just felt like hands. "He wasn't exactly hurting anyone," she said. "And he didn't seem too keen on giving up his powers, either."

With Charlotte it had been easier. She'd wanted out. She'd been desperate for Melanie to help her. Lars Milo had been different. When they'd knocked on his door, the first instinct for this sketchy individual with a nervous twitch had been to try to jump out a back window. Mr. Richardson had been waiting for him. Milo thought they were some kind of law enforcement. He was resigned to the idea of losing his powers; he didn't fight it. In fact, it was almost like he expected it to happen one day. He'd had a good run at making a profit off his abilities, and now it was time to go back into the real world.

Was that what Juliet's organization was? Some kind of police force for super-powered individuals?

Even if he did deserve to have his abilities taken away, Melanie would never forget the look in his eye as she drained him—the sadness and disappointment was enough to make her queasy. She'd left the apartment as quickly as possible.

She'd been sitting on the curb ever since.

"Lars Milo was making a profit off of others by tricking them. Eventually someone would have gotten hurt, most likely Mr. Milo. Would you rather that have happened? We likely saved his life. The path he was on would have led him to the wrong type of people, and they would have seen his act for what it was, an act. Those kinds of people would have taken his life for payment."

"I guess," Melanie mumbled. Then louder, "How many powers can I take?"

"Hmm?"

"You know, until I'm … full."

Juliet studied her a moment and then laughed. "You're not a flash drive, Melanie. You don't get full. Your storage space is infinite." A feral glint came into her eye. "You could take all the world's powers and still be hungry for more."

Melanie dropped her gaze.

That's what she was afraid of.

Chapter 27

Melanie sat with a paper towel pressed firmly against the heel of her hand as she waited outside Sydney's animal clinic. She'd agreed to meet Joel here after work and caught the first bus she could. She was early, but that was fine with her. She stood outside, the sun beating down on her, warming her chilled flesh after she'd been cooped up in a frozen yogurt shop all afternoon. One of the machines had gotten stuck and Melanie had tried giving it a good smack, but only succeeded in slicing the heel of her hand on a corner of the metal. Luckily, it didn't bleed all over the place and had happened near the end of her shift.

She stared down at the bloody paper in her hand. The bleeding had all but stopped. She examined the wound for the fifth time, squinting to see if she needed stitches.

A shadow fell over her, causing her to jump.

"I didn't mean to scare you," the figure said. "Are you lost?"

Melanie's eyes adjusted and she blinked at the stranger.

He looked to be in his early thirties. The crow's feet in the corners of his eyes gave away the fact that he spent a majority of his time smiling. His green eyes sparkled against his tan skin and dirty blond hair. He looked like a bona fide surfer, only the outfit was all wrong. He wore a white shirt, white pants, and an apron covered with red stains.

Melanie's eyes went to the shop twenty feet away. Tom's Pizzeria. It didn't take a genius to make the connection.

She shook her head. "Not lost." She gestured with both hands to the clinic. "I'm waiting for Niella."

He followed her movement, his eyes lingering on the clinic. "Ah, the mysterious receptionist."

"Huh?"

He pulled his gaze back to Melanie. "I'm sorry, that's very rude of me. I'm Tom Larkin. I've been working next to Sydney for quite some time."

She took the hand he presented with her unbloodied one and shook it. "Melanie."

He smiled, eyes crinkling handsomely. "Nice to meet you, Melanie. So I take it you are a friend of Sydney's?"

"I'm Joel's … " She drifted off. Not sure what she was. Girlfriend? She doubted Mirror Mate would fly with this guy, or soul mate. "I'm friends with Joel."

"Ah, and here I thought I'd be able to get some information out of you," he teased.

"About the mystery receptionist?" she teased back.

He gazed out into the parking lot. "I have to admit it's very strange that as long as we've worked near each other, I've never met her."

"Is she new?"

"Not that I'm aware of. She'd been working with Sydney for years, ever since Sydney took over the clinic from her parents. I've known Sydney since she worked with her parents, and I've met everyone in Sydney's clinic, even the new young man, Luke— everyone except the receptionist."

"Not even once?"

"Every time I go over there or poke my head in to say hi, the front desk is mysteriously deserted. If I didn't know any better I'd think I was being avoided. Strange, isn't it?" He shook his head and laughed.

Melanie peeked back at the clinic doors, tinted too dark to see inside. "Very."

"The best I have is rare glimpses here and there."

Melanie grinned. "Harboring a secret crush, are we?"

Tom jerked his chin toward her hand. "What'd you do to your hand there?"

Without warning, Tom pulled on her wrist until her hand was cradled in his. His hands had a faint white sheen to them. Flour. It reminded Melanie of Felix. Was that why she didn't reflexively pull away like she usually would? She didn't know why, but she got no bad vibes from this man.

He carefully removed the paper towel and handed it to her.

"Are you some kind of doctor in your spare time? Hitting the medical books between cooking pizzas?" she poked fun at him.

His lip twitched. "Something like that. It doesn't look too bad." He fanned out her fingers to allow better access.

Joel's truck pulled into the lot and Tom released his hold on her hand.

"So what's your diagnosis? Do you think it's infected?" Melanie asked as she rewrapped the injury.

A spark of amusement in his eyes. "I think you'll be fine in a couple of days." Tom inclined his head to her. "It was great to meet you, Melanie. Hopefully I'll see you around." With one last devastating smile he turned and headed toward the pizzeria.

She watched him leave, wondering why her heart wasn't racing after this encounter with such an obviously attractive man.

Because no matter how good-looking Tom was, he was missing that spark of mischief in his eyes, the one that would tease her about country music or challenge her to a video game shoot-out. She couldn't see Tom sitting with her for hours, painstakingly helping her get control of a power she wanted nothing to do with, dealing with all her drama and still looking at her without judgment.

Footsteps drew Melanie's attention. Joel came up beside her, keys still in hand. Her heart rate sped up. "Not you, too," he whined. "Damn that guy."

"What are you talking about?" She turned but Tom had already disappeared from sight.

"Your future fan club membership."

Melanie tilted her head in askance.

The door to the clinic swooshed open and Niella poked her head out. She scanned the sidewalk, as if looking for anyone who might jump out at her. "Are we ready?" she asked, still not coming farther out into the waning sunlight.

Sydney's golden blonde head popped up over Niella's. "Not yet. Joel, can I talk to you for a minute?" Her emerald eyes rested on Melanie and she smiled. "Hi, Melanie!"

"Uh … " Melanie lifted a hand and waved. "Hi." She didn't realize how much Sydney and Tom looked alike. The two could have passed as siblings.

"I'll be right back," Joel told her and went into the clinic.

Melanie expected Niella to come out and keep her company. But the clinic door closed, leaving Melanie to her thoughts.

•••

Joel followed Sydney into her office. She shut the door behind him, trapping him in her bright yellow sunshine room. Joel hadn't been in here for quite some time. It hadn't changed much; there were still pictures of the guild littered around the room. A frame that used to house a picture of him and Sydney was now replaced with one of her and Merrick.

Joel walked over to it and picked it up. "I got demoted, I see," he tried to make light of the situation. This was the first time he'd really been alone with Sydney since their breakup, and he hated to admit it, but he was antsy.

Sydney's face fell. "I didn't mean anything by it—" she started, gesturing to the picture, but Joel held up a hand.

"I'm teasing, Syd. I guess it's still a bit soon, huh? Look, I'm right there in one of the group shots; I have nothing to complain about. Now, why did you want to talk to me?"

"Right." She buzzed around the room, too much energy for that tiny little body to contain. "I know you and Felix are having a fight right now—"

Joel gaped. "How do you know that?"

She stopped her buzzing to stare at him.

"Right. Cali." He should have known.

Sydney nodded. "But I don't want to have to pick sides. We're all a team and I think you should be aware of our plans as much as anyone else."

"Plans? What plans?"

Had the guild made plans without him? Son of a bitch!

He clenched his hands into fists. "Felix," he grumbled. "What did he do behind my back?"

Sydney shot her hands out. "Joel, calm down. He didn't do anything. This was a group plan."

"And where the hell was I?"

"I think you were, uh, busy"—her cheeks flushed—"with Melanie."

Joel cleared his throat. Well, this was awkward. Nothing like talking about sex with your ex. "Okay," he said calmly. "So I was … busy." Adopting her word didn't stop the urge to run away from this conversation as fast as possible. It was worse than when his father had asked him about his first time. He shook the thought away. "What was this meeting about?"

Sydney looked relieved to be back on safer conversational ground. "We want to go back to the building, compound, whatever. The documents we took weren't enough. We want to question someone, to know what they're doing with these people on the list, if anything."

"You're going back? All of you?"

She nodded.

"When?"

She looked away. "Tonight."

"Tonight?" he exploded. "And no one thought to involve me?"

"I'm involving you right now," Sydney shot back. "Look, Felix was worried that you might tell Melanie what we were planning, but I figured you deserve to know what is going on. I did a poor job of letting you in on things before, and that's going to stop now."

And there it was.

The root of all Joel's anger. He exhaled loudly. "Hell, Syd—"

"I know you don't want to talk about it. I know now isn't the ideal time, but I wanted to let you in on this because if I didn't, the rift between us would continue to grow and I don't want that, Joel. Felix has his reasons for not wanting to involve you. I don't agree with them, so I'm telling you, but the last thing I want is for you to harbor ill feelings toward Felix because you think he's doing to you what I did to you. I was a coward. Felix is trying to protect those he loves."

"I know." Felix's reasons made it all the harder to be angry at him. Joel would do anything to protect Melanie and the guild.

He let out a huge breath.

"Thanks, Syd." He didn't know what to make of his situation with Sydney, but he did know he wanted to find out more about this organization. "Does this mean I can go with you guys?"

"Aren't you hanging out with Melanie tonight?"

He shook his head. "It just so happens that I'm free tonight. I'm taking Melanie to Niella's, then I'm all yours."

Sydney frowned. "Niella wants to hang out with Melanie?"

"Yeah," Joel said quickly. "You know … girl stuff." He didn't want anyone else to know about his plans with Niella. "I'll see you later tonight, Syd. And thanks."

He left her standing there, a perplexed expression on her face.

•••

"Wow, this is your house?" Melanie could do nothing but stare. The entrance hall had a small ramp to the right and opened into a huge living room. Hallways branched left and right, but Niella rolled into the living room. Melanie descended the few steps, taking in the tall ceiling, complete with a skylight, and all the potted plants that lined the walls.

The living room was connected to a large, stainless steel kitchen.

"You want anything?" Niella called as she took out two glasses and held them up for Melanie to see over the island.

"Water's fine," she called back and proceeded to the large entertainment system. The shelves were bare, but on the floor, packed into cardboard boxes, Melanie found what had once decorated them.

Trophies, medals, and pictures were thrown into the boxes, some of the picture frames cracked where the packer hadn't taken care to place them in the box gently.

She took one out and stared at the young, smiling face.

It was Niella. Her oak-brown hair was still short but a few inches longer than it was now, held back with a neon green fabric headband. She held up a first place medal, her other hand holding out her index finger for number 1. She stood in front of a sign that read San Diego State University.

"No way." Melanie stared at the newspaper articles and magazine clippings hidden beneath the picture frames.

> Souveray favored to win next summer Olympics.
> Niella Souveray, next Olympic legend?

Melanie squatted and sifted through the articles. There were dozens. Stories of Niella being the next track and field star, her success through high school and college, interviews about her goals and aspirations, and then the articles changed.

Terrible car accident wrecks Olympian's dream.
Souveray crashes under the pressure.
SDSU Track and Field star, Niella Souveray, paralyzed after horrific accident.

Melanie stifled a gasp at the black-and-white image of a car wrapped around a large tree.

The caption beneath the photo read: *Rising Olympic potential Niella Souveray crashes her car while falling asleep at the wheel after what rumors say to be a hard week of training.*

Melanie stared at the article, unseeing.

Fell asleep at the wheel?

Her hands tightened around the paper, her heart constricted.

She'd bet her entire life savings that Niella hadn't fallen asleep at the wheel. She'd had a Dream.

"Oh, Niella," she breathed.

The paper was ripped from her hands. Melanie jumped, falling on her ass. Niella stared down, her hazel eyes hard. "Don't you dare go through my things," she warned. "And don't you dare feel sorry for me." She thrust Melanie's water at her, liquid sloshing out the side onto the carpet.

Melanie fumbled for it, afraid if she didn't reach it in time Niella would simply drop it to the floor, not a care in the world.

"I … I didn't mean to pry. I saw it there—"

"And thought that because it was out in the open it was available for public viewing? Well, guess what? You thought wrong. Now, because you have no qualms about invading my personal space, let me return the favor." She leaned over, her chest nearly resting on her knees as she stared down Melanie. "What the hell are you really doing here?"

Melanie's fingers tightened around the glass in her hands. "I'm sorry?"

Hazel eyes narrowed. "Your reason for being here. What is it? And don't lie about it either. I'll find out. I may not be able to control my Dreams, but if I concentrate hard enough on something, I can sway them."

Melanie started. "You can?" That was news to her. At Niella's look she swallowed her curiosity. "I'm here to help you. Honest! You're like my brother, a Dreamer, and I see in you the same struggle he went through. I thought I could help."

Niella continued to study her before finally leaning back in her wheelchair. "And how exactly did you help your brother?"

Melanie could read Niella's skepticism in every line of her body. She had only one shot to convince her and she couldn't screw it up. Niella's life might rest in the balance. Tonight was the night, if she wasn't mistaken, and she needed to do everything in her power to keep Niella from leaving.

"It was an accident, really," she started. "I got scared when Nathan started to have another Dream. He looked as if he were in pain and I panicked. My powers flared. I didn't have much control at the time and I absorbed them. It tore him right out of his Dream and sucked me straight into one." Niella eyes went large. Shit. She shouldn't have added that last part. She waved her hand. "That doesn't matter though; I was fine. The fact is that my brother was … relieved of his powers. I don't know how long it lasted, but it gave him a break. I can only imagine how much you ache for a break. To have a guaranteed amount of time to call your own, where you don't have to fear—"

"I'm not afraid of my powers," Niella snarled.

Melanie jumped.

Damn, she did it again. She needed to stop assuming everyone in Joel's guild thought like she did.

Niella looked away and lowered her voice. "Not anymore. I've accepted my lot. I might not be the most joyful one in the bunch, but I've learned to cope." She stared at the cardboard boxes that lined the floor. A few heartbeats later she spoke again. "You said you took your brother out of a Dream and fell into one?"

Melanie instinctively reached for the leather band on her wrist, but the water in her hand stopped her. "Yeah."

Niella's attention turned back to her. "It was of me, wasn't it? That's why you acted the way you did at the hospital."

Melanie stared into her lap, her throat growing thick with emotion. "Yeah."

"That's the main reason why you're here, isn't it?"

Melanie felt the tears burn the back of her throat. She nodded.

"Do I even want to know what you saw?"

Melanie bit her lip and shook her head.

A moment of silence.

A resigned sigh. "In this Dream you had, do I accept this help that you volunteered to give? Does it help me?"

Melanie shook her head miserably. "I don't know." She swallowed past the tears, "I'm trying to change what I saw."

"Ah," Niella said, as if she understood, which Melanie guessed she did.

They were quiet for a few seconds more.

"Does Joel know about this Dream?" she asked.

"No. I haven't told anyone. I don't want to worry anyone else. I promised myself I would deal with it and I am."

Niella let out a heavy breath. "Well, I see Joel's hero complex has rubbed off nicely on you."

A laugh escaped Melanie. She looked up to see Niella smirking at her and she laughed even more.

"I guess it was bound to happen, all those superhero t-shirts he wears … "

Niella groaned. "Oh God, don't get me started on his horrible fashion sense. It's awful, isn't it?" They laughed. "I can't believe Sydney dated that for three years."

Melanie's laughter cut off abruptly. "Sydney and Joel … dated?"

Niella expression froze. "Shit. I thought you knew." She snapped her mouth shut as if attempting to stop any further rambling.

Melanie was only half listening as her mind went back to earlier that day when Sydney had wanted to talk to Joel. Alone.

A flare of jealousy.

She quickly stomped it down. That was impossible. Sydney had Merrick, and even in the short time Melanie had with them she could tell the two were crazy about each other. When they weren't talking to anyone else their eyes were constantly on one another.

But there was the first time she'd met Joel. At the bar, when he'd been drunk and depressed.

Like someone who'd just gotten dumped.

Her stomach twisted. Was Joel still pining over Sydney?

Was she nothing but a rebound? A temporary fling, despite his claims about soul mates?

She had to admit, hanging out with an ex after breaking up with them was strange behavior. Though she supposed belonging to a guild where everyone had powers made for certain exceptions.

But still …

"Are they … " She cleared her throat. "Are they still close?"

Niella squirmed in her chair. "Look, Melanie, I'm not really the gossiping kind." She held up her hands. "Not that there is any gossip to begin with. Any questions you have about Joel and Sydney need to be directed to Joel, not me, but I will tell you this. They're over. And they most definitely aren't as close as they used to be. In fact, Joel has been pretty scarce around the clinic. We're hoping that'll stop soon. After all, he's a part of our guild, probably the most enthusiastic about it too aside from Felix, and we need him." She took a swallow of her water. "Now, should we get started on whatever treatment you had in mind that's supposedly going to save my life?"

Melanie hesitated. "What makes you think it's supposed to save your life?"

Another smirk. "Life and death would be the only reason someone would want to seek out *my* company."

"Why?" Melanie asked. "Why do you push them all away? They're a great group of friends that clearly care for you, so why do you act the way you do?"

Niella took another swig of water, looking as if she wished it were something harder. Like vodka. "It's a protection mechanism."

"Protection against what?"

"Against caring, okay?" She finished her water and wheeled herself into the kitchen. Probably in search of something alcoholic.

Melanie heard the fridge open and the sound of liquid pouring into a glass. Niella came back moments later, glass full of a cream-colored water.

"Is that white wine?"

Niella knocked it back. "I have boxed in the fridge, and before you judge, it does in a pinch and that's all that matters."

"Fair enough. Are you going to elaborate on what you said earlier anytime soon?"

Niella glared at her and finished the glass of wine. "Out of everyone, I would have thought you'd figure it out fastest. Guess I overestimated you."

Melanie locked her jaw to keep from snapping. Niella was just falling back into her defensive mode. She decided to do as her mother always did: cross her arms and wait.

Their staring contest lasted about two minutes before Niella sighed and stared into the bottom of her glass. "It won't hurt as much when I Dream something terrible happening to one of them if I don't care."

Melanie wanted to reach out but knew this was the wrong person to do it with. Instead she sipped her water, letting the words tumble around in her head for a bit.

"It's normal to worry about seeing something you don't want to. Lord knows Nathan was terrified, but I'm sure nothing horrible will happen to them."

Niella laughed humorlessly. "You don't know the guild. They search for trouble, have been for the last eight months or so now. We're stuck. They won't stop and there's nothing I can do. It'd be different if I was out there helping them break into buildings and rescue others, but I can't." She punched her own thigh. Melanie winced at the sound. "I'm left at home like a spouse with a husband in the forces, waiting for that one phone call, only it won't be a phone call, it'll be a Dream and I'll have no way of stopping it. There's only so much you can do to change the future. I think some events were just meant to happen."

Her gaze bore into Melanie's. The image of Niella getting hit by the vehicle flashed through her mind, over and over.

She squeezed her eyes shut.

No. She could change that future. Niella would never be hit if she didn't flee from her house, and if Melanie stopped her from fleeing, it would stop her death.

She reached for her powers, felt the familiar tingle in the back of her neck and held out her hand to Niella. "There is only so much one can do to change the future. So let's start changing it. And if you could promise never to leave your house after dark for the next week, just as a precaution, that'd be great."

Niella's lip twitched.

She stared at Melanie's open palm for a long time. Indecision, fear, hope—it all swirled in her hazel eyes. After a few heartbeats she tentatively reached out and grasped Melanie's hand.

Chapter 28

"What the hell is he doing here?" Felix jerked his chin at Joel.

Syd stepped between them and put a hand on Felix's black thermal-covered chest. "I invited him."

Felix's blue-green eyes widened. He opened his mouth then closed it. He shook his head at Syd, finally returning his attention to Joel. "Where's Melanie?"

"With Niella."

This caused quite a few of his guild members to stare at him.

"With Niella?" Cali asked.

Joel clenched his fists. "Yes, with Niella. I asked her to keep an eye on Melanie." His stare bore into Felix's, daring him to say a word. Felix was still full of shit, but that didn't mean he'd risk the guild.

Something in Felix's eyes changed and he gave an imperceptible nod.

Felix launched into their plan of attack. The building was still being occupied, according to Merrick. Despite the guild's first attack, this new group wasn't worried enough to flee. They were either exceedingly cocky or dumb as fuck.

Joel really hoped for the latter.

Felix, Cali, and Sydney would head in through the front while Joel, Merrick, and Luke took the back. Everyone was to keep in contact by the walkie-talkie app they'd all downloaded onto their phones. If anything suspicious happened, they were to alert one another immediately.

Felix was through the front door before Joel and his group even reached the back. Damn Eraser abilities. Joel didn't have the luxury of waving his hand and making the door lock disappear; instead, he had to wait for Merrick to jimmy it.

"We're in," Luke radioed to the others.

"Copy that, Skywalker," Felix responded. "Alarm has been disabled."

The three of them crept quietly through the darkened hallway. That was another thing that sucked about being split up: if they were with Cali, they wouldn't have to worry about making a sound. But, unfortunately, they weren't all together so Joel had to tiptoe through the hallway, checking each of the door locks as quietly as possible.

"Do you really think anyone is going to be here this late?" Luke whispered as he checked a door farther ahead.

Joel was about to respond when Merrick came between them, hands up to halt further conversation. He held his index finger up to his lips to signal for quiet and pointed to a door up ahead that had a faint light showing beneath the crack of the door.

Bingo.

Joel nodded and together they crept to the door. There was still no sign of the others, which meant they'd either found something more interesting in the front of the building or they were taking their sweet time.

Joel pulled out his cell and texted Cali a quick message.

She got back to him instantly.

Felix says to wait. Almost there.

Joel ground his teeth but knew better than to rush into a situation without the appropriate backup. He placed his hand on Merrick's shoulder to stop him. He showed Merrick Cali's text message and together they set up around the door and waited. Joel strained to listen for any sounds of movement but couldn't pick up anything.

A heavy hand came down on his shoulder.

Blue-green eyes stared at him.

Joel stepped back. Felix got into position, turned to Cali She nodded in confirmation. He waved his hand, the doorknob vanished, and the door swung soundlessly open.

The office wasn't very big. A faint desk light was all that illuminated the place. There were two chairs sitting opposite a wooden desk and behind the desk—

Merrick stepped forward. "Juliet?"

Juliet Arden's head snapped up from where she pored over some reading material.

Sapphire-blue eyes widened at the sight of them.

Joel could only stare.

Juliet?

Juliet was working with whoever these people were?

She'd been a part of the group of kids he and Sydney had rescued last fall that had been on the run from Vander together. He'd taken care of them—of her. His gut sank even further—Juliet was most likely the one who had compromised their identities.

"It was you," he said and stepped forward. "You told this organization about us, that's how they know of our existence."

Juliet licked her lips and shuffled the papers on her desk into a folder. "It's good to see you all again." She tried for a smile, but it failed.

"Juliet … " Luke took a step closer, but Merrick's hand on his shoulder stopped him cold. "Why?"

Juliet flinched under Luke's gaze. "To protect the human race from your kind." Her chin rose and she stared them down without an ounce of fear.

"We trusted you." Sydney clutched Merrick's free hand in hers. "We protected you, took you in … "

"Told me everything I needed to know," Juliet finished for her with a nod. "It's nothing personal. I appreciate all you did for me back then, but I've been doing this long before you came into my life. Loyalty to my family cannot be overridden by one quick rescue mission."

Sydney's green eyes shimmered with unshed tears.

Merrick tucked her into his side. Very slowly he looked up at Juliet. "*This* is what you were referring to when you talked about your family?" A beat of silence. "Where's Hazel?" he demanded.

Pain flashed across Juliet's face.

"No," Merrick breathed. Rage flooded his eyes. "What have you done to her?"

Hazel Benedict had been another Joel and Sydney had saved last fall. A nineteen-year-old foster child with electrokinetic powers, she'd easily wormed her way into all of their hearts, Merrick and Luke especially, with her quiet tendencies. The thought that anything horrible had happened to her made Joel sick. It was a cruel fate to have saved her from Vander all those months ago only to hand her off to Juliet, who'd lied about having a family that would take Hazel in.

Well, she hadn't lied about having a family that wanted Hazel— it just wasn't what any of them would have expected.

Luke started to shake. "Juliet, how could you!"

Merrick's hand tightened around Luke's shoulder and Joel winced at the force. Luke didn't even seem to notice.

"She trusted you," he continued to rant. "We all did! Where is she?"

Juliet's hands shook and she hid them beneath her desk. "She's safe."

"Yeah?" Cali asked sarcastically. "Safe and sound in her cell somewhere? Wishing to be free? Wishing she'd never trusted your lying ass?"

Juliet's eye twitched; it was the only thing that gave her away.

"So it's true," Joel said. "She's locked up somewhere and you're to blame. Does she even have her powers anymore? Or did you strip her of those as well as her freedom?"

She swallowed. "I don't have to explain myself to the likes of you."

Merrick disentangled himself from Sydney and Luke. He stepped forward menacingly. "Oh yes, Juliet, I really think you do. Where's Hazel?"

Juliet shrank farther back in her chair.

Joel knew Merrick would never harm a woman, but the feral look in his ice-blue eyes made Joel second-guess himself. "Easy, Merrick," he whispered. "We'll find Hazel again, but we need to find out about what's going on right now more."

Merrick's jaw tensed. Joel waited for the fist to come sailing his way, but it never did. Instead, Merrick gave a curt nod and stepped back to where Sydney hugged one of his arms to her side.

Joel took the lead. He stared down Juliet, sitting in her leather chair, chin raised defiantly. Her so-called bravery was undermined by the way her body shook from time to time. Good. She was scared of them. She should be. It wasn't every day one managed to piss off six super-powered people in the span of five minutes.

"Tell us what we want to know, Juliet," Joel said, "and you won't find yourself in a cell wishing for freedom."

Her chin rose higher, jaw trembling. "You wouldn't dare."

"Oh yes, we would," Sydney spoke up, emerald eyes blazing. "I usually clean the largest kennel for people we need to lock up, but for you, I'd make an exception."

"I'd listen to her," Joel said. "She's also overdue for some more vacation time. The last thing you want is to be forgotten in the back of some vet clinic with only a bowl of water and some Kibble 'n Bits. It'd be days before you could bathe, and forget about having a toilet. I'm sure some newspaper would do, but the smell—"

Juliet's eyes burned with anger. "What do you want?"

Joel smiled. "Answers. We visited this building once before and came across some interesting paperwork. Detailed reports of people with powers, almost like a dating site profile, if you ask me.

Some of the people had 'stripped' next to their names, others were just crossed out. Did you kill those people?"

Juliet jerked back. "We do not kill people. We're not Vander Donahughe."

"No, you're *so* much better," Cali drawled. "Not."

Juliet's cheeks flushed.

Joel continued. "If you don't kill them, what are you doing to them?"

Juliet glared at him.

"Well?" he pressed.

"They're detained," she told him. "Until a reasonable method for dealing with them can be found."

"You mean until you strip them of their powers," Merrick said.

"If I meant that, I would have said it," Juliet snapped. "We do not have the resources to strip every supernatural we encounter, so we deal accordingly and figure out best where our resources should go."

"And the rest, what?" Joel asked. "Get to rot until you brainwash them?"

"We help them!" Juliet hit her desk with one fist. "We keep them from hurting others or themselves. It's not their fault they've been cursed with these powers. We give them back a normal way of life."

"You cow them," said Felix.

Juliet shot her nose into the air. "Like I said, I don't have to explain myself to you."

There were a few more scathing remarks from the guild, but Joel hardly heard them. One word kept going around and around in his head.

Cursed.

His stomach flipped. Juliet sounded just like Melanie.

Or was it Melanie who sounded just like Juliet?

"Why have you been hanging around Melanie Vyntra?" he blurted.

Juliet's attention snapped back to him. "I don't know what you're talking about."

She's lying.

He fisted his hands. "Are you using her? Trying to brainwash her into joining your little quest for power extinction?"

"Melanie Vyntra is a dead end. She has no control over her powers and is just as much a threat as you and your guild."

Joel wanted to believe her so badly. Had Melanie told Juliet to fuck off? Rather than waste her time trying to recruit Melanie, had Juliet brushed her off as a lost cause?

He wanted to ask her more, but Luke beat him to it.

"Where's Hazel?" Luke asked.

Juliet pressed her lips firmly together. They'd get no more out of her.

At least they'd gotten what they wanted, clarification on the documents they found. That was enough for a new purpose: they needed to save those Juliet's organization had taken.

"Where are you keeping the others you have detained?" Joel asked.

Juliet smiled. "You can find out for yourselves." Her gaze landed on something behind him. The guild turned and found Man in the Suit, along with five others, all broad shouldered, filling out their suits with layer upon layer of muscle.

Joel cursed under his breath.

Behind the men in black was the Asian woman from before—the one with multiple powers.

"Guild of Truth," said Juliet. "I'd like to introduce you to the head of security, Mr. Dallas Richardson. I'm sure you'll have plenty of time to become very close."

Dallas Richardson bared his teeth at them.

"Was that supposed to be a smile?" Felix mock whispered to Cali.

She shrugged. "I think maybe he's constipated."

Mr. Richardson's face darkened.

"Oops, I think he heard us," Cali said.

Joel sidled over to Sydney. "At the first sign of powers, shut us all down," he said to her. "The woman at the back has numerous abilities, some we're not even aware of."

Felix, clearly having overheard, nodded. "We can fight our way out without powers."

Mr. Richardson laughed. "I'd like to see you try." He cracked his knuckles. The five men behind him got into a fighting stance.

Joel's heart kick-started.

Sydney placed a hand on Cali's arm. Something passed through their gaze, then Cali nodded and Sydney's lips started moving. Cali nodded more, but no sound came from them.

She took a deep breath and closed her eyes in concentration. When she opened them her face looked strained.

"Did it work?" she asked. "Can you all hear me?"

Joel and the others exchanged glances. "Uh, yeah. Why wouldn't we?"

Cali gave him an exasperated look. "Because they can't." She jerked her chin at the men in black.

"Really? Well, that's convenient," said Joel brightly.

"I'm glad you approve, but in case you haven't noticed, this is a little tough to do for a long period of time with so many people. So can we get on with it? What's the plan?"

"We can't fight our way out of this," Merrick said. "Felix, Joel, and I are trained and have experience in hand-to-hand fighting, but the rest of you don't. Our attention would be too divided worrying about you guys too." His gaze touched down on Sydney and Cali.

Cali winced in pain.

Felix's hand darted out to rest on her shoulder. "What is it?"

"We need to hurry. This conversation isn't going to remain private much longer. That woman is trying to push her way in." She winced again, her jaw clenched shut.

Past the sea of confused men, the Asian woman's face was pinched in concentration. "They're planning an escape," her cultured voice spoke up.

"No shit, Sherlock," Joel mumbled. "Plan?" he asked the others.

Mr. Richardson pulled a dart gun from his pocket.

"This is gonna hurt," Luke said before he charged him.

"Luke!" Sydney cried out, but it was too late.

Luke crashed into Mr. Richardson. The two fell backward, knocking a few other suits with them. The ones who stepped out of the way pulled Tasers. One took a shot at Luke.

"Don't think so." Felix Erased the Taser before it had a chance to hit Luke.

Felix might've saved Luke from being electrocuted, but Mr. Richardson threw a punch that caught Luke right in the jaw. He flipped onto his back, his hand going to his bleeding mouth.

"Fuck this noise." Cali shot out a sonic wave that threw the men on the floor onto their backs again. The few remaining in the hallway staggered. Except the woman. She smiled at Cali.

Cali stepped toward her. Challenge accepted.

Despite wanting to watch the showdown, Joel tore his gaze away and shot into action. He threw himself into the hallway, making sure all the men on the floor stayed down. He Locked Mr. Richardson, blew him a kiss, and moved on to the other two. The rest followed him out of the room as Cali kept the multi-powered one occupied.

They all raced for the back door.

A loud, resounding *boom* shook through the hallway, followed by Cali's scream.

Felix sprinted back the way they'd come.

"Felix!" Sydney called in a vain attempt to keep him back.

"I'll go after him," Joel said. "Get clear."

Sydney hesitated, but Merrick caught her and led her and Luke out the back.

Joel ran toward Juliet's office. He nearly collided with Felix, who had Cali tucked protectively against his side.

Screams and crashes echoed behind them.

"What the hell did you do?" Joel ushered them past him and risked a glance farther down where the woman and what men remained standing fought off—

Joel blinked.

The demon cat.

It perched on the edge of one of the computer desks, screeching at the woman. It was the size of a Labrador, only its body was all wrong. Joints shot out at weird angles, and its skin—no, fur?—was a dark maroon, its paws covered in the faint mucus that lingered on all the things Felix brought back.

"You summoned that spawn from hell?" he asked Felix.

"Yup. And I don't feel the tad bit remorseful about it either." His hands tightened around Cali.

Joel gave a low whistle. "Damn, is it safe to leave it in … our world?"

"I'll put it back," he said as they beat feet to catch the other guild members.

They met the others in the parking lot, Luke and Sydney already packed into the Hummer. Merrick stood by the open door waiting for them. Felix helped Cali into his car and jogged back toward the building.

"Where is he going?" Merrick asked.

Joel watched Felix disappear into the building for a second time.

"To leash his pet demon."

Chapter 29

"What the hell happened here?" Melanie studied the destruction of Juliet's workplace. The large workstation set up outside her office was in shambles. There was a faint trace of sulfur in the air. "Did someone try to build a campfire?" She meant it as a joke, but Juliet's hardened expression dried up any and all humor.

Melanie cleared her throat.

"No campfire, though what caused this did appear to come from hell." Melanie frowned but Juliet continued. "We had a nice visit from your beau."

"Joel?"

She nodded. "And his friends."

The guild? Joel had looked tired when he picked her up at Niella's last night, but she didn't question his activities. She didn't feel the need to.

And he hadn't felt the need to share.

What other secrets was he keeping from her?

You're one to talk.

Her inner voice made her cringe. "What was he doing here?"

"It appears that the Guild of Truth has noticed our activities and came to investigate."

Melanie's blood went cold.

"Don't worry," Juliet said, easily reading her face. "I told Joel you weren't working for us. Your secret is safe with me."

Melanie couldn't breathe. "He asked about me?"

"This is their second break-in; in their first they stole some documents. They put it together that we take people's abilities away from them and that we need people like you to do that, so it was only natural to make the connection between us. I made sure to sever that connection."

Melanie didn't know whether to feel relieved or anxious. Her body was going for anxious. Was this the fate she'd chosen for herself? Leading a double life?

No. This wasn't forever. Once her debt was paid, Juliet would leave her alone and she could go back to her life. The sooner she finished her next mission, the sooner she got to her end goal.

"Where are we going today?" she asked Juliet.

Juliet finished packing her bag and gestured for Melanie to follow her. "Let's take a ride."

"An herbal shop?" Melanie stared out the tinted car window some time later. Korean and English covered the windows, boasting anti-aging teas and anti-wrinkle cream. "What are we doing at an herbal shop?"

Juliet opened the car door and stepped out. "This is where our next con artist works."

Melanie followed, a trickle of unease racing up her spine as the two men in the front of the car opened their doors.

"What're they doing?" she whispered to Juliet. "I thought they stayed in the car."

"It's fine. Just play along."

The jingle of bells cut off any further conversation. A short Korean woman looked up from behind the desk that sat in the middle of the room. The four walls of her business were covered with different bottles of every shape and size. The air stunk of burnt tea, or maybe that was incense. Melanie couldn't quite tell.

"Good morning." Her accent was heavy. She got up from her chair and came over to them, her face crinkling as she smiled. Up close, Melanie could make out the streaks of gray that hid in her short, black hair.

"Good morning," Juliet returned.

"How can I help you?"

Juliet held her hand up to her heart. "Well, you see, I've had this terrible cough as of late, and the doctors might be worried it's cancer, but I don't think it is. I'm far too young, so I was wondering if you had any pills that could help my lungs."

Melanie balked at the lie.

The old woman held her hand out, close to where Juliet's rested on her chest. "May I?" she asked.

Juliet dropped her arm. "By all means." Her eyes met Melanie's and glittered with triumph.

Melanie shifted nervously.

The woman placed her hand on Juliet's chest and closed her eyes. "Just breathe deeply," she instructed Juliet.

Juliet went along with the farce and did as she was told.

The woman frowned after a few moments and dropped her withered hand. "I will show you something that should help." She shuffled past Juliet to the far corner, where she pulled a bottle with a picture of lungs on the front. "Take this twice a day, it will help."

Juliet took the bottle and turned it over in her hand. "Hmm, $72. That's a hefty price, don't you think?"

The woman waved away the comment and shuffled back behind her desk. "It's good. In a few weeks your cough will be gone."

The bell jingled and in came the two suits from their vehicle. They both stopped and stationed themselves by the door.

Melanie's pulse spiked.

So did the old lady's, if her face was any indication. "What's going on here?"

Juliet slapped the pill bottle down on the desk. The sound made Melanie jump.

The old woman's attention snapped back to Juliet, who smiled sweetly. "Is this what you tell all your customers after you heal them?"

The woman's dark brown eyes widened fractionally. Her gaze darted to the door and back. "I don't know what you're talking about. Please leave."

This apparently wasn't the correct answer. One of the suits locked the front door and closed the blinds. He kept his back to them, watching outside the window.

"Let me ask something different then," Juliet said. "Did you notice that nothing was wrong with me when you touched me? Didn't you think it odd that you couldn't find anything to fix? I bet you tried anyway, right?" She inhaled deeply and exhaled. "My lungs have always been in perfect order. I just wanted to see what you'd do if I claimed to be ill. This is how you make your living, isn't it? You get customers with ailments, you fix them with your powers, and sell them some expensive sugar pills, telling them it will heal them, when you've already cured them of their sickness."

"Please," the woman said, clasping her hands out in front of her. "I don't hurt anyone."

"I'm afraid your time has run out," Juliet stated coldly. She turned to Melanie.

It took Melanie a moment before she understood why Juliet stared at her so intently. "Me?" She shook her head. "I—I." She gulped and started over. "Can I talk to you?"

Juliet sighed and nodded to the man at the door. He came over and stood behind the old woman, a heavy hand on her shoulder, keeping her in place.

Melanie tried to block out how frightened the Korean woman looked, how small she appeared next to the hulking man next to her.

Melanie turned her back on them to whisper to Juliet, "What are we doing here? This old lady wouldn't hurt a fly! She wants to keep her powers, and like she said earlier, she's not hurting anyone. In fact, I'd say she's helping people."

Juliet stared her right in the eye. "Not everyone we come across is going to be willing to part with their powers. This is your last training exercise. The last type of person you will encounter—the most resistant."

"I can't. She's helping people," she hissed.

"And making money off of them by selling them sugar pills! There is no black and white, Melanie. This job operates in a whole mess of gray."

"Well, maybe I don't like gray," she shot back.

"Boo-hoo. I've got news for you, Miss Vyntra. No one likes the gray. Sometimes the gray makes you question your actions, your morals, what's just and what's not, but you do it anyway because the overall good is what is at stake here."

Pain and remorse swirled in the blue depths of Juliet's eyes along with more secrets than Melanie could probably ever count. Could it be possible Juliet didn't want to do this job either? Was Juliet questioning her sense of right and wrong every day like Melanie? What horrible deeds had Juliet done in her past to get to where she was?

She shook her head again. "I can't."

Juliet locked her jaw. "If you don't, someone else will. There's no other ending to this scene except the one we came for."

Melanie's throat tightened. "I refuse."

"Fine." Juliet huffed. "Samuel, call for Trina."

Two minutes later, a knock sounded at the door. The suit opened it to let in another Asian woman who looked to be in her late thirties, early forties, with a delicate bone structure and pale skin. Her dark eyes surveyed the scene, resting on Melanie for a heartbeat. She sneered at her. "You are weak."

Melanie jerked. "Now wait just a minute—"

"Enough," Juliet cut in. "Trina, your target." She dipped her head to the herbalist, who was now silently crying.

Melanie stepped forward, but a strong hand fell to her shoulder. She looked up to find a pair of pitch-black sunglasses staring back at her. "Unhand me." She tried to squirm away. His fingers dug further into her flesh. Melanie winced. "You can't do this." She twirled around to face the others.

No one paid her any attention.

Trina loomed over the old woman, who now sobbed freely in Korean. Melanie's gut wrenched and she struggled again. The hand on her shoulder turned into two hands clasped around her upper arms.

When Trina placed her hand against the woman's forehead, Melanie wanted to turn away, but she couldn't. It was like watching a horrible car accident.

Trina remained motionless, eyes closed, while the old woman thrashed, trying to sever the connection between them. Shouts burst from her lips, heavy with tears. "Please," Melanie could make out in between the Korean. "Please!"

Suddenly her body bowed, like someone was sucking the heart right out of her chest.

Melanie knew it was the end.

Trina jerked back, the old woman falling into the man at her back. "It is done," she said curtly.

"Good," Juliet said.

Melanie twisted from her captor. He let her go.

Trina left without a word, leaving Melanie with Juliet and her two suited friends.

She stomped to Juliet and drilled her finger into the woman's ample chest. "This is not what I signed up for," she seethed.

Juliet knocked her hand away. Despite being a handful of inches shorter than Melanie, she stared her down. "This is exactly what you signed up for— you just failed to read the fine print." She stormed out, leaving Melanie to either trail after her or stay in the shop with the unconscious woman the guard had placed in her chair behind the counter.

She went after Juliet.

"Fine, I resign." Melanie dogged her every step.

"It doesn't work that way," Juliet said in a tight voice as they took their seats in the back of their vehicle that was parked outside the herbal shop. "You refused orders. You made me look like a fool in there."

"I wasn't refusing orders. I was acting human."

Juliet scoffed. "I let you spend too much time with Joel. It was necessary, but I underestimated his ability to brainwash you."

"You think Joel made me feel this way? Joel had nothing to do with this. This is my moral compass telling me you guys are screwy."

"You failed your assignment."

Melanie threw herself back into her seat. "Oh, goody."

Juliet glared at the back of the headrest in front of her.

The rest of the ride continued in silence, giving Melanie plenty of time for her guilt to eat away at her. Twice she had to blink back the tears. She wanted out. She'd been wrong, so wrong about so many things.

When they pulled up to their building of operation, Mr. Richardson was already waiting for them.

Juliet saw him. "Great," she mumbled.

"What the fuck happened?" he roared as they made their way inside. "What is she still doing here?" He jerked his chin at Melanie.

She was done listening to this dickhead. "You think I want to be here? Well, guess what? I don't, so if you're dismissing me, I'll be on my way." She spun on her heel, but Juliet's words stopped her short.

"We're not finished with her. She failed her assignment, true; she's not for us. That means our time here is nearly over. We have one more target to hit."

Mr. Richardson crossed his arms over his massive chest and grunted. "The Guild of Truth."

Melanie's blood turned to ice. "What?" She spun. In the back of her mind, she always knew this was coming. It's what Juliet had said from the beginning, but somehow she'd convinced herself that they would leave it be—let the guild be. Juliet had dismissed Joel before when Melanie had brought him up in conversation, so why go back to him now?

Mr. Richardson spoke over her as if she didn't exist. "What do we do about her? She knows too much; she'll warn them."

Juliet turned on Melanie, a feral smile tugging at her lips. "I don't think she will. In fact, I think she's going to help us. Call it our last payment."

Melanie stood her ground. "No way."

"Did you think our services were for free? We had an agreement and you voided it. But I have another payment plan in place."

"You think I'm going to help you out of some obligation I feel?" Melanie laughed.

Juliet didn't look perturbed in the least. "If you don't pay up, we take back what we gave you. In this case, your brother."

Melanie's nails dug into the palms of her hand. "Is this how you get your cooperation? Blackmail? Is this how they got you?"

Juliet remained silent.

"What do they have on you?" she demanded.

"What'll it be, Melanie?" Juliet cut off any further questioning. "Your brother or nothing at all?"

Melanie's mouth snapped shut. "You can't do this."

Juliet rolled her eyes. "Please, we can and with our resources you know how easy it would be. We probably wouldn't even have to resort to supernatural methods. Nathan was overjoyed when we helped him. He feels as we do and would love to come to our aid. He'd work for us in a heartbeat, but that's not the only thing he was interested in when we visited. He had quite the gleam in his eye when he looked at me." She grinned. Melanie ground her teeth. "I'd even go so far as to say he fancies me. Getting him to go on a date would be child's play, and as much as I'd like to have him as an employee, sometimes sacrifices have to be made. You know better than anyone, Melanie, how horribly wrong dates can go."

It took a second for her meaning to hit.

"It was you?" Her voice came out barely above a whisper. "You're the ones who rammed us off the bridge in Newport?"

Juliet shrugged, neither denying nor acknowledging the act.

She thought back to her training after the accident. "You wanted me to become … full-forced or whatever."

"You were supposed to be our newest weapon."

Melanie cringed at the way Mr. Richardson said weapon.

Juliet nodded. "And while we would have loved to add you to our roster of employees, it appears you are unwilling to do so. In that case, I'm offering you a deal. You help us with this final mission, we tick the last big organized group of supernaturals we know about off our list, we leave the Orange County area, you have your brother just like you wanted, and everyone goes back to their normal lives."

"You missed the part where I said 'go to hell.' I'm not helping you strip Joel and his entire guild. I'd never do that to him. I lo—" She cut herself short, shocked at her slip.

Juliet seized the opening. "You love him."

Mr. Richardson gave an exaggerated sound of disgust. "Who cares?"

"What if we spared him?" Juliet bartered.

"What?" Mr. Richardson exploded. "You can't—"

"Silence!"

Mr. Richardson clenched his jaw but refrained from speaking.

"I'm in charge here." Juliet's face was flushed. "Is that what it'll take, Melanie? If you agree to turn in the rest of his guild, we'll let him go. You can have your brother and your lover. That's my final offer. Take it or leave it. And please take into consideration that if you leave it, you won't be leaving here."

Melanie's stomach flipped. Bile rose in the back of her throat.

She opened her mouth to seal her fate.

Chapter 30

"You look horrible," Niella said as she opened the door for Melanie a few days later.

Melanie didn't bother with a response. She brushed past Niella and took a seat on her luxurious sofa. The soft cushions were heaven, and Melanie wanted nothing more than to drift to sleep, but every time she closed her eyes she was haunted with images of the Korean woman. Her red-rimmed eyes as she'd sobbed, the fear in her face when Trina had come for her.

Melanie didn't even know her name. How horrible was that?

"Melanie?" Niella rolled to her and in a rare show of concern, touched her arm.

"How're you feeling?" Melanie blatantly avoided her question.

Niella's gaze narrowed. Clearly Melanie wasn't fooling anyone in this room, but luckily for her, Niella dropped it. "Better," she admitted. "Less visions, more periods of lucidity. Even the guild has noticed my increased mood."

She swallowed back the sickness she felt rising.

"Shall we get started?" She held her hand out to Niella. She was anxious to get the Dreamer's power. Niella had mentioned that Dreams could be focused if the user concentrated on a specific person. Melanie wanted to know if the Korean woman would be okay. She wanted to give herself some kind of peace of mind, even if she didn't deserve it.

Niella held out her hand but drew it back fractionally when Melanie reached for it. "If you need to talk, you know I'm probably the only one in the guild who can actually keep a secret, right?"

Melanie smiled. Her first genuine smile in what felt like ages. "I sure hope so."

She grasped Niella's hand.

...

Joel paced in the lobby.

"Cut it out," Niella snapped. "You're giving me a headache."

He shot her a dark look. "Have you noticed anything odd about Melanie?"

Niella seemed to focus harder on her paperwork. "Not a thing," she said blithely.

Joel frowned. "Then why are you avoiding my gaze?"

"I'm not. I'm working. Sydney pays me to work. I work. I don't get paid to look at you, now do I?"

He resumed his pacing. "I don't like this. Juliet's little group has abandoned their building, and I bet all my Star Wars collectibles that they didn't just get up and leave. They moved. I've checked every day for the past couple days and not a peep."

"And you look like hell for it," she conceded.

Joel grumbled under his breath. "Aren't you the least bit afraid of them attacking us?"

"Terrified," she said without feeling. "But there's not much I can do about it." She jiggled her wheelchair to emphasize her point.

Joel paced some more. He didn't like this, and he didn't know if his unease was rubbing off on Melanie or if something else was bothering her. The last few days he'd hardly seen her. When she wasn't working the night shift, she was over at Niella's. And whatever girl code they had going on between them meant he couldn't join in on their plans.

The one time he and Melanie hung out, she'd had large circles under her eyes. She claimed she was fine, but Joel knew it was a lie. And that hurt too. Why would she lie to him?

But what really drew his curiosity was the phone call he'd received from her yesterday. She told Joel to assemble the guild, like he was Nick Fury calling forth the Avengers. Melanie wanted to speak to them and needed them all in one place. He didn't know why, but his Spidey sense was tingling, which was ridiculous. Juliet had put his suspicions to rest. If Melanie wanted to talk to them, maybe she learned something of importance?

"You know, you didn't have to come so early," Niella eyed him.

He froze and took the nearest chair. "I can't help it. This doesn't feel right to me, Ell."

Her face softened into sympathy. "Look—"

Felix and Cali marched through the door. Joel glanced at the clock: 6:01 p.m.

"Where's the fire?" Felix asked.

Joel stood. "There is no fire. Melanie wanted to meet us tonight. *All* of us," he pointed out in case Felix felt like cutting out early.

Joel expected more resistance, but Felix only nodded and led Cali over to the chairs to take a seat and wait.

Merrick arrived shortly after. Sydney and Luke came out after they finished cleaning up in the back. The whole guild crammed into the lobby, like some secret AA meeting.

Melanie arrived six minutes later. She stopped short in the entrance at the sight of them all. Her eyes were red rimmed and her nose pink. He got another creeping sensation.

Joel went over to her. "Hey," he whispered so the others wouldn't hear. "Are you sick? Allergies?"

Melanie sniffed. "Yeah, allergies."

Joel dug in his pockets for some kind of tissue but only produced some change, a mini screwdriver, and a flash drive.

Melanie smiled. "I'll be okay."

He stepped back and followed her to the center of the guild circle. She swallowed thickly as everyone's attention zeroed in on her. Joel took his place in the circle with the others. They all stood, probably in an attempt to try and ease Melanie's obvious nerves. It was easier to talk to a group of people if everyone was standing, right?

"Um." Melanie waved and dropped her hand, embarrassed. "Hi."

Joel coughed behind his fist. He half expected the guild to burst out unanimously with "Hi, Melanie."

They remained silent, waiting for her to get to the point.

Melanie cleared her throat. "I asked Joel to bring you all here tonight because I wanted to apologize."

"Apologize?" Sydney's delicate brow furrowed.

Melanie nodded and walked over to grasp Syd's hands in both of hers. "Yes, I'm afraid I've been keeping my distance because I've been scared of my newfound powers." She dropped Sydney's hand and moved to Merrick, placing a hand on his bare forearm. "I know you guys all accept your powers, and for me that has been a hard pill to swallow." Sydney frowned at her hands. She opened and closed them. Merrick's gaze snagged on the motion, his eyes quickly darting to where Melanie touched his arm. He opened his mouth, but she was already moving on. She laid a hand on Luke. "I've kept my distance from you because it's intimidating to be around people who are so comfortable with who they are—what they are." She smiled up at Luke. His neck turned red. Felix was next. "I've seen what some of you can do, and I envy the kind of comfort you have with yourselves." Felix's eyes were locked with Melanie's, searching. Melanie broke contact first, hastily moving to Cali. Cali leaned back, as if trying to avoid the contact, but Melanie placed a comforting hand on her upper arm. "I'm here to apologize because it took me this long to see what I really wanted. All this time I thought powers were a curse, but you guys have helped me see things differently."

Joel felt a swell of pride in his chest. Melanie was finally coming around to view powers as a gift. Relief washed over him. All his worry wasn't necessary. Everything was going to be fine.

Cali jerked away from Melanie, her arm tucked tight against her body. "What the hell are you doing? She took my powers!"

The fine hairs on the back of Joel's neck stood up.

"I felt it, too," Merrick said with a slow nod. "I've never experienced anything like that. A numbing sensation?"

Cali nodded.

Sydney and Luke shared nervous glances.

Felix frowned. "What gives, Joel?"

What the fuck? Did Felix honestly think he was behind this? "I … " He didn't know what to say. He hadn't known what Melanie was going to do. He certainly hadn't told her to do this.

She stepped forward. "Joel has no idea what's going on."

The sound of car doors slamming came through the eerie silence of the lobby.

Sydney peered through the glass door. Her face whitened. "Um, guys?"

Joel's stomach turned to lead.

Juliet and her goons came through the front door. Salt air blasted into the lobby, heavy and wet, sticking to Joel's skin, chilling him to the bone. Or maybe that was the feeling of utter betrayal he got as Melanie stepped away from the guild to greet Juliet.

"I'm sorry," she said to them at large.

Felix's eyes glittered with repressed rage.

Cali's face was red.

Merrick remained impassive as he stepped in front of a shocked Sydney and a nervous-looking Luke.

Joel glanced behind him and quickly stepped in front of Niella.

"You turned us in." it wasn't a question. Joel's whole world spun on its axis. All he could think was that he'd been so wrong—and he'd endangered them all.

Melanie's eyes filled with tears. Now he knew why they were red.

"Allergies, huh? Just another lie you let me believe?"

"Joel—"

He broke eye contact. He didn't want to hear any more of her lies. A part of him was dying inside and it hurt like a bitch, but he wasn't going to let her see that. He didn't want her to see how much she'd hurt him—how foolish he felt.

"Take them." Juliet pointed to the others.

Another salty blast of air. The door opened and in came the Asian woman.

"Syd," Felix said. "Shields up."

"I—I can't." Sydney's green eyes widened in fright. "Nothing's happening."

Felix frowned and waved his hand. Nothing.

Bile rose in the back of Joel's throat. They were helpless.

No, not everyone.

She didn't take his powers.

Without another thought Joel lunged, but it was too late. The Asian woman threw out her hand, a sonic boom blasting him into the reception desk. His neck snapped back with a resounding *crack*. Melanie screaming, warmth at the back of his neck, and then darkness.

He awoke to a throbbing pain in the back of his skull. He groaned, wishing for unconsciousness to take him again.

"Joel? Joel, stay with me. Come on, I need you to wake up."

Something cool pressed against his forehead. The scent of copper hung heavy in the air, but underneath he could pick up the traces of white chocolate and strawberries.

Melanie.

His eyes snapped open. He struggled into a sitting position.

"Not so fast." She gripped his shoulders as his world took a dangerous turn.

He took stock of his surroundings. He was still at Sydney's clinic, the hard lobby floor beneath him, but he'd been moved to the center of the room. He reached for the back of his head and his fingers came away red, his hair sticky and wet with blood.

He felt a bandage covering the source of the throbbing and only vaguely felt the pressure of the tape around his forehead holding it in place.

The lobby looked undisturbed other than a few chairs moved out of perfect alignment. No sign of a struggle.

If Joel didn't have a chill in his bones and his head injury, he would have thought nothing had transpired, that somehow what he'd seen earlier was just some horrible nightmare, but he knew better.

"You betrayed my guild." It came out hoarse.

Melanie winced. Her arms dropped away from him and she took a step back.

"You betrayed me." His voice grew in strength. He rose onto shaky arms.

Melanie reached for him but stopped herself short. "Joel, I—"

"You lied to me! In the worse possible way."

His throat clogged with emotion. He felt like someone was squeezing his heart—killing him slowly. He pushed the pain aside, let the anger take over. It felt better—stronger.

"Why?" he spoke again when he was certain his voice wouldn't shake. "Was it all a sick game? Lead me on, make me feel for you, and stomp around on my heart a little bit until you had your fill?" Something clicked in his brain. "You used me to become full-forced, didn't you?" He reached out for a chair to keep himself standing. He needed to get away from Melanie—far away. Now.

"Joel, please, it wasn't like that. Let me explain."

"Explain what? How I lost the Mirror Mate lottery by a landslide?" He snorted. "I think we've already established that." He took a tentative step. The world spun. Still woozy, but not as bad.

"I did this for you," she called after him.

He paused and slowly turned to face her, his vision going red. "You did all this," he spread his arms to encompass the clinic, "for me?"

She sighed in exasperation, glancing at the clock. "Look, we don't have time. You have to—"

"You took away my entire guild—probably sentenced them to a fate worse than death, and it was all for me?" He spat the last words.

"Yes," she said desperately. "Juliet would have taken you, too, if I didn't cooperate. I had to go along with it, but if we hurry we can make it in time and save them!"

"How the fuck are we going to storm a castle in this condition?" He pointed to himself, disregarding her statement and the flare of hope it brought him.

She looked like she was torn between crying and smacking him upside the head. "Because I took the entire guild's powers! I have them all inside me and I can use them, if we hurry."

Joel blinked. That spark of hope inside his chest flared. Could Melanie be telling the truth? Could he be wrong about her intentions? Had she been playing Juliet the entire time, working as a double, double agent?

His head spun.

He had no idea who to believe.

He had no idea what to do.

He stomped that little flare of hope right out.

"Why the hell should I even think about trusting you? You betrayed us all."

"Because I didn't have a choice," she nearly yelled, clearly trying to hang on to what little patience she had left. "This was the only way I knew I could stay in the loop with Juliet and keep you safe. If I had warned you of the attack, they would have tried again. But they're done in Orange County. I know where they're taking the rest—it's a small pit stop before they load up their trucks and drive away. If we hit them now, they'll cut their losses, turn tail, and run. Plus, Niella mentioned you guys are looking for another girl, Hazel Benedict? This might give you another chance at finding any information about her before it all disappears."

"Niella is in on this?"

Melanie gave him a small smile, some of the tension and sadness leaving her face. "Yes. She helped me plan."

His jaw metaphorically hit the floor. "Seriously? Niella? Why didn't you come to me? I would have helped you in a second. I would have protected you."

Her hands fisted and rested on her hips. "I don't need saving all the time. I'm not that Zelda princess to your Link."

"Wait." Joel held a hand up. "You actually know who Zelda is?"

Melanie fumed. "That's not the point!"

"Right," he said hastily. He rubbed his temples, trying to concentrate and ignore the pounding in his head.

Some of his pain must've shown because Melanie went to her purse on the floor and dug around inside until she produced a small pill bottle. She held out two tablets for him. "Here. This should help."

Joel swallowed them dry and grimaced. Hopefully, they'd kick in soon so he could focus better. His mind was a jumbled mess. He didn't know what to feel.

Maybe that was for the best. If the terrible pain in his chest was any indication, he was being ripped apart from the inside out and the only cure was space apart from Melanie. But if what she was telling him was true, that wasn't an option right now.

"Say I believe you. What then?"

"You need to believe me, otherwise your friends are screwed. And what we need to do, *now* I might add, is drive to this address." She thrust a small piece of paper at him.

He stared down at her bubbly script and had to blink a few times.

She took the paper back. "You know what, I'll drive. You focus on getting better. I'll need you as strong as possible. I'm not sure what Trina can do, but right now I'm powered up on eight different abilities."

"Eight?" Joel narrowed his eyes at her. "You only touched five of us, and if you add in your own powers, that brings the total to six. I may have hit my head, but I can still do simple addition. Where did the other two come from?"

Melanie avoided his gaze. "Missions with Juliet, before I realized what a monster her organization is."

His heart kicked against his ribs. "How do you have them for this long?"

She reached for the leather around her wrist and the action wrenched his heart even more.

No. Anything but what I think she did.

"Melanie?" It came out hesitant, nervous.

She looked up at him through guilt-lidded lashes. Tears threated to fall on her cheeks. "I took them. Permanently."

He knew that answer was coming, braced for it even. But hearing her say it hit with the force of a wrecking ball. The air left his lungs; he wrapped his arms around himself because what he really wanted to do was wrap them around Melanie, but he couldn't allow himself to.

"I told you I had secrets," she said. "I wanted to tell you all of it, but I couldn't. I was going to when it was all over. I never knew it'd escalate to this."

He didn't know who this woman before him was. She was a stranger, deceiving him from the beginning. She was worse than Sydney.

"Did you ever believe any of it?" he asked softly.

Melanie frowned. "I don't understand."

The pain in his gut turned to anger. He fisted his hands to keep them from shaking. "Everything you told me, about free will, about making your own choices, was any of that real?"

She blanched.

"You're a hypocrite," he accused. "Have you ever stopped to realize that what you're doing is taking away other people's free will?"

Her mouth opened and closed. The tears fell this time, but Joel refused to be moved by them.

"You're worse than Juliet." He held up his hand to stop her from speaking. "Save it," he told her. "The only thing I'm interested in now is helping my guild. They're all that matter to me." He stared at her without blinking as he said the words. But instead of feeling satisfaction at the hurt in her crystal-blue eyes, he felt an answering pain.

Chapter 31

Melanie thought for a moment they weren't going to make it. Mrs. Kegler's crappy car had rumbled and protested all the way as she'd driven with the pedal flush to the floor. But it was worth it. She had only one shot at this, and she had no idea how much time she had with these powers. She needed all the advantages she could get.

In the passenger seat, Joel shifted uneasily.

The wound in Melanie's soul cracked open and bled a little more.

He hated her.

Did you really expect anything else?

She knew what she was getting herself into from the beginning. She wouldn't bitch and complain about what couldn't be fixed. She had only right now, and she was going to right as much of her wrong as possible. Starting with putting an end to Juliet's plan with the Guild of Truth. Then she was going to promise to use her powers only for good, like Joel and his friends, because the last thing she wanted to do was hurt anyone else.

Melanie knew Juliet wasn't going to strip any of them that night. After Joel was knocked out, they'd tranquilized the rest of them. She'd watched as they loaded them into their van, careful that no one saw. Melanie had kept an extra eye out for Tom. The last thing she needed was some innocent witness harmed for something he shouldn't have seen. But, thankfully, Tom stayed in his pizzeria and the rest of the shopping plaza had closed up for the day.

Juliet's plan was to take them back to their headquarters in L.A., where Melanie bet Hazel was being kept too. Juliet didn't want to risk giving Trina too many powers. It appeared that the woman was already getting too cocky, which had been precisely why they'd wanted Melanie so much. She was a newbie, someone with no other powers, and who hated abilities to boot. If everything had gone to plan, Melanie would have been Juliet's perfect little weapon, doing what she wanted—helping strip others of their abilities but never using those powers, until eventually—from what Melanie understood from little bits she'd overheard—she'd be stripped of all her abilities by another newbie when she became too hard to handle.

It was a vicious cycle. It ate her up inside that she'd had to pretend everything was okay after that stunt in the herbal shop. She felt dirty, but she'd needed the information. It was the only thing that could help the guild now.

"I need a quick run through of everyone's powers." She turned to Joel.

She hated how his eyes stared at her with no flicker of amusement, no affection—just emptiness. Whatever fresh start she'd thought she'd be able to have with him was crushed. She'd screwed up. Joel might never look at her again, and she couldn't blame him. She never knew it'd come to this, but that wouldn't matter to him. Betrayal was betrayal no matter how one painted it.

He held up one finger. "Felix, Eraser—pretty self-explanatory. He concentrates very hard on an object he wants to vanish, waves his hand, it disappears." He held up two fingers. "Cali, Silencer—she can manipulate sound. Hers is more complex, but think of it as a sound vacuum; she can make herself soundless and sneak anywhere she wants, and also can project sound into a physical element, like that woman, Trina." Three fingers. "Sydney, Shielder—activate her powers and no one else will be able to use theirs. If you need some kind of visualization, think of erecting walls all around you. Merrick, Decoder—he can learn information from an object when he touches it. Luke, Rejuvenator—used to be called the Generator, but he didn't like it, thought it sounded too much like terminator." Joel's face softened momentarily. "He can heal faster than any normal human, making him pretty resilient when it comes to fights." All five fingers were raised by then and he wiggled them before dropping his hand. "That's everyone you touched."

Melanie quickly committed everything to memory.

"What are the other two powers you have?" Joel asked, his voice carefully neutral.

"Super strength and the ability to enlarge anything I touch."

For a moment the nerdy little boy inside of Joel came out. His mouth opened in awe, his midnight eyes wide with wonder.

She couldn't help it. She reached out and cupped his face.

Wrong move.

He jerked away, his expression shutting down instantly.

Her heart squeezed painfully in her chest, the hurt radiating through her body with every beat.

"We need to hurry." Joel stepped from the car and Melanie was happy to see that he didn't topple over. His equilibrium seemed to return, and she hoped he was strong enough to help her. She hadn't counted on him getting injured at the clinic.

Maybe that had been Juliet's plan all along, a safety measure to make sure Melanie didn't stick her nose into their business anymore?

Well, too bad, bitch, 'cause here I am.

Juliet didn't know Melanie knew the whereabouts of this place. That's where Niella had come in handy. The last couple of sessions together had been devoted to Melanie forcing Dream upon Dream on herself in an effort to glimpse as much of today's events as possible. Including where they would be taking place.

Melanie made sure to park a safe distance from the location to avoid detection, and together she and Joel walked the half block to the warehouse. A semi-truck took up most of the front parking lot and the warehouse stood dark and empty, the wooden exterior worn and weather-beaten. It looked ready to collapse with the slightest breeze. No lights shone in the windows, but that didn't mean no one was home.

"You're sure this is the right spot?" Joel stared up at the abandoned building. The smell of fish greeted them, and Melanie quickly switched to breathing through her mouth.

Joel gagged.

Melanie reached the front door, which was actually a large, wooden planked slider with a padlock.

Game time.

She reached for her powers, felt the tingle in the back of her neck, and focused on the lock. Taking a deep breath, she held it and waved her hand.

The lock vanished.

She exhaled in relief.

"Nicely done." Joel's voice held a hint of reluctant admiration. Melanie ignored it. She couldn't let her fantasies of winning Joel's trust sidetrack her concentration.

"Thanks. I had a pretty amazing mentor."

Joel's eyes glittered. "Flattery will get you everywhere."

"That's what I'm hoping for."

Maybe there was still a chance for them after all.

Inside the stench of fish was worse. Twice, Melanie had to stop and breathe into the sleeve of her shirt. The warehouse had been divided into different sections using large, pleated metal sheets; from the back she could see a faint yellow glow and hear voices. She kept her powers on high alert, using Cali's at the moment to keep Joel and herself quiet as they crept over wrappers and dried fish bones and God knew what else that littered the floor.

A long conveyor belt lined the right side of the building. Melanie used it as cover and hunched down to walk along it. Her heart raced in her chest and she turned some of Cali's abilities on herself so that she couldn't hear her own heart. She was grateful for the silence; it helped her think. But she could still feel the pounding against her ribs.

The voices were growing louder.

Joel's hand on her shoulder gave her pause.

"What's our plan of action?" he whispered.

Melanie thought for a moment. "I'll surprise them, distract as many as I can, you sneak around and free any of the guild you find."

"What? I'm not going to leave you to take care of everyone."

"I'll be fine. I have super healing and super strength, so I'm pretty much—"

"Golden," he finished for her in a defeated tone. "Fine, but as soon as I'm capable, I'm helping you. Got it?"

She nodded. "Fair enough. I have a score to settle with these people, and just to give you a heads up, I'll be using Sydney's powers from time to time."

"I'll try to keep my power usage to a minimum."

They reached the end of the conveyor belt. The back of the warehouse was a large empty space, probably where most of the fish packing happened if all the broken box pieces were any indication. Melanie could make out Juliet and the others standing on the opposite end.

Shit.

There was no way she'd be able to reach them without being seen. Behind them was more metal sheeting and beyond that the sound of metal being shaken. "Let us out." Felix's strong voice was slurred, as if he were pumped full of too many drugs. "We're not fucking animals." Whatever cage they had him in rattled again.

Juliet massaged her temples. "Would you take care of that?" she ordered Mr. Richardson. "And give another dose to Luke. His system has probably already burned through the other shots by now."

Mr. Richardson smiled and picked up a large tranquilizer gun that rested against a nearby box. "My pleasure."

At least Melanie knew the guild hadn't been stripped of their powers. They wouldn't be keeping them sedated if they didn't. Trina hadn't gotten to them yet, which meant they were only suffering from the lingering effects of her powers. Their powers would come back shortly, giving Melanie a small window for the different abilities to run in her system.

Melanie could feel the waves of rage coming off Joel. "We act now." He started to move.

"Wait, I'll make a distraction then you run in, okay?"

He hesitated. "Make it snappy."

"Right." She glanced around to find something of use. Her eyes landed on a large fish head below the conveyor belt. Her stomach turned over.

Well, if it made her squirm, she could only hope it'd freak Juliet out when enlarged to five times its size.

Melanie squatted down even lower and reached for the head. It squished under her fingers and she swallowed down the food that rose up her throat. Once she had it firmly in hand, she dropped Cali's powers and focused on making the fish head larger. Slowly at first and then progressing in speed, the head grew. Joel watched in sick fascination until it was the size of a watermelon.

"How are you going to throw that?"

"Super strength, remember?" And luckily for her, growing up with an older brother made her a little more athletically inclined, which meant she could aim.

She threw the fish head, but no one noticed until it got within a few feet.

"What the fuck is that?" one of the suited men near Juliet shouted. He pulled a Taser and fired.

The small electrodes embedded themselves into the fish head and together they crashed into Juliet.

She screamed.

Melanie smiled as the fish hit its target, splattering all over Juliet's immaculate blouse and dress slacks. And if she got a few electrical shocks, all the better.

"Go," Melanie ordered Joel as she pulled at one end of the conveyor belt. The metal groaned beneath her strength and a large piece broke off into her hand. "Now!" She launched the object, catching a guard in the shoulder and sending him flying.

Joel took off at a run. Melanie left the cover of the conveyor belt as the back door sliders were thrown open.

Trina came into view and Melanie instantly imagined shooting up those invisible walls.

Trina's eyes lit on Melanie. "Now you will get what you deserve for your cowardice."

"Bring it." Melanie charged her. She had a lot of rage to let loose.

Trina shot an arm out. Nothing happened.

Confusion registered on her face before Melanie dropped her Shield and called forth her strength. She punched Trina right in the jaw, heard a satisfying *crack*, and sent her flying.

"What in God's name?" A man next to Trina pulled another Taser from his jacket.

Looked like they weren't carrying anything lethal.

Good.

Melanie didn't even have to think. She waved her hand. It disappeared. She punched him and sent him spiraling through the air.

"End of the line, bitch," a voice spoke up from behind her.

Melanie started to turn, but something sharp stabbed into her shoulders and suddenly pain tore through her body, causing her muscles to convulse as shock after shock went through her.

She dropped to the floor, spasming.

A new suited man dropped the Taser. The electrical shocks stopped. Melanie lay there, trying to catch her breath.

The new suit ran to Juliet. "We need to get out of here, ma'am."

Juliet grabbed the lapel of his jacket. "I am not leaving here. We haven't finished loading the cargo."

"B-but … " The young man started to stammer out reasons why they needed to leave. Melanie lost track of their conversation.

Cargo.

There were people in the semi-truck. She had to get out there.

Repressing a groan, she rolled to her side and flexed her hands. Her muscles were coming back under her control.

That was fast.

Then she remembered Luke's ability.

Grinning to herself, she pushed up to her hands and knees and crawled her way toward the door. She heard commotion coming from the back, where she prayed Joel had freed some of the prisoners.

The sea air slapped at her face when she exited the warehouse. She got to her feet and ran for the semi. The doors were closed but not locked. She wrenched them open and stared into the dark recesses.

A few faces lifted at the sight of her.

Then a chorus of "Help!"

Melanie didn't waste any time. She tore open cage after cage.

"Is that all of you?" she asked of the last prisoner. There were still more cages deeper in the semi, but none looked filled.

The man stopped. "Yeah, there's an old guy at the very end, no one was supposed to go near him. From what I've heard, you should leave him." The man took off.

Melanie stood alone in the back of the truck.

The sound of the ocean echoed inside the metal container. Melanie hesitantly made her way farther down. The hair on the back of her neck prickled and thrice she turned to find no one there.

Her senses were on high alert, palms sweating, heart thundering.

She stopped near the end of the cargo bin where she could see the last prisoner. The man she'd freed had been right—it was an old man in the last cage. Why was he being kept isolated? He certainly didn't look terrifying.

White hair and deep wrinkles around his eyes, forehead, and mouth placed him somewhere around the eighty- to ninety-year mark if Melanie had to guess.

Still, she would heed the other prisoner's warning. She eased closer.

"Sir?" she called to get his attention. His chin was resting on his chest, possibly sleeping.

Her voice echoed off the metal walls and Melanie shivered at the sound. She wrapped her arms around herself as the wind swept inside the storage unit.

"Sir, are you awake? I'm here to help." Only a few feet separated them now.

His head jerked and a pair of dark, ancient eyes stared back at her.

Melanie stumbled to a stop. Something in his eyes shot a bolt of fear straight to her toes.

Leave him.

She shook her head. She was not like Juliet and her group. She would never leave someone to whatever fate Juliet had in store for them.

Pushing one foot in front of the other, she wrenched the door of the cage open.

The man watched her with those worldly eyes, still sitting.

"Come on, we need to get you out of here before some of those goons come back. Can you stand?"

The man shook his head.

Melanie ducked into the cage with him and bent in front of him. "Okay, put one of your arms around my shoulders—"

He moved like lightning.

His hands grasped either side of her face.

Melanie tried to jerk away, but he held tight. "What—?"

Her words cut off as pain ripped through her body. She choked on a scream while a strange sense of fatigue took hold of her.

Her eyes locked with the old man's.

Her lips parted.

No words came out.

As suddenly as it had started the man let go. Melanie staggered back and fell into the bars of the cage. She grasped them like a lifeline, her heart racing a mile a minute. She blinked a few times to clear the spots that had appeared in her vision.

When she could see clearly, the old man stood before her, his face unreadable. He nodded once. "Thank you for freeing me. In exchange I will spare your life."

Was it just her or had his wrinkles faded?

Melanie didn't know what to say. Out of nowhere a young man suddenly appeared. Melanie jumped with a squeak.

The old man didn't even blink. The young man held out his arm and the old man took it. Together they walked out of the semi-truck, but not before the young one spared a glance over his shoulder, his mismatched eyes connecting with Melanie's before they were both gone.

She shivered.

She touched her face where the old man had grasped her. Something Joel had said niggled at the back of her mind.

Those powers.

Her heart ceased beating.

Vander Donahughe.

Could it be possible that she'd just rescued the Guild of Truth's most hated enemy?

Her evening was just getting better and better.

It took her a few moments to collect herself. When her legs stopped shaking and could support her weight again, she stumbled from the semi-truck.

Only to be blasted off her feet.

The force hit with a *whomp*, causing her ears to ring.

Disoriented, Melanie shook her head and found Trina standing a few feet away, revenge blazing in her eyes.

She started to advance on Melanie.

Melanie shot her Shield up, but nothing happened.

The powers are fading.

Trina was upon her, her hands grasping Melanie around the neck.

Instinctively Melanie's hands wrapped around Trina's. She reached for her super strength, but the next second her entire body froze.

Panic flooded her and she reached for Sydney's Shield. Again, nothing.

"What's the matter?" Trina drawled. "Terror got you immobilized?"

Her eyes, the only thing Melanie seemed to be able to control, latched onto Trina's smirking face.

This was all her doing. She could immobilize Melanie with nothing but a touch!

Then something worse started to happen. Melanie's neck started to go numb, the pins and needles sensation climbing down her throat, along her arms, into her chest, everywhere.

Horror gripped Melanie. She knew this feeling—was usually on the other end of it. She reached for her strength, willed it into her fingers, willed her fingers to move, but couldn't.

Helpless, tears pricked the backs of her eyes.

Just as the pins and needles became unbearable, her back bowed off the floor, the air leaving her lungs, as she felt something torn from her body.

Her vision went black. All sensation left her body and she floated down into the comfortable abyss of unconsciousness.

Chapter 32

Joel watched as Melanie's body rose off the ground like someone being possessed. Her bright, crystal-blue eyes were wide in terror.

His chest burned and he put his hand over his heart were the bond between him and Melanie usually radiated warmth.

Something was wrong.

He scanned for something to use as a weapon but found none.

Without thinking, he charged the Asian woman holding his Mirror Mate and tackled her. Melanie's body dropped to the ground with a *thud*. The woman screamed and clawed at Joel's face. He Locked her to the asphalt and scampered off of her, his cheek stinging where she'd got in a swipe.

She tried to lunge but didn't get very far. She screamed in rage and fought against his Lock over and over again.

Good luck.

He crouched next to Melanie, his gaze snagging on the open end of the semi-truck and all the open cages within.

She'd saved them all.

He gathered her into his arms. "Melanie?" She didn't respond. He shook her. "Melanie, come on, open your eyes for me." His heart lodged in his throat, he turned to the Asian woman. "What did you do to her?" he barked.

She smiled at him, seeming to have given up on breaking his Lock. She sat back and feigned nonchalance. "I did to her what she didn't have the courage to do to others."

His heart stuttered in his chest at the implication. "No." The word slipped out of him as he rocked Melanie in his arms.

Not Melanie. Her powers …

His arms tightened around her. All she wanted was to save the guild. Something Joel had been too preoccupied to notice. He'd been so obsessed with his own grief, his feelings of betrayal, that he'd shunned Melanie, let her go off on her own and now she paid the ultimate price.

"Joel." Merrick's voice rang out behind him.

The rest of the guild made their way from the warehouse, a few of them unstable on their feet, clinging to one another for support.

Niella wheeled over to Melanie. "What happened?" Her hazel eyes shot to the Asian woman and narrowed.

Joel looked down into Melanie's pale face. The circles under her eyes stood out against her skin. She'd been losing sleep, worrying about Joel and her plans against Juliet, no doubt.

"I think she was," he swallowed, "*stripped* of her powers."

The guild remained silent.

"Do you need help carrying her?" Luke offered, stepping forward. He swayed on his feet.

Joel repressed a smile. "I can manage. Thank you, though."

He scooped Melanie into his arms, tucking her head safely beneath his chin. Her skin was sticky from the moisture in the air, the awful scent of fish from the warehouse clinging to her clothes, but he pulled her close anyway.

"Were you able to find out anything of use?" Joel asked Merrick as they made their way to his mother's car. Eight people in five seats was going to be fun.

Merrick shook his head. "I got bits and pieces off Juliet, but once she realized what I was doing, she shut down completely. I got a glimpse of their headquarters in L.A., a flash of Hazel, but nothing more substantial. I could have given chase, but in the condition we're in, I thought better of it."

Joel nodded.

Sydney, still drowsy from the drugs, patted Merrick's shoulder but missed about half the time. "It's a start. We'll find Hazel again."

Luke, who clung to the back of Niella's wheelchair for balance, turned and nodded. "We won't stop until we find her."

They all stopped once they got to the car.

"You didn't think to bring my Hummer?" Felix stared at the sedan with a horrified look on his face.

"Shotgun!" Cali and Niella shouted at once.

It turned out that Felix and Cali both shared shotgun, Cali in Felix's lap. Merrick, the least drugged of the bunch as they didn't need to suppress his powers, drove. That left Sydney, Niella, Joel, and Luke to squeeze into the back with Melanie laid out over their legs. It was a miracle they weren't pulled over.

Joel cradled Melanie's head in his lap, running his hands through her silver-blonde locks.

Niella nudged him with her shoulder. "For what it's worth," she murmured to him, "she wanted to tell you her plan."

He stopped mid-stroke. "Why didn't she?"

Niella looked uncomfortable. "She knew working with Juliet would be a betrayal to you no matter what after I told her everything we've been through. Why didn't you tell her about all the times you went to find the guys in suits?"

Joel stared into Melanie's face. "Because I didn't want to scare her off. I was trying to protect her, and instead I just shoved a wedge between us. I fell too hard, too fast, like usual." He sighed. "I'm an idiot."

"Just a little," Cali called over her shoulder.

Joel reached forward and pulled on her ponytail.

"Hey!"

"No comments from the peanut gallery," he said. He turned back to Niella. "She was frightened because her last boyfriend was stalking her, she was wary of men, and I thought if I told her suited men were following her, she'd freak out. Like I said, I screwed up."

"No one's perfect, man," Felix piped up. "Whether it's you, me, Melanie—we all have some kind of demon to overcome."

Felix was right. God, he hated how Felix was right. Melanie was only trying to protect him, like he'd been trying to protect her by keeping her in the dark about the men in suits—about pursuing Juliet. If he wanted someone to blame, he only need look in a mirror. Maybe if he were open and honest from the beginning, she would have felt comfortable with him and gone to him instead of Niella. He knew they had a rocky start, that maybe Melanie wasn't looking out for him in the beginning, but in the end she'd chosen him. Shouldn't that count for something? She'd stepped up and got over her fear of losing Joel by admitting the truth.

A small hand reached around Niella and touched him on the wrist. Sydney's emerald-green eyes locked steady on his. "She's not me, you know," she said softly.

The words penetrated all the way to his soul.

Melanie wasn't Sydney.

Melanie might have deceived him, but her back was against a wall. She'd wanted to help her brother. She hadn't meant to hurt Joel, that much he saw from her expression after Juliet's attack. Just like Sydney hadn't meant to hurt him.

Silence descended upon the tiny, stuffed car for a few blocks.

"It's up to you now," Niella spoke up, "whether you can forgive her, put the past behind you, and move forward."

•••

Melanie awoke to the sound of running water. For a moment she froze, her mind putting her at the last place she could remember. The warehouse.

But the smell of fish was gone and she wasn't on the hard ground but on a soft mattress that smelled like Joel.

Her muscles were already starting to relax when her brain caught up.

She tensed. Joel had brought her here because she was injured. That didn't mean he'd let her stay. In fact, he'd probably kick her out as soon as he found out she was awake.

She'd betrayed him—betrayed the guild.

The running water stopped.

She sat up and her eyes darted to the closed door that connected to the bedroom. She looked down at herself—she wore one of Joel's t-shirts and nothing else. She didn't see her clothes anywhere.

How long had she been out?

The windows were dark around the blinds. Joel's alarm clock read 10:52 p.m. She'd been unconscious for a few hours.

Shuffling from the other side of the door made her heart stutter. Her mind told her to flee, to escape before she had to confront Joel, but her body didn't listen. She didn't care if he hated her, she wanted to see him at least one more time before he ended it between them. Besides, she would not cower from the consequences she brought upon herself by her actions. It was time to face the music.

The handle jiggled and her pulse spiked. She pulled the bed sheet up higher against her chest. That didn't mean she liked facing the music nearly naked. It took away a little of her bravado when she thought too hard on the fact that her bare bottom was on Joel's smooth sheets.

Joel stepped out of the bathroom, clad in sweats and a Star Wars graphic tee. She would miss his shirts. She would miss him.

He toweled his damp hair as he came out of the bathroom, stopping when he noticed her sitting up in his bed.

The towel dropped. "You're awake."

Her mind went blank. She couldn't think of anything to say. "Hi" sounded too lame. She opened her mouth to try, but in the next instant Joel pulled her into his arms.

His warmth and strength triggered the tears she hadn't known she'd kept at bay. She clung to Joel as they fell.

He stroked her back, murmuring words of comfort the entire time.

When she was finally able to get a handle on her emotions, she pulled away. "I'm so sorr—"

He cut her off with a fierce kiss.

The taste of him melted her insides. She opened herself up to him. He fed from her like a man starved.

She knew the feeling.

Her mouth moved under his, giving, taking, until she was breathless from it.

Finally, he pulled back. "You don't have to apologize. I understand that I didn't exactly earn your trust. And I'm sorry for that. Niella told me about your plan to attack Juliet. How you wanted to tell me but didn't. I'm glad you had someone in the guild you could confide in."

She took his hand in hers. "Joel, I made a mess of everything. The situation with Juliet, Alexander, your guild." She shrugged. "Like I said, everything. I was lost and confused and that's no excuse. You tried to help me, but I was too stubborn to listen, and I understand if you want to end things between us. I ruined it all. You probably hate me. Along with the guild."

She tried to disentangle her hands from his, but he hung on. "I don't hate you. The guild doesn't hate you either. Niella explained to them what you were planning after they were kidnapped. They might be a little grumpy, but they know why you did it. And you were right, Juliet left after the attack. There's no sign of her, and even though we didn't get all the information we would have liked on Hazel's whereabouts, we're a little closer because of you. Trust me, the best thing you could have done was align yourself with Niella. She wouldn't defend just anyone. She's hard to win over and the guild knows that."

The tears were back in her throat, but she held them at bay as she smiled at him.

He returned her smile and tucked a lock of hair behind her ear. "Can I ask why you were suddenly so interested in Niella?"

The urge to tell him something different rose, but she beat it back. The time for lying to Joel was over. If she didn't give him everything, she would lose him, and she knew without a doubt that she couldn't lose him, not now, not ever.

"I had a Dream about her," she confessed, already feeling lighter after that short sentence, like a weight had been lifted. "I Dreamed that she was killed."

Panic flashed across his face.

She squeezed his hands. "It's okay, I fixed it. She was hit because she was fleeing her house in a confused state. Her Dreams were overwhelming her, bombarding her thoughts—that's why I wanted to help her. I took her powers, giving her periods of calm without risk of her powers flaring. Her mind was at peace, at least for a little while.. She said she was doing better at our last one, so I can only hope that means her future is going to be a good one."

His expression turned solemn. "But now you'll never know."

"What do you mean?"

His fingers tightened around hers. "I mean, you'll never be able to take her power and look into the future. Your powers … they're gone," he said gently.

Her blood froze.

Memory flared.

Trina. The warehouse.

She remembered fighting her, struggling to move but being locked in some kind of living rigor mortis.

Her mind must've repressed those last moments before her world went dark.

But the one thing she did remember was being lifted from the ground as if something were being torn from her body, ripped away from her very soul.

Her powers.

She pulled her hand from Joel and wrapped her arms around herself. She should be happy, shouldn't she? This is what she always wanted. A normal life.

Then why did she feel like throwing up and crying at the same time?

She went back to that moment before unconsciousness took her. Remembered the fear, the terror.

Her neck tingled from the memory.

She blinked back her tears.

Joel cupped her face, one of his thumbs wiping away a stray tear. "It's okay," he soothed. "Don't cry. You're not hurt and that's all that matters."

"But I'm nothing now." She stared down at her lap. "I'm not one of you any longer. I'm a regular human. I'd only get in the way."

He lifted her face; she stared at his neck, refusing to look into his eyes.

"Melanie," he chastised.

She lifted her gaze.

Her breath caught at the love and affection in his eyes.

"I don't care if you have warts and boils. I love you. Powers or no powers."

She sniffed, holding back the tears. "Really?"

A warm tingle filled her, strongest at her neck.

Joel frowned.

His midnight eyes shifted to his hand and back to her face.

"Are you doing that?" he asked.

"Doing what?" She turned her focus inward.

It took her a moment, but she finally identified what he meant. She gasped and Joel dropped his hand, shaking it out as if he'd lost feeling in it.

"My powers?"

Hope flared. She snatched the pillow from behind her and pushed it down into the mattress, concentrating.

She released it seconds later, heart in the throat. "Pick it up."

Joel complied. The pillow didn't budge.

Joel stared down at the bed in awe. "I don't understand."

Melanie didn't either. She distinctly remembered Trina holding on to her, taking her powers. She remembered it all, how she'd tried her hardest to move her hand, to use her super strength to break free—

"That's it."

"What's it?" Joel asked.

"When Trina was taking my powers, I was concentrating with all my might to use the super strength to break free from her. She must've taken that power instead of my siphoning powers." She opened and closed her hands. "I still have my original gifts."

Her lips curled into a grin. She threw herself at Joel.

They tumbled right off the bed and landed on the floor with a *thunk*.

Joel groaned.

Melanie reared back. "I'm so sorry!"

He chuckled, rubbing his head where it hit the floor. "I'm fine. Bruised, but fine."

She stared deep into his eyes and couldn't imagine any other future other than being with him.

"I love you," she blurted.

His eyes widened. Beneath her palm, his heart kicked against his ribs.

"I love you, too, Melanie."

Her heart soared, radiating heat like a mini furnace inside her chest.

"We might've sped through the Bonding process"—his chest rumbled beneath her as he spoke—"but I have faith that if we build this relationship on trust—truth, that's what the guild stands for after all—we'll be just fine. No more hiding secrets from one another. I want to be honest with you, and on that note I think it's time I told you about Sydney and I. When I found out about you working for Juliet, it hurt, a lot, but I don't think all the pain I felt was because of you. I was holding on to the deceit I felt because of Sydney." He told Melanie of their relationship and how Sydney found Merrick. "I hung on longer to that pain than I should have, and I let it poison me. It made my reaction to you worse. And I'm sorry for that. I want to start anew. Does that sound good to you?"

She leaned forward until their lips nearly touched, her breasts pressed firmly into his solid chest. "That sounds amazing."

His hands slid down the sides of her body, reaching the hem of his t-shirt. He dragged his fingers along the smooth skin of her thigh and cupped her bare bottom in his hands. "Are you ready to be inducted into the Guild of Truth as a Siphoner?"

She rubbed her pelvis against his, only half listening as his hands began stoking a fire within her.

"If you'll have me, I'm all in," she breathed and pressed her lips to his.

He growled low in his throat. "I'll have you, all right."

He rolled her beneath him.

Acknowledgments

A big thank you to all my family and friends who've supported me in my writing career. To all the Guild of Truth fans out there who waited patiently for this book. Thank you to Crimson Romance for believing in this series, and a special shout out to my editor, Julie, for making this book the very best it could be!

This was so humiliating. After moving out seven months ago, Cali was already crawling back to her parents.

That's what you get for trusting anyone.

Jessica had been her roommate, her sort-of friend, and she'd stolen Cali's painting and hawked it to the highest bidder to get the money and run.

Cali exhaled. "Figured." She'd been working on that painting for two months. It was supposed to pay for this month's rent. It was a little too convenient that it was Cali's turn to pay the full brunt when Jessica decided to take off. Her parents were going to love that.

Don't think about that. Remember the job offer you got back in April. Vander said you were all but hired. Use that to lure them in, then when their defenses are down, pounce.

It was as good a plan as any, but that didn't stop the nagging voice inside her that said her parents wouldn't do a damn thing to help her. While she knew her parents weren't the harshest out there, she still thought it a little heartless for them to force her to pay rent at eighteen or move out when neither her brother nor sister had to.

Jared and Garnet never got arrested.

It didn't matter. Her parents never helped her when she'd been behind paying them rent. Why would they help her now? She'd once had to pawn off a gold bracelet they'd bought her for her sixteenth birthday so she could make her payment. Granted, she'd splurged that month on new oils and brushes, but her parents never approved of her art.

And that bracelet was hideous, so maybe they did you a favor.

Either way, she'd see this through till the end. She kept her head high as she unlocked the front door.

The drapes were pulled shut, casting the house in darkness. She squinted against the sudden change in lighting, giving her eyes a second to adjust.

A lone shadow lay hunched in the hallway.

The back of her neck prickled. "Hello?"

The lump didn't move. Gripping her side bag, she pushed the door open wider with her shoe. The sun spilled into the hallway, not quite reaching the far end where it led into the kitchen.

Get a grip, Cali. How do you know that thing isn't a new piece of furniture Mom and Dad bought?

She squinted against the sun's reflection cast on the wood floor and hesitantly made her way in.

Her heart stopped. "Whoa."

The body slouched up against the wall was surrounded by a pool of bright red blood.

That's a lot of blood.

She was going to be sick.

Don't panic, don't panic, don't …

She sucked up her fear and approached. What if he was still alive?

With all that blood? Yeah, right.

The man couldn't have been any older than thirty-five. He had brown hair and plain features, nothing to make him stand out in a crowd, unless one factored in the current piece of wood sticking out of his chest.

Dropping her bag, she inched closer. Was that a stirring spoon?

All panic fled as concern took root in her gut. She called out, "Mom? Dad?" The prickling at the back of her neck intensified, and nothing but dead silence greeted her.

Movement at her feet had her jumping back with a shriek. The dead man slumped forward, his body caving in on itself. The skin started to sink in as if aging decades right before her eyes. This most definitely wasn't a sign of rigor mortis, and with morbid fascination she watched as the body continued to shrivel until all that was left started to crumble and turn to ash.

Cali wanted to scream, but her throat closed up, her eyes fixed to the sight before her.

She had to find Mom and Dad.

Trying to control the trembling of her limbs, she edged toward the kitchen, keeping as far from where the man had been as possible.

"Don't freak," she told herself. "There has to be some sort of reasonable explanation. You're not going insane."

But how did she know that? Didn't all the research say that a person never knew when they were crazy?

She shook her head and stopped dead in her tracks as she entered the kitchen. "Mom!" She rushed to her mother's prone form on the floor, her father within arm's reach. "Holy shit." She checked her mother's wrists, felt no pulse, cursed and fumbled around at her neck.

The pulse was slow but steady.

Cali sagged in relief, her muscles turning to jelly. She crawled to her father and checked his throat. She'd never been good at taking radial pulses.

"What the hell happened here?" The kitchen hadn't been touched. There was no sign of a struggle. It was as if some kind of assassin had snuck in, incapacitated her parent's and then gotten stabbed in the chest. But by whom?

The light coming through the open threshold flickered.

With a sinking sensation, she realized she'd left the front door wide open.

• • •

It couldn't be real.

Felix took the next corner a little too sharply. He'd always hoped — hell, he'd dreamed of finding the one woman who was meant for him. That one person he wouldn't have to hide himself from, but after so many years he'd simply given up. He'd stopped looking for any sort of companionship ever since Collette —

He cut the thought off as soon as he'd had it, but that didn't stop the memories.

Jasmine. Dead.

The bullet scar along his left shoulder stung. He ignored the phantom pain and sped through a yellow light. He'd learned the hard way that his life would never permit him to date or get close to any normal girl.

And if this girl was another *normal* person to save?

Was it possible Niella had Dreamed wrong? He doubted it, but it tempered his excitement. He needed to stay level headed. There was no point getting riled up over a fantasy that'd been haunting him for four years. The only living proof he'd been given had been shot down the very same day. By him.

He turned down the last street and scanned the houses for their numbers. It wasn't necessary. The house had the front door wide open.

His hands tightened around the steering wheel.

Was he too late?

He parked on the curb one house up and ran from his car. His eyes caught a large, navy blue van two houses down. The hair prickled at the back of his neck.

He stepped through the front door.

Silence greeted him. The drapes were drawn shut, casting the house in shadows, the sun carving a shaft of light through the dim hallway.

Something shimmered at the end of the hall. He gently shut the door. He took measured steps deeper into the still house. No matter how quiet it was, that didn't mean he was alone.

The hallway led into a kitchen but before he stepped through the threshold he squatted down next to the shimmering pile of ash. He passed his hand right through it. "Illusionist."

A chill swept down his spine. This was not another vigilante rescue mission. The seriousness of Ell's prescience crashed down on him. He'd just run head first into something he had no concept of.

Other people with powers were involved.

Movement darted past the archway that connected to the kitchen. The shape female.

Felix jumped to his feet. "Hey." She was reaching for a drawer, and he had a pretty good idea what was inside. He grabbed her before she could get her hands on something pointy.

Her body jerked. Felix hissed as a jolt went straight through his system.

"Don't touch me." She started to struggle but he dropped her instantly, having no idea what had ripped through his body.

She stumbled. Dark brown hair covered her face until she whirled on him, her hands held like claws near her chest, ready to strike.

She faltered when she caught sight of him. He was pretty sure his face held the same expression.

She was tall.

It was the first thing he fixated on. And why not? Sydney didn't even reach his shoulder, and Niella was bound to a wheelchair. He'd met tall women before, when they came into the bakery, but none of them was this tall.

Not without high heels, anyway.

She had to be at least five-ten. Her shoulder-length, dark chocolate hair was cut in an edgy fashion with side bangs. Her eyes were polished onyx and her skin had a faint golden tinge, as if she'd just begun enjoying the So Cal summer sun. She had on a loose-fitting tee and jean shorts with sneakers. It emphasized her lean build. Felix's whole body tightened. It looked as if she'd been made for him.

Her eyes finished their own appreciative assessment of him. His appearance had caught her off guard. The thought made him smile.

When she noticed his attention all emotion was wiped from her face. She regarded him coldly. "Who are you?"

He gave a bow from the waist, making sure to keep his eyes locked with hers. "Felix Del Valle."

Her eyes raked him again. His blood rushed south.

Calm. Stay calm.

She took a step back from him and glanced down the hall toward the front door. "Did you kill that man?"

He frowned. There was no man …

Then he remembered. The Illusion.

He ground his teeth. Niella was right. This was some kind of trap. Someone was setting her up. But for what, he didn't know. "No, but I need to get you out of here." Every instinct inside him raged for him to protect her. "You're in danger. This is a trap, some kind of set up. There was a dark blue van parked two houses down. I thought I might have been too late, but either way I don't think we have much time."

She looked at him like he was crazy and stepped back. He wanted to follow. He wanted to be near her, to smell her hair and touch her skin.

She glanced over her shoulder. Felix followed the movement and spotted a man and a woman on the floor.

Shit.

"There's no way I'm leaving my parents," she said.

He didn't blame her, only now his chances of getting her to leave with him went from slim to none. There had to be something he could —

His gaze shot back to the girl's parents. He stared hard, knowing he hadn't imagined it.

It came again. The slightest shimmer along their shoulders, like an image struggling to stay in focus.

An Illusion.

The air left his lungs. "Son of a bitch."

That could only mean two things. One, the Illusionist was getting tired. Two, he was still close by.

He swung his attention back to the girl. She jumped back.

He ran a hand through his hair. How the hell was he supposed to explain this?

"Look, your parents aren't real."

Her eyebrows rose and her foot darted out behind her, seeking an escape.

Great start, Felix.

He took a hesitant step sideways, trying to ease his way over to where the Illusion of her parents resided. If he could get her to reach out and touch them then she'd see that they weren't real. The Illusion was fading, the power draining, which meant they were going to lose their solidity.

She watched his progress with blazing eyes, but she didn't retreat. He took that as a good sign.

When he got within a foot of the Illusion he stopped. She looked ready to strike if he so much as sneezed at the Illusion wrong. "I'm not going to harm them," he tried soothing her. "But you have to believe me when I tell you they're not real. If you'd simply touch them you'd know." He started to lower himself. All he'd have to do was show her, then she'd see …

"I've already touched them. I felt for a pulse. It's there — faint — but there. And if you so much as harm one hair on my father I'll make that trick you pulled with the stirring spoon on the man in the hall look downright enjoyable."

Felix halted his hand where it was inching out to touch the shoulder of her father. "Stirring spoon?" What the hell had been back in that hallway?

She didn't elaborate on what she had seen and Felix didn't ask. There was no time. He could sense the minutes ticking by.

There was another faint glimmer from the Illusion. Time was running out. If the Illusion dropped then he had a feeling their time was up.

"Would you just watch?" he bit out. "Nothing is going to make sense to you right now but if you'd simply watch, it would really cut down on all the explaining I'd have to do."

He looked up and found she'd retreated a few steps.

He lightened his tone. "Please."

He didn't wait for her to respond. He eyed her father and slowly lowered his hand. If the Illusion remained solid, he was so totally fucked.

His hand slid right through the back of her father's shoulder blade. He sighed in relief and kept his hand where it obviously sat in the middle of the Illusion's body.

He looked up to explain. "I know it looks —"

She'd made a break for it.

He exhaled. "Fucking hell."

• • •

Cali didn't wait. As Felix's hand reached out for her father she took it on blind faith that he bore no malicious intent toward her dad. Besides, it was the perfect opportunity. Felix was distracted, and Cali had spotted the portable phone on the bench by the front door. As much as it pained her to turn her back on her parents, she had to contact the police. Her parents were unconscious and defenseless, and she was alone with a murderer.

And just what the hell had happened back there when she'd first laid eyes on him? God, when he'd introduced himself with that elegant bow, his brilliant blue-green eyes locked with hers … the effect had been positively electric.

Her fast-acting lunge only carried her as far as the hall before a pair of warm, firm arms wrapped around her waist. "Yeah, I don't think so." His breath brushed against her neck, causing a shiver to run down her body. Her knees buckled.

Felix's arms locked around her as they went down with a grunt. He twisted at the last minute, his firm chest cushioning her fall. One of her hands landed on his sternum. She felt his heart kick start beneath her palm.

She snatched her hand back as if burned.

His eyes locked with hers. "You don't understand — " he started to say but she refused to listen. She needed to get out of his arms. His touch did something to her, made her feel things best left unnoticed.

That strange prickling at the back of her neck started up again.

She'd never been very good at fighting, but she'd spent a lot of time with her older brother when she was little. He'd been a wrestler, and she'd been famous for her flexibility that allowed her to maneuver out of his holds.

Felix must have seen the determination in her face because he quit talking. His arms wrapped tight around her back. She ignored the flutter in her chest and twisted her limber body out and under his arms.

He swore. "Look, I don't want to hurt you," he pleaded as Cali shot to her feet. He was behind her in an instant, his fingers curling around her wrist like a vise. She ducked the left side of her body, going down to one knee while simultaneously turning her torso and arm out and around, breaking his grip. His other hand shot out in an attempt to make up lost ground. She pushed up with her bent leg, throwing her right shoulder back to pivot out of his reach.

She collided with the stair banister, and pain spiked up her spine as the wood hit one of her vertebrae.

Felix winced, hesitating in his pursuit.

It was all the opening she needed. She dove for the phone. Her fingers closed clumsily around it as her momentum drove her into the living room. It was one of those sunken rooms that she swore she'd never get in her own home specifically for this reason. She'd forgotten the drop-off was there. She tried to stop herself from landing on her face but her foot met nothing but air.

A yelp whooshed out of her as her stomach smashed into the hard back of her dad's favorite leather chair. She took in a pained gulp of air and rolled as Felix grabbed for her.

"Would you stop already?" He sounded beyond frustrated. "You're my Mirror Mate. I'm not going to harm you."

Ignoring him, she hit the *talk* button on the phone, her finger shaking over the 9. The button gave the appropriate *beep* before Felix caught her in his arms again. Cali swirled around, having no qualms about fighting dirty, and kicked him in the shin as hard as she could. His blue-green eyes widened in pain.

She expected him to release her, but instead her kick must have disrupted his equilibrium because he lost balance, and together they fell onto the beige leather couch.

She kept the phone above her head to keep it from getting crushed between them. She squirmed against him but only succeeded in pressing her body closer to the hard planes of his.

Heat pooled low in her gut.

She brought the phone close to her face and hit the 1.

"I said stop." One of his arms snaked out from under her, giving a showy wave, and just like that the phone *vanished*.

"Holy shit."

Cali stared at her hand, waiting for the phone to reappear. It didn't. Her shock started to diminish as the realization that Felix was still atop her sank in, his tall, powerful body pressing hers into the material of the sofa.

He was a magician.

It was the only explanation her mind could come up with.

"How — ?"

Her mouth went dry as her eyes bored into his oceanic ones. The prickling on her neck increased as all sound seemed to fade from existence except theirs. Her breathing was loud and harsh, and she could've sworn she heard the pounding of Felix's heart like thunder.

A look of awe came over him as his gaze fell to her lips. She licked them instinctively but they continued to tingle. "What's your name?" he asked her.

In the strange stillness of the house, his words reverberated in her ears louder than normal.

She found her own gaze dropping to his mouth and forced her eyes back up to his. They met with a spark.

"Cali Crazar," her traitorous mouth spoke.

A boyish grin tugged at his mouth. "Cali." He seemed to test her name on his tongue. "Cali from *Cali*-fornia."

She glared daggers at him and he laughed.

"How did you make the phone disappear? Are you a magician?" A murderous magician, she tried to remind herself. *Don't forget you still have no idea who this man is.* But she couldn't dispute the fact that if he wanted to hurt her he would have done it by now.

Amusement sparkled in his eyes. His thumb reached out and brushed her lips. Her heart pounded against her ribs, her nipples hardening where they were pushed against his firm chest. "No, I'm most definitely *not* a magician."

She didn't believe him. He had to be. Phones didn't simply vanish, and dimly in the recesses of her mind she recalled that there had been no sign of the dead body in the hallway when she'd gone for the phone.

Strangest. Day. Ever.

Felix's head dipped close to hers.

Alarms shot through her brain.

Pull away. Spit in his face. Do something!

She couldn't, even if she wanted to. Something inside her simply responded to him. She couldn't resist. She'd wanted him as soon as she'd laid eyes on him, and that want frightened her.

The warmth of his lips ghosted over hers. Heat rolled through her body.

The front door burst open.

For more books by Mary K. Norris, check out:
Shield from the Heart

In the mood for more Crimson Romance?
Check out *Sanctuary by Rachel James* at *CrimsonRomance.com*.